Goddammit Goldsmith My Real Name's Rosenberg! - A
Tenderloin Tale

By Tim Fulmer

I0517426

Party Crasher Press
Los Angeles, California

"Goddammit Goldsmith My Real Name's Rosenberg! - A Tenderloin Tale," By Tim Fulmer

ISBN-13: 978-0692504499 (Party Crasher Press)
ISBN-10: 0692504494

Text Copyright ©2010, 2015 Tim Fulmer, Party Crasher Press

Please direct any enquiries to:
partycrasherpress@gmail.com

Table of Contents

PART 1 Amber

Chapter 1

Greetings from the Arab surrealist movement!

I'm the cofounder. I'm the writer. The first and last name's Rosenberg. I'm serving our country, volunteering for everything in sight. I've murdered someone I intimately know. I've reversed the laws of motion. I ../../../../. I can't wait to say fuck you on national TV.

I'm here to stay forever. At least. 'I' will delineate a recognizable through-line that links this story's episodes, providing some measure of coherence to the proceedings. 'I' am present at least once in nearly every paragraph. That fact alone should ease the listener's mind at the outset. If I begin to mumble or scream inconsistently or speak paradoxically and things become muddled, readers can backtrack to the last sentence containing 'I,' working forward again from there, doing their best to generate a meaningful chain of events that meets their personal standards of literary coherence.

The cities of San Francisco, Reno, and Tel Aviv will figure prominently in this story's setting. Rather than spend time describing those cities, I'll refer readers to the many pictures of them available online. That not only helps reduce the story's length, saving us valuable time, it also allows me to focus on the sweeter-smelling interior aspects of the events I experience.

Tonight the city's air reeks of dog shit and diesel fumes. Car horns blast repeatedly. Across the street a homeless man wrapped in a tattered sleeping bag roasts weenies over an open fire. Cars line up in geological formation to display their many strata. Headlights, windshields, side windows, taillights. It's like an old foreign movie. Luis Bunuel or Jacques Tati? Six-dollar admission, lime-green modular furniture, an ancient limousine parked in a no-parking zone.

Damn! I see cops are butchering male baboons out here in the field tonight. Lay off the meth pipe man! Cops are beating the piss out of that seventeen-year-old girl over there. Good riddance. A cop car turns the corner. I wouldn't say those bastards lack ambition. Watch where you're walking! Manners are important out here on the sidewalk. You? Yes I'm dying to buy drugs off a total stranger. Why are those other strangers lining up at the ATM? Their credit reports require lots of paper's why. Got your plastic wafers handy? For the bank, the paint store, the Safeway, the tattoo parlor, for a stale cappuccino-fudge cake. Later I'll price water pistols at Wal-Mart. At a salon I'll get my hair colored. Off to the first wedding reception of my life. If tomorrow's not a holiday why is Starbucks packed with customers at this late hour? Caffeine addicts are so afraid of falling flat they never aim for the next big thing. You're not gonna die from drinking soy milk that expired six days ago people!

Boredom is the main cause of my writer's block tonight, along with disgust, a bad haircut. Very bad memories. Writer's block drives me out into these alien city streets, inspires me to mutter obscenities into a mini-cassette recorder while I pace the cruddy pavement. The taping's begun. Part 1. Chapter 1. Help me celebrate this night. A writer with a month to live sets out to find his creditors in San Francisco. He'll obey the orders of a greedy psychotherapist and strangle his daughter, mistress, and estranged wife. Those poetic mementos will outlast the memory of this tirade's sloppy transcripts.

Two summers ago on Martha's Vineyard writing fiction was more important to me than muttering into a tape recorder and murdering someone tonight. I went to bed in broad daylight. No whores, no meat, no liquor. Nothing provoked panic. No Coca-Cola, no beans on rice. My cock and balls were easy to describe. I had a different girlfriend, a young woman named Bianca who was blonde, knew lots of tricks, and didn't care I needed a girlfriend around. Four legs were better than two. Alone with nothing to do, no one at our sides, we lived in symbiosis unaware of who occupied the dramatic roles of Dominant and Submissive. I remind myself Thou shalt NOT commit adultery tonight or early tomorrow morning. My hands are trembling as I speak into the recorder.

Trust me not to make this story overly complicated and unnecessarily confusing. Something's wrong. I detect literary interference-patterns trying to destroy every idea for a story. Twenty-two different pedestrians dash in forty-seven different directions, each of them out for blood. The paragraphs go by quickly. Very quickly. You'll see. Who am I kidding when I'm not enraged at myself? I might never survive another night in the neighborhood they call the Tenderloin. It's much too spooky around here. The walls and ceilings are painted a dull institutional gray-green.

I open the door, step inside the diner. A bit later in a small smudged mirror behind the counter I watch the waitress vigorously massage a booth's cushions with Lemon Pledge. I know her nametag reads PENNY. She's got fiery red hair. She's not good-looking or anemic enough to be a model. She's got parental qualities too and a rather large bosom. Her nails look like a four-year-old painted them. Her eyes resemble tiny erasers. Escorts, hustlers, strippers, drama critics, other non-legit types. I bet she remembers every face. I bet she's on ecstasy. At the counter two sleazy idiots from the East Bay are talking 49ers football and who's gonna win next year's Super Bowl. The jukebox plays Madonna's Lucky Star, an incredibly depressing song.

I've had far too much chicken-fried steak and gravy at this late hour. I get up from the booth, walk inside the restroom where I glue a beard and mustache to my face. Note to self. Get some sleep. Having done absolutely nothing tonight I've accumulated vast amounts of potential energy.

The incredible pressure building inside my skull forces me to adjust the beard before I return to the sidewalk. My sightings are mythic around here. A red leatherette booth at the back of a diner. A sighting on a fishing boat out there on the Bay. What's that got to do with anything? Nothing. The reader's other questions are unanswerable. Sightings in a dim corner at the back of a diner. Those Polaroid snapshots of unrecognizable things that are possibly disgusting.

At address no. 2 Goldsmith holds out an open manila envelope. When I take the cash I imagine he's frightened to death of me and my many manuscript pages. He smells like coconuts. I think he's a depressive tonight or at least a neurotic. How can he recognize me in this get-up? My sightings are mythic around here. I'm like an alien in a bad sci-fi movie. These melodies are campfire songs. Complete stupor is a mere hairsbreadth away.

Lately Goldsmith and I have become very good friends. Our friendship's the most inexplicable sort of transformation if not an outright disaster.

"Why you carry around that old mini-cassette recorder Rosenberger?"

"It helps me confront writer's block."

"Confront? Speaking a lot of nonsense helps you write larger quantities of better nonsense? I don't see the connection."

Goldsmith yanks the recorder from my hands.

"You son of a bitch give that back to me! "

"Your first task is to find out what happens when you're rendered speechless."

I pat my jacket pocket.

"I have two bullets left in this revolver Goldsmith, one for you, one for me. If I were you I'd give that back this instant!"

"You're gonna kill us both over a shitty tape recorder? You outta your mind?"

"That's a different matter."

"Take the goddamned thing. You don't know what you're doing. Those descriptions of human conduct are nonsense. They're insufficiently disturbing, far too realistic."

"I'm getting the work done!"

"Have you forgotten you give me your documents to read?"

"Those are first drafts!"

"By the third or fourth draft you've grouted the plot holes, which takes a toll on your hands and knees. No wonder you're exhausted when you reach that final draft. What's worse, the editors require the whole thing be re-grouted anyway, putting you back on your hands and knees to work on another final draft."

"Are we having the same conversation here?"

"Nonsense never makes sense no matter how hard you attack it. If you don't have a firm grasp on reality you'll never become a surrealist. You're living in a dream world. You're a psychopath. There's nothing surrealistic about that."

"You're the world's expert on what's real?"

"Tell me what you do for a living Rosenberger. How do you earn money when you're not stealing it off drug dealers and robbing strippers?"

"Look in the mirror you bastard! You know what I do for a living and I'm not responding to the rest of that. You can't get my name right half the time. Yourself what do you do?"

"I chase girls mostly."

"How inspiring. What types do you specialize in?"

"Neurotics, neurotic from screwing too much."

"That sounds very surrealistic and irrational Goldsmith. You do what you want. I don't care. I'll kill us both if I have to. Like the other ones."

"Other ones?"

"I'm moving to Reno to finish this writing assignment. After that, the deserts of the Middle East. How's that for movement?"

I wave the mini-cassette recorder at him.

Goldsmith frowns.

"San Francisco's not disturbing enough? You gotta move to Nevada? Gotta add gambling and pimping to your list of psychopathic accomplishments? You've got three months to make the cut or your dream's finished Rosenberger!"

I leave the club.

Cash in hand, hand in pocket, mini-cassette recorder on pause, I return to the diner. Penny reminds me she gets off work at midnight. It's a straightforward answer to a straightforward question. I won't bother putting it in quotes. Turns out she's not on ecstasy tonight. Her feet are no bigger than a child's. The two sleazy idiots from the East Bay have cigars jammed in their mouths. Everything I see in the diner's essential and at the same time a chance occurrence.

First thing I do when Penny's shift ends is take her aside, show her the mini-cassette recorder, explain I'm trying to protect myself from a severe case of writer's block. She laughs. She gets the joke. We'll soon be at each other's throats.

We go back to my place, a two-bedroom flat I share with my teenage daughter Amber that's situated above a pawnshop. If all goes as planned, and it must, I'll write lots more about Amber and the pawnbroker in subsequent chapters. Right now, before we retire for the night, Penny and I need to discuss a few things, in particular Goldsmith's distortions of my plans for the Arab surrealist movement. That will conclude our first nocturnal session.

Rest assured I never fail to perform what I've promised.

Chapter 2

A throbbing pain dragged me out of bed quite early and forces me to resume writing. Outside the smudged window it's a foggy Monday morning. Strangers walk past on their way to work. Perhaps they're exercising. They have a pleasant kinetic energy about them. Dogs are chained to their wrists.

I sit at a wobbly writing table in the breakfast nook praying to Allah or Yahweh, what have you, to intervene and prevent last night's writer's block from taking hold. I've placed the loaded revolver right beside the keyboard and mini-cassette recorder. If things get bad, a stray bullet should keep me from surrendering to restlessness and distraction. My lack of susceptibility to inertia isn't something I want to dwell on. I'll write about Penny, Amber, and Goldsmith.

As a general rule I'm careful to observe Amber's early morning silence. The materialists once called it beauty sleep. I'm haunted by memories of yesterday's conversations with Amber and her precocious-sounding laughter.

"You know I love you. You're my only daughter. You respect me. Would you like to skip school and go somewhere new and unusual today?"

Amber's calm and silent face reflects back my gratitude.

"I hate it when you and your Mommy have problems. I won't call it anything other than problems, big problems. Your mommy and I are separated."

Amber laughs. "I'm stuck living with you Daddy?"

"Let's reason together on this. Don't we have everything we could want right here?"

"You don't understand a word I'm saying!"

"I'm not the one who's angry."

"You'd never get angry about anything."

"Maybe you should Amber."

"Do what?"

"Get angry."

"Why should I be angry if you're not? You said we both have everything we could want."

"I'm talking to you and you don't understand a word I'm saying. You're not a good listener. Like your mom."

"The real reason you don't understand me is you're too hungover to make any sense half the time."

"That's what the school counselors tell you? Something insane and psychotic like I'm hungover or high? My daughter can't understand her father?"

"Go to hell!"

"Drugs and booze keep me from living a proper life, turn me into an obsessive writer. I'm not the one getting angry right about now."

"I said go to hell!"

"Seems to me the lack of imagination is more your problem than mine. I guess I have the drugs and booze and word processor to blame for that one too."

"When do you stop or can you?"

"I can stop. Is it so surprising I don't have your genuine attention right about now?"

"How genuine is this Daddy? Shut up!"

"I'd prefer not to."

Amber begins pouting.

I resume writing.

Why can't the reader see why I'm so infatuated with my seventeen-year-old daughter? You might think it a pity Amber was born without fake arms. It might explain why I love her so much more, why our love is more secret, more hidden than my love for Penny ever can or will be, even with Penny's pair of fine full breasts, that high forehead, those shining eyes, the fiery red hair, all of it bathed in harsh fluorescent light. I imagine a desperate sort of trembling holds the three of us together. A magical bit of attraction exists for me, what the pornographers used to call a threesome. I imagine this big ruddy face creasing into laughter every time my flesh pierces theirs. Amber wrinkles her forehead. Penny closes her eyes. I tell myself I'm the one in charge here. I'm the writer. My body relaxes.

I'll do my best not to impose myself perversely on any single episode. That should ensure smooth transitions between sentences, paragraphs, chapters, parts. Don't be alarmed if I pretend the entire tale's one form of surmise, a persuasive conjecture based on incomplete evidence. I'm recording observations here. I won't offer the reader good news or literary convention. Nor will this tale become a philosophical argument we're having. I'm a grotesque troublemaking writer who's bad in the morning, a bit worse in the evening. That's quite early for me.

You ask what I've accomplished by the end of a given day. I've tried to clarify a difficult situation with less groping about in the dark as it were and fewer children playing about the monument to Saint Francis. Invisible hands brush against this word processor as if nothing remained or no word were lost. My fingers flex nervously. I blush like a schoolgirl. If I never get to the bottom of this difficult situation I'll nonetheless write about Penny and Amber and Goldsmith again and again. And again I'll see that succession of faces amid the stupefying routine of everyday editorial work and avoidance of writer's block. No edges, no beginning, no end.

No wonder I dig my teeth into the flesh of these fingertips before beginning to type. I know any story risks meeting some level of incomprehension on the part of a reading public whose interest in literary fiction has dwindled over the past decade. Writing fiction remains an art. I do it exceptionally well. For that reason alone I've made a concession to the average reader's bad habits by relating this autobiographical story through a first-person narrator in the present tense. That should maximize the impression of realism. If all goes as planned, and it must, the reader will forget these are recollections and experience the story as 'I' experienced these events when they were present.

"Let's back up for a minute Amber. Mom got you a doll for your birthday. You brought it home. After that it started moving around, changing places by itself?"

"That's when I realized I wasn't imagining things."

"You mean the doll would be there one instant, gone the next?"

"That's right."

"Where did this happen?"

"All over the flat, in my bedroom, sometimes in the bathroom, the kitchen. Once it was suspended in midair."

"The doll levitated?"

"If that's what you call it. Mostly it moved around."

"You saw the doll turn up without you carrying it there?"

"That's right. Stuff started coming out of its mouth."

"Stuff?"

"Lots of slimy mucous material."

"Vomit?"

"Sort of. Later there were voices, depressed and confused voices. Bizarre spirit entities maybe."

"I'm not sure what that is."

"I don't know what to call 'em!"

"What happened next?"

"When the doll wasn't looking I grabbed it by its neck and squeezed hard."

"You throttled your doll?"

"Its eyes popped out of its head. Its face got purple. A weird hissing noise came from its mouth."

"Was that good?"

"I don't know. My hands got tired and I let go. The voices started up again louder this time. That's when I got scared."

"You stuffed towels down the toilet?"

"I thought the voices would stop if I jammed up the toilet with towels. The voices got more muffled sounding. Helped a little I guess."

"What were the voices saying? We're they commanding you?"

"More like a big crowd of people mumbling under their breath. I had to concentrate to hear separate words and got a headache."

"Where was the doll during this time?"

"In the flat I guess."

"You ignored the doll after you strangled it?"

"What was I supposed to do?"

"I don't know, throw it out the window, rip it to pieces, light it on fire, anything! Where's it now?"

"Can't you see it wouldn't have mattered! The voices were everywhere, coming from all sides, the walls, ceiling, the carpet. Once or twice there was knocking on the door and footsteps."

"This was loud?"

"Not as loud as a rock concert. Loud enough to keep me awake at night."

"Jesus Amber how could you let this happen?"

"It's not my fault!"

"How can you be sure you didn't bring it on yourself? Maybe to get back at me for something I did or get my attention. You wanna be famous is that it? There could be many reasons."

"You think I'm making it up?"

"I don't know what you're doing. Why did you first go to the pawnbroker with these stories instead of me?"

"He listens."

"He'll listen and put a bunch of weird shit into your head about spirit possession."

"I babysit for him. We're friends. We talk about things. I mentioned it to him one evening. He said the voices are memory tracings."

"A recording?"

"Something like that I think. Like an engraving."

"That guy's fifty years old, not married. He's got a two-year-old daughter. Doesn't that strike you as a bit odd?"

"Why should it? He never forces me to do anything I wouldn't want to."

"That's reassuring. I suspect the guy's a weekend queer."

"You might like to know he thinks you're pretty creepy too!"

"He hardly knows me!"

"He says Penny's a bad influence on me."

"What the hell does he know? He spends all day downstairs in that worthless junkshop."

"I guess he notices things."

"I'm sure he does. My theory's the guy's a world-class perversion freak. Why the supernatural nonsense? Are you trying to prove you're independent? Can't you do something more conventional like run away from home or smoke pot or get a lizard tattooed on your hip? You never do me a favor!"

"I will run away!"

"To Alaska no doubt. You can say the voices are telling you to work as a deckhand on a salmon boat. You wanna die is that it? You got a death wish?"

"I could move in with the pawnbroker. He said he's got an empty room with a bed in it."

"I'm sure he does, along with weird devices and toys and nylon rope. Pawnbrokers in this neighborhood see lots of bizarre crap, French tickler's, albino rattlesnakes. You can imagine. He ever put a burning cigarette on your arm?"

"Go to hell!"

"I'm saying that man's no parade in the park."

"He's the only real friend I have around here."

"Everyone likes what they like don't they Amber?"

"I'm going down there right now to hang out with him!"

"Your teenage idealism is gonna get you killed. You may think you got a big heart. To every pervert out there those are two firm little titties!"

"Spare me your sermon!"

I spend the rest of the morning alone with a hangover and a head cold. I daydream. The hours pass. A sinking feeling forms in my gut. I daydream some more. The hours pass. I draw in deep breaths, trying to shoo away the weird images. Again that succession of faces appears. My how big they are! Their mouths don't say anything much. I'm partial to the blonde ones with big tits and the young men in those Texas-sized hats standing in a Texas-sized circle-jerk, their crotches shaved and glistening, their chins tilted above their chests. Their hands work away. Their lips are pursed. I experience no reaction when Goldsmith walks into that scene to join them. He must sense something ominous is developing. A crisis or perhaps a closure. When I ask for another drink Goldsmith says truth is the searchlight that liberates. Silence I reply. Magicians and thieves.

Far more than another eccentric genius from North Beach, Goldsmith's the very model of English middle-class propriety. He's earnest, well-mannered, pipe-smoking, tweedy. He takes The Times to keep up with English cricket scores. I know he abandoned his childhood Christianity to become an adult Muslim. The subject of graphology flies right out of his mouth. He can speak of Spinoza. I could layer detail upon further detail if I so pleased.

The pedestrians in this story are not phantoms though the cities are real, too real if you ask me. I remember Goldsmith once saying the Tenderloin is the great wine-press of love. I think of it more as a demon in a bell jar. I field the same questions time and time again from the same curious bystanders. I wonder if these scenes exist in the mind of God or somewhere else far more predictable and less interesting.

They ask me what kinds of stories I write.

"That's hard to say."

You're a journalist?

"Not exactly."

At first I thought you might be a student. There are so many college kids around here. How do you like living in San Francisco?

"I like it okay."

I see you've got plenty of free time on your hands. I have to get up early every morning to work at the docks. You can sleep in. That's an ideal arrangement for a writer.

"I couldn't write constantly even if I wanted to."

Do you have any books printed?

"Published? Nothing much. One story."

A detective story? A love story?

"Not exactly a love story, not exactly a detective story, something in between. I write stories that describe how I deal with difficult situations on the alien city streets of the Tenderloin."

Alien? It's very fascinating!

In a flash the mind's eye projects a thousand dust-tormented rooms jammed to the rafters with thousands of ragged-looking literary personae. They render the imagination helpless in the face of such overwhelming possibilities. I see endless permutations of character-driven drama, chance crossings of paths, conspiratorial forms of domination and control. de Tocqueville said chance does nothing that hasn't been prepared beforehand. Pynchon said you can never touch the Master but you can tickle his creatures. Freud said I'm accustoming myself to the idea of regarding every sexual act as a process in which four actors are involved. I assure you I'll have lots more to say on that last point.

Around here I'm prepared for high vulgarity. I appreciate its character when I find it in fortress-like museums, used-book shops, out-of-business video rental outlets, gentlemen's clubs. Digressive, sensuous, intrusive, Brechtian, jarring in tone, coldly aglow in harsh fluorescent light, sinister yet surreal. You request it, the vulgar list continues. If you're ../../../../ it's too easy to sneer at the streets of the Tenderloin. I only gotta describe those urban forms. Often under incredible strain I desperately write prose to ensure the resulting literary patterns exist with proper variation and many different states of consciousness leaping from dimension to dimension. Digressions are the essence of these city blocks. I've read street names off signs more than a hundred times in various states of consciousness and undress. Eddy. Market. Geary. Turk. Montgomery. Those names are world famous. You've heard them mentioned in movies. The pedestrians who roam those streets appear small and ordinary and inconsequential even while making important-looking gestures when they cross an intersection. Those pedestrians are the funniest little actors I've ever seen. For that reason alone they appear throughout this story.

Goldsmith towers over your average Tenderloin pedestrian who prefers to take refuge from the swiftly changing world rather than engage it. Goldsmith's curious and confrontational. He's embarrassing. He claims to suffer from a form of greatness that cannot find application in the arts or sciences and is doomed to wreak havoc in daily life. Unlike me he knows how to get along with intellectuals without being tarred by their brush. When I write about him I feel myself sinking down into this chair with a weary groan as I try to evaluate the intensity of the glint in the pupils of his eyes and penetrate those hidden motives. I've come to realize my often misguided literary enthusiasm's has created a one-sided portrait of the man. You'll see that's par for the course. Goldsmith's guilty of serious misconduct even if he's a man of good family and his company's easy to enjoy. He might've had a successful career in the Army or as a journalist in some remote outpost of the British Raj had he not decided to wear Arab clothes half the time, 'gone Arab' as we used to say. Otherwise he dons those gray suits two sizes too small, those battered brown canvas shoes. Doesn't 'artistically sound' mean 'commercially feasible'? No wonder I want Goldsmith's female friends to be well-bred and have nice legs, including the foreign-exchange students. They should live well, travel first-class, drink freely. Why not?

Chapter 3

The afternoon's erased the morning. Events keep improving. A Buddhist
monk walked past my window followed by a ridiculously attractive girl in
a tracksuit. Who gives a shit about the recession. I'm in favor of people
finding new ways of getting off. Anyone hiring a writer delusional beyond
repair? I can bench-press 300 lbs. I don't smoke anymore. I throw Penny's
iPod at the bathroom mirror. I flush Amber's Xbox down the toilet. The
three of us learn Cantonese from a Korean soap opera dubbed in
Cantonese. We agree to buy a puffer fish.
  Why can't I fall asleep for an afternoon nap? My obsession with the
pawnbroker's babysitter's unhealthy. She's deadly quiet. I believe her
mother washes dishes in Chinatown.
  I throw open the window to the gorgeous afternoon. Lovely sky-blue
explosions. My creativity reading's off the scale. Vodka mixed with orange
soda. Not bad. Penny says I don't act my age. What's my age? I love
writing with the windows open before allergies kick in. Why do I brush my
teeth after deciding I'm still hungry? I crave Turkish food instead of a BBQ
pulled-pork sandwich on cornbread. Delicious! I'll start the 48-hour literary
fast tomorrow. Penny brings me two servings of biscuits and gravy. Damn
I forgot to update the Netflix queue. They've shipped the Clint Eastwood
movies I don't wanna watch. There's wine on the ceiling too. Oops I'm a
very bad Jew. No wonder Penny's a cranky bitch this afternoon. Doesn't
she remember last night? She'll spend the rest of the day cleaning the
hardwood floors or reflecting on the cable TV installation fee. She says
boardgames are fun, CNN's overkill, Top Chef sucks. She's glad we have
hardwood floors. Cleaning the blood off wood is easier than from carpet.
  I sit down, resume writing. I imagine a clean-shaven Englishman in
shirtsleeves. He reminds me of someone I know. I can't quite place the
high-pitched voice and effeminate gestures. I ask him to recommend a
motel. A lofty eternal idea. To request a motel room and the company of a
strange Englishman. Not Christ, nor the Prophet, nor the cramped hall of a
mortuary. Nearby stands a tan-colored chapel, the largest of its halls done
up in gray, green, and brown. An icy shiver runs up my spine. I know that
place. Worshippers lie naked, crushed, bloody, barely breathing on the
checkerboard marble floor. God looms useless above the dirty hair and
muddy fingernails. A musical sadness fills the air. I didn't invent that
phrase. Nor will I write another story about Costa Rican babysitters
roaming the streets amid San Francisco explosions.
  "Checked out did you say?"
  The Englishman nods in agreement. It's impossible to determine his
state of dress in the room's dim light. The odors of cheap cologne barely

obscure his need for a bath. I'm not letting the fat slob give me writer's block again. I'm astonished when he tells me his mother's Jewish and multiple items are missing from the Arab surrealist movement's documents vault, including the Telefon Buch and the Gelb Pages. This time I'm the one who nods in agreement. Something needs to be done here. The Englishman ignores me, glances over at a robot standing in the corner. He takes several deep breaths, makes multiple effeminate gestures, appears ashamed. That's crazy. I recognize the robot by its flat nose and fat thighs.

The windows rattle every time a bus or streetcar roars by, breaking my concentration. I pause, gaze outside at the tops of the buildings across the street. Pedestrians move past duty-bound to their suspicions and cups of caffeinated drinks. They're suspicious of everything around them. They remind me of a scene from Invasion of the Body Snatchers. They're troubled in some way, lame or afflicted, godless. I imagine they've arrived from a different unhealthier planet. They wear blue sweaters, light brown T-shirts, yellow scarves, terrycloth towels. Their pants hang too low on their waists as if fitted for someone three sizes bigger. Their white sneakers have Velcro clasps instead of laces.

I turn my attention back to the computer screen. I need to resume writing about the Englishman. Yet I can only imagine God on the other side of that wall stranded on the alien streets of a suspicious-looking city. That's how writer's block begins, with musings on Allah or Yahweh, what have you. I'm not sure why it works that way. These thoughts return again and again to a supreme being who's monotheistic, detached, alternately bored and enraged with His Creation. Again I see that succession of faces, this time against a backdrop of high-rise fixtures and inexpensive air travel.

WORD OF WARNING Penny will soon sense something's altering me, changing the course of the Arab surrealist movement. Amber knows. Goldsmith suspects.

I imagine the pawnbroker's shop downstairs as the wildest dreary grandeur. Never been so long. The air inside bears the stamp of an ancient seal. Arched objects over causeways open up to gates lit by torches into slaughtered inexhaustible dumps where rusty metal shunts the sunlight. Tunnel pipes shudder up to toilet stalls through narrow-shafted bales of wire. The phantom double's done gone out inside a futile maze of masonry fragments as the remote portion vanishes into the bells of obsession. Soon ocean waves will rise up to chip away the smallest pieces. Palm trees will lean in cracked cement. Shipmates will run rail to rail on the decks while blue-black bell buoys clang in the damp laundry air. Clouds of ragged rain hold still. Penny craves the things she craves the most. Amber pouts. I discover hundreds of Goldsmiths listed in the San Francisco phone directory. The four of us are so crazy for one another.

Outside on the street, Hollywood stuntmen inside automobile props huddle up against their own cold indifference. One of the drivers ominously honks the horn. The hell does he want? More proof that daily feedings never fail to bring out the baby alligators? The Tenderloin's starting to make no sense to me. They should've shot the goddamned scenes in Golden Gate Park. No third parties are allowed here. What's the point? You'll rent the film adaptation on home video. The critics say you gotta see the film in a theater for maximum impact. Which theater and why can't I find it?

I find a bloody hacksaw beneath our favorite sofa. I'm stunned. How does Penny have adequate time to murder anyone?

"Penny I need to have a word with you!"

Silence.

"Penny!"

The out-of-place unnecessary window air-conditioner kicks on. I walk into the kitchen. Penny's standing at the sink. Vegetables are lined up along the cutting board. I'm forced to look around and remind myself the kitchen is real. Seeing Penny there also reminds me that preparing supper and lunch is often a problem in this reality.

"Didn't you wash those dishes once today?"

Silence.

"You're not tweaking again are you?"

Silence.

"Who gets the reward me or the person who turns you in?"

I watch the expression on Penny's face change in the window reflection. It develops new highlights and textures. Strange how her complexion develops those textures! I stare at the textures awhile longer before deciding not to bring up the issues of murder and drug abuse after all. If it's true, it's too late to turn things around, too late to squirm at the bottom of a fishbowl like a guilty crab. I wouldn't do that though I've had forebodings.

The spell breaks, the miracles never come, the afternoon's inexplicably over. I find myself in the next room consoling Amber.

"Do you feel nothing, Amber? It's those voices again isn't it?"

"I'm saying that things seem desirable until they're acquired. Everything's alike, empty, worthless."

"I can't understand your impatience. Everything here suits me fine."

"Including the meals, the food?"

"What are you talking about? If you're hungry go in the kitchen, get a snack!"

"I'm saying things are desirable until they're acquired."

"That's a sophisticated idea. You're a very precocious girl Amber. Your teachers are threatened by you. I appreciate nothing interferes with our pleasures more than boredom."

"You agree with me?"

"I don't agree with you. I think you need a therapist or a counselor less than a boyfriend at this point in your life."

"I'm saying we make these things seem desirable until we get them. They're alike, empty, worthless."

"I appreciate you feel nothing at all. That's your basic problem. I don't agree with you. I understand you. You think the true nature of things is temptation. You think life's about resisting those things. Every time you resist them you feel nothing afterwards."

"I do resist them."

"Where does that leave you except feeling like crap? Do you feel a sense of accomplishment?"

"It leaves me with nothing."

"What kind of life goal is that?"

"It's a goal."

"Christ! You have an answer for everything."

"That makes me irrational?"

"Irritating."

"Unfair! We're having a conversation. We're both complicit in this."

"Drop the big words."

"Now you've vindicated your ego. You wanna drop the topic altogether."

"There's not a topic here! Since when do you use words like 'vindicated'?"

"Unfair! You think you figured it out. Now you won't give me a chance to rebut."

"You've responded to everything. What's that if not rebutting? I wouldn't call it rebutting. That makes it sound like we're having an actual debate. We're not."

"Boredom gets the last word. Boredom's what ends every conversation with you Daddy. You're bored, your attention wanders, you start looking for other things to do. Wandering the streets. Daydreaming. You haven't reached a meaningful conclusion."

"I'm leaving now Amber!"

"Isn't that what the counselor calls avoidance behavior? Isn't that denial? You turn your back, walk away. I've seen that before!"

Chapter 4

Why am I so smart? How do I have so much free time to battle writer's block? Where do I get this money? How do I spend it so quickly, with an abundance of good cheer and humor? Stay tuned!

This evening Penny and I are shopping our brains out at the Embarcadero Center. We've bought jewelry, belts, wallets, a jean jacket, a winter coat, new Converse shoes, three iPod skins, cheetah-print hoop earrings, Vitamin Water, even pastries at Starbucks. I'm wondering if I should do more of my hair pink or keep it this way or go natural next time. I did it way too much damage when I went platinum. Every time I washed my hair whole clumps fell out. The front looks great. Who cares how the back of your head looks right?

Much like me, Penny has a weakness for women in tight suits. We're at one of those specialty big boob bra stores. The checkout girl's frowning. She smells sweet. I smell like I mean it. How much longer will I last here? These cashiers are driving me mad, brainwashing me in some astounding way. My money's supposed to vanish yet I cling to the reality of cash. Perhaps my inner self's emerging at the end of a section of the Law of Credit. My credit report will become unattainable as a result of a difference in debt levels and subtle shifts in obscure financings. Truth be told, and it shall, I can't believe these cashiers want my worthless cash. Don't they recognize my expertise, my genius at developing disciplined shopping strategies? Old ways of shopping are no longer relevant here. I'm lucky in that regard. I should stop doing these things without concern otherwise my death is in the barrel, leaving mock execution as the only indignity left to undergo.

Standing in the rain at a bus stop loaded down with heavy shopping bags is an awesome way to spend the rest of the evening. I wonder, Is Nude the New Black? Sounds like a solid shopping strategy. I don't care if he's moving to Lubbock. Your drummer needs to join our band. I can salvage his hard drive. If that dog barks at me one more time I'm gonna lose my shit. Monumental! Some fool call an ambulance! Dumbass pedestrians walk past the recycling bin to put paper in the garbage cans. It smells like dog shit out here. The chickens are fed. The pawnbroker's babysitter's dead. Have some balls and apologize for the crime!

"I don't feel contempt for anyone Penny. I'm soaked to the bone under a streetlamp. I didn't plan on it when I woke up today. Something altered the weather."

"Let's figure out how to get back home rather than argue about the weather."

"We've been out here awhile. We're soaked to the bone. I don't feel contempt for anyone or anything."

"I have to prepare dinner too!"

"Even when we're soaked to the bone, eating occupies a central place in our lives. It's charming the little things we do to evade that underlying impulse to..."

"What?"

"Food tastes good is all. The air smells like something's burning. That's more than enough for now. We'll have to postpone the wild extravagance of dying for another day."

"Christ you're getting on my nerves!"

"I don't feel any contempt. One way or another we're lost in the corridors of our own failures."

"That's sure poetic. I'd get more satisfaction out of listening to the rain for awhile."

"Rain makes a sound."

"Doesn't sound like words."

"Words you don't like? My literary voice is dangerous."

"Annoying. Can we please listen to the rain?"

"What's the rain telling you? Something's dripping from your shopping bags! Look!"

I point at the dark red pool forming at our feet. I squat down, touch the dark fluid with the tip of my index finger before bringing it up to my nose.

"Nothing more than a dark red fluid's dripping from your shopping bags."

Penny laughs. From down here Penny's eyes are dark hollows. I stand back up.

"You don't have the slightest concern about your dripping shopping bags. You're disconnected from reality."

"I've done a lot of shopping today. I'm tired."

I look down again. The dark red pool is more viscous now. The sidewalk's forming a scab in spite of the rain.

That's where the distortions begin.

"I said I'm worn out is all."

"If that's how you feel, let's get home and dispose of whatever's in those shopping bags."

I taste copper on my tongue.

This latest episode's rapidly become a lesson in how to reverse the laws of nature. How many more days do I have left in this city? With each attempt at literary disclosure less and less of my presence remains. I feel disconnected and detached. My odd behavior continues to get the city cops riled up. I'm learning to expect the unexpected.

Perhaps I'll soon become the best friend of a patient with a terminal disease or better yet a delivery boy who fantasizes about his dream girl only to discover she's a holographic projection of his daughter's consciousness. Well-acted. The very ordinary story runs out of steam halfway through, becoming a tedious tease of a film. Or perhaps another movie involving a long train journey through India, or a character study of a colorful Confederate soldier, or an escaped convict undergoing plastic surgery, or best of all a corrupt lawman pursuing cattle rustlers in end-of-the-world Wyoming. I'm thinking give me the computer-colored version. Everything about this city has sequel written over it. A pleasant, forgettable farce with a large off-Broadway cast putting in their cameos, hitting their marks, while reality exists only in the trash-choked corners of the alleyways. So much for murder and suspense at a Lake Tahoe ski lodge. Around here the catering sucks. Unremarkable boneless-skinless chicken breasts, black-eyed peas, golden ripe pineapples, mangosteens, Carthaginian apples, the maudlin slip-slop of compotes and marmalades, Tostitos chips, two-liter bottles of Coca-Cola, six-packs of Budweiser. The salads consist of large chunks of romaine lettuce. For dessert a brownie tray with the standard 25 pieces. Everyday I perish in the furnace of bottomless appetency. O tempora! O mora!

The bus never arrives. I manage to hail a rare street-roaming taxi. The driver expertly steers us past law firms, investment banks, computer companies, gasoline stations, second-hand clothing shops, three-story Victorian row houses, large-scale intermediaries, past truckloads of air-conditioners, televisions, DVD players, past limousines with diplomatic license plates, past lifting cranes, past men staring into drugstore windows and scores of pedestrians held together by dentures, hearing aids, fake gold earrings, softening chemicals, Coke & popcorn, past firing ranges, training grounds, dark places with lots of floors, stairways, exits, dripping chains & slimy metal edges.

I roll down the window to listen to the streets. Twenty five fatally wounded by an explosion at a cartridge factory, blown to bits or drowned in the Bay. Another man falls from his bicycle, tries to save himself, breaks his neck and several ribs. A panic follows. Uncertainty as to how a third man's coat caught on fire. One theory is he was smoking his pipe and, thinking it out, placed it inside a coat pocket where loose matches were set on fire. Another theory is that while walking along the trolley tracks in a path much used by mechanics going to and from work, the man stepped on pieces of the roadbed's stone ballast, falling down, igniting the matches in his pocket. The truth will never be known. A streetcar blazes up, its occupants riding on a fiery apparatus, screaming for help. One of the badly burned tourists starts on a wild race before tangling up with a lamppost.

Nowhere to be seen are uniforms of eccentric belief, violence on the far rocks, mean sons of bitches at the bottom of the social ladder, street-corner reefer deals. Unable to cultivate an optimum angle from the backseat I recoil from the nervus sympathicus of symbol-overload, surrendering to the cabdriver who takes me and Penny the rest of the way home.

Chapter 5

Tonight a second bout of writer's block drives me and the mini-cassette recorder back onto the alien city streets. With one foot in compulsory delusion, the other in secret reality, I stroll down these vast hilly boulevards. I feel like a drink tonight. Drinking won't be shameful. Rest assured I'll never ../../../../.

I've hardly slept in four days. Nighttime's become an illusory form of bedtime to me. I'm decked out in magic lizard-skin pajamas. I make no apologies, give no quarter or nickel, plunging on, abolished by writer's block. I'm excellent at what I do, vigorously arguing for the free exchange of ideas relating to the creative psychosomatic process. Mine's the face of a worn-out literary refugee who politely listens, never offering advice. I feel the weight of my neck. I hold in my midsection. I straighten my back. Once I'm on you can't turn me off in sooner than twenty minutes. I have the scar tissue and tattoos to prove it.

Everywhere I look in the Tenderloin I see lips moving in prayer. I see spasms of torment, faces gorged with blood. A musical sadness fills the air. Like a sort of monkey. Like a kind of lion. The harmonious sounds of buses and streetcars and signal-calls cry out to awaken what's barely fallen asleep. I'm no psycho. I'm the patron saint of manic depressives. I'm a spokesperson for the disturbed and disenfranchised. My words are tender, lustful, bestial. I'll spend the whole night walking around and around the same few city blocks, a fraction of time as it were, though insomnia's never my fault. I'd rather not describe Penny's naked bottom or pull at her overly tight skirt. Rest assured tomorrow I'll write stories throughout the day until evening pushes the two of us back onto the alien city streets where our nostrils will fill with the stench of rotting leaves, garbage, dog shit, what have you, and we're forced to become a naked couple trapped in confounding darkness.

I feel pedestrians approach me like individual events. That isn't a big hill over there. None of them crosses the timberline.

Last Thursday someone strangled the pawnbroker's babysitter. I now have a bright red stain on this scaly nightshirt to illustrate the state of the art of forensic science. I'm not sure of the babysitter's status. I don't have the answer to everything. If you have too many answers, you can ruin the element of surprise life might otherwise offer you.

Right here I'll open these doors and enter my favorite gentlemen's club to resume the monologue inside there. First I must put on the customary sunglasses, fake mustache, and beard.

I follow the petite redhead down a familiar narrow hallway into a single-stall women's restroom with harsh fluorescent lighting. I play with her tits for awhile. She tells me she's got a great ass and a tight pussy. Right now it's time for more drugs. Hillbilly stuff. Tons of money, classified documents, nothing left to chance, pretty surreal though not exactly jihad. I'm Bachelor Number 3. She starts jerking me off, says nothing, her eyes focused on an intermediate point in the distance. I'm starstruck. My cock's like a Louisville Slugger. My asshole tingles. My knees swell. She rubs something between my balls. I notice her red hair has a bluish tint to it. While I ponder that distracting bit of nonsense my mind starts to race in Hebrew. That's good for the cardiovascular system. Like open-heart surgery. Like trips to the moon. Soon paranoia creeps in. Be sure to get rid of that tattoo infection pronto! I'm not impressed with the shitty hard-hitting electro beats I'm hearing right about now. Smells like someone lit the goddamned place on fire. My asthma worsens. I have to plan for each breath. A=B B=C C=D. I realize I need new clothes. Last stuff I bought was last year at the Army & Navy Store in North Beach. My fingernails are a disgrace. I can't handle this toothache. I push the girl away from my cock, zip up, resume my walk down the black-painted corridor. When I reach the first door on my left I open it.

The fake boobs sit too high on the chest, obscuring portions of the pectoral muscles. The trapezius is too prominent for a woman's body. I don't like any of it. Most stripper judges are idiots. They'd never know the difference.

Beads of sweat are forming on her brow. She's nervous.

"Relax girl shake it out."

I begin the weekly inspection. First thing I notice is clogged pores on the tip of her nose and fissures in the corners of her mouth. No signs of jaundice.

"Your complexion's shot to hell."

"I'm working on it."

"You've got angular cheilitis. Are you taking your vitamin pills, the vitamin Bs?"

"Yes."

"Remember I don't work with losers. I expect total commitment. Turn around."

The bikini bottom's bunched up in the crack of her rear. Otherwise her muscular body looks nice and firm, with meaty genitals to match.

"That bikini's not exactly a G-string is it?"

"What?"

"I'd love to have some pictures of you, your best shots, the masochistic ones in the shower with Goldsmith scrubbing your ass. I'd put that in my wallet."

"You know about those pictures?"

"Relax girl shake it out."

She relaxes her pose, closes her eyes, takes a deep breath, turns to the mirror. I examine her paraffin-coated nipples. I give them each a little squeeze. She moans, grabs my erect penis with her right hand. I nod. She takes a big scoop of Vaseline from the container, smears it over my groin.

"This will make it better Rosenberg."

I'm thinking this isn't the first time I've committed adultery. I do it quite often. She knows how to make it last.

I moan and nod. "Squeeze it now!"

She cleans the semen off her hands with a Johnson's baby wipe, sprays the air with a floral room deodorizer. She puts on an oversized sweatshirt and baggy workout pants.

"You're taking the testosterone twice weekly?"

"Yes."

"Any health problems? Inflamed clitoris?"

"No."

"Abnormally high blood pressure? Palpitations?"

"No."

"Goldsmith doing your injections?"

"I do my own injections."

She puts on black leather weightlifting gloves.

"Keeping to a high-protein diet?"

"Red meat, chicken breasts, eggs, steamed vegetables, grilled fish."

"Raw eggs?"

"Sometimes."

"Watch out for salmonella poisoning. That could set you back weeks."

"I hard-boil them."

"You have time to train between meals?"

"Yes."

"Hungry right now? Can I get you something?"

"I'm fine. I've got food in the car."

"What's next?"

"Stripper pole training."

"You like jewelry?"

"Yeah sure."

"You smell something weird?"

"The room deodorizer. Your Old Spice."

"Have you seen Goldsmith around here today?"

"I saw him earlier. He was with Kathleen."

"Fat chicks turn him on. He likes 'em big. He never bothers you much. Are you sure you don't smell something weird like someone tracked dog shit in here?"

"I don't."

"I'm imagining it. Good to see you. I'm off."

I pick up the gym bag and leave. I walk down the black-painted corridor to the next room. It's very dark in here. I can barely make out the walls. I crouch down on the floor, forcing myself to take deep breaths and stay calm. My heart's pounding faster and faster. I remove a flashlight from the gym bag, turn it on. Gym mats cover the floor.

The two of us become a boy-girl couple looking for wild adventure in a private booth. A handsome Jewish Englishman on a date with a much younger Jewish American girl. Thigh Killer and Mommy Robot. We meet at this club on alternate nights. She's dolled up in a silver lamé baby doll dress and black-and-silver-high-heel-lace-up boots. A pee-wee chain collar encircles her slender neck. My face is covered in blue saran wrap. I like to choke girls while I screw them. The bouncers have beaten me to death over it. Mommy Robot's rusty from disuse. She needs to get constantly screwed. Everything coming in she shits right back out. Her limbs are lost in little PVC pipes. No wonder the club owners named her after American icons. Part Mommy, part sex kitten, part robot serial psycho-sinister twin. Complete with dangly girl fingernails, long red shiny hair, a tiny vertebral column, thick mucousy secretions, the filmy wings of insects. Not too much alcohol or sunlight.

The private booth's got nice tobacco patterns and mesmeric geometric designs that have little to do with the original ../../../../. The dancer winks at us from the other side of the glass. She's alternately bored, enraged, ready, sexy. Her tits are tilted too high as she rubs at something between her legs. Suffocation under a pile of shit before the grubs start feeding on pussy influences? The beefy Bedouin dancers arrive with telephone cord to tie off Mommy Robot's legs. They slide back the oily panties. I watch them gang-rape Mommy Robot. She becomes the star in a brutal game of tug-o-war. A muddy bog's the wrong place to squat tonight. Mommy Robot's sweater pocket will hang forever in a bamboo cage.

Ever get the feeling you're stranded in the wrong gentlemen's club? Hours later I'm snorting meth off the back of a lesbian hooker. Like in the movies. Like in the Reagan administration. Is anal bleeding okay with you? Anal bleaching? Too much to ask for the video feed? I can be a dick sometimes. I can spend $500 on strippers in a single night. Penny would laugh. Man I need to poop. I hate public restrooms when men are pooping in the next stall. I keep waiting for the next shoe to drop. Imagine how you'd look if that bouncer watched you poop on a video monitor. With Latex gloves. He'd need press credentials.

Here we have two ultra sexy Jewish lesbians from the university. I'm so tired I've lost sense of what to say. I can only abuse them. In sweatpants. Art's pain. The ICU sucks. Damn platelets. God I'm sick of shoving square pegs into round holes. I'll spend tomorrow hiding, pretending I'm nothing less than a miserable writer. No truth can abolish writer's block like the restless days of spring. I'll sleep throughout the daylight hours. I'll daydream. Like a sort of monkey. Like a kind of lion.

Chapter 6

Yet I'm up early this morning to help Amber get ready for school. She's eating cereal with chocolate soy milk. She smells like a piece of cake. I'm drinking orange juice, playing with our puppy's pubic hair. Amber's wearing striped satin panties or a thong. I'm not letting her have any more Mountain Dew and raspberry Pop-Tarts. She's a spazz. She's trying to exit her own head. She says she'll fall asleep tonight. I'm skeptical. On Friday she played hooky, got a nose-ring, got her teeth whitened, left her purse in the lady's room at the cinema. This morning she looks sexy. It's a good hair day.

"You got rid of that doll right?"

"I gave it to the Salvation Army."

"We're finished with that episode?"

"The voices are more like a low buzzing now. The problem's they seem to clog up my throat sometimes, like I'm choking on something."

"Jesus Amber! What's next, the Heimlich maneuver, an emergency tracheotomy? School's not keeping you occupied enough?"

"The voices never happen at school."

"Your psychic skills only come out at home? I bet you get this psychic crap from your mom. We both know she's bat-shit crazy. Suicide runs in her family."

"You think I should go to a doctor? Or a priest or rabbi?"

"I think you're getting back at me for something. That's what's going on here. You're jealous I'm spending too much time with Penny."

"I don't give a crap what you think. I want it to stop!"

"You're not going crazy Amber. You're making my blood pressure go up."

I bring a handkerchief to my lips. I sense I'm losing Amber. She's pulling away from me. What can I do about it? I suspect her mom's the main problem here. The half-wit bitch is intent on ruining our whole family. If I could destroy her before she messed with Amber anymore the outcome would be irrevocably altered. How does that work? Where the hell's her family stashed her anyway? I imagine Amber's mom sitting on a threadbare sofa in front of a blank television screen. She's clipping her nails. Beside her a cigarette smolders in the ashtray. A KFC bucket overflows with chicken gizzards. You could put your whole dick in that bitch's mouth. I wouldn't recommend it. Leave that to the stale cinnamon rolls and bottles of cheap whiskey.

An ambulance drives past, sirens wailing, red lights flashing.

"Your mom's behind this nonsense. She gave you the doll as a birthday present remember?"

"I tried to tell her what's happening. Her phone's been disconnected. She's not replying to emails. Is it okay if I go to line-dancing lessons with the pawnbroker tomorrow?"

"Line-dancing? Hang out with bikers and cowboy types and shystery old fat guys? What's that pawnbroker's gig anyway, taking the neighbor's seventeen-year-old daughter out dancing? You gonna wear those tight cut-off jeans and eel-skin cowboy boots?"

"If I want I will."

"That man's what they used to call a satyr, a sex maniac. He's a functioning alcoholic too."

"He's never laid a hand on me. We're good friends is all."

"He never tried to put a napkin in your lap while you ate lunch?"

"He's got good manners!"

Another ambulance drives past, sirens wailing, red lights flashing.

"What else have the two of you done together?"

"You want more reasons to call him a pervert? We played miniature golf down on the Peninsula."

"You got in a car with that douche bag? That's not kosher! Your behavior's scaring the shit out of me Amber. Next thing you know he's giving you twenty bucks to blow him in the backseat."

"Another time I helped him load several bags of quick-dry cement and containers of insecticide into his car."

"What the hell's this guy up to?"

"Once we spent Sunday afternoon in the Tenderloin with a six-pack of beer and a pair of binoculars."

28

"You're paying for your own funeral."

"He told me tough neighborhoods are America's last advantage."

"You smell something? Like burning. Forget it. It's nothing, another endorphin high."

On the way to school we stop at Starbucks for a venti iced mocha and apple fritter. The barista's face is covered with pus-filled boils. His index finger's stuck up his nose. Cool. Maybe he'll break out a speech impediment or call the cops.

We sit down. Amber asks me to help her cheat on a take-home sociology exam. Hell yeah! She's not old enough to legally vote. I wish I were seventeen again. That was an awesome summer. Profound pangs of nostalgia are the scariest things that happen to me. I ought to invest in a cotton candy machine or an Andrew Wyeth painting. I feel so accomplished I ought to start paying my taxes again rather than plan an imaginary suicide bombing.

I tell Amber she's lucky Prozac doesn't kick in for the first three weeks. She's still got time. And a sunburn from the tanning bed. Back in the car I rub her smooth back with aloe to take the sting out. Her legs look fine. I tell her to slap me if I ask silly questions about her sex life. She says she hates acne and CSI Miami. Her new tattoo itches. She's decided life consists solely of random moments. Earlier this morning she spilled orange juice on her laptop. Dear tech support you suck! Nothing worse than being drunk and distracted. Decisions, decisions. Amber tells me her latest boyfriend was suspended from school for meth possession and pulling a knife in the cafeteria. She's infatuated with a strange silent Arab-looking boy. I imagine the two of them enjoying a five-dollar foot-long at Subway. They're such dorks. I remind her I'm nervous our car won't pass the emissions test tomorrow.

I'm an accomplished father. There's no point in planning an alternate strategy here. I'll keep true to these diurnal progressions and stroll right back into the gentlemen's club. Must I? It's early. Amber's safely at school. I'm the accomplished cofounder of the Arab surrealist movement.

Look at me as I proudly even luxuriantly stretch out these arms and legs and stride down the black-painted corridor. It suits my taste to stretch out these old legs. I stop, draw in a deep breath of alarm. Do I have a legal right to look at these young girls in bikinis? They share the same hair color and collapse to the floor as if they're stoned. This time I have nothing to say to Jack the Bedouin bouncer when a haggard-looking woman begins stimulating her clitoris with the three fingers of her right hand. She's like a piece of sculpture with an unnatural color. Her tushie looks too big in that tight skirt. She moans a bit to prove she's not unconscious. Her nipples rise and fall. Her eyes are slimy as silverfish. I walk past her, look for a table near the bar. My real purpose here is to enjoy hatred at very close range. I light a cigarette, stare intently into the amber depths of a bourbon on the rocks. I imagine bugs crawling up and down the club's walls. I'm so far behind the times I catch myself sneaking looks at the bartender's wristwatch. I feel like a poor old man selling shoelaces to the wrong fans of Velcro.

At this morning hour there's standing room only. I first glimpse her sitting down at a table reading a newspaper and eating an apple. She shares the table with two old men playing chess. The club's flooded with light and music. I almost overlook her, the woman I came here to see. I recognize her from last night. There she is! I push my way through the rich and variegated crowds of stoned diplomats and consulate-generals. The closer I approach, the better I appreciate the individual elements of her magnificent beauty. With those long flexible forefingers, she reminds me of a race of giant man-eating queens who are born of tragic philosophy and die of the vapors. Her stillness and concentration fascinate me, as does the way she handles that apple core with the long flexible fingers of her right hand. By the time I reach her table, one chess player has mated the other, leaving a chair open for me.

"How do you do?"

"Excuse me I have to leave now."

"Wait! What did you say your name was?"

"I said my name was Guinevere before I changed it to Candy."

"It's so loud in here I didn't catch that."

"I said my name's Candy!"

"That explains your sweet smell!"

Candy's very thin and blessed with a firm vertebral column. The secret behind her success is a tremendous idleness. I imagine she lives only on produce imported from the rest of the world, from Egypt, the city of Alexandria. I suspect she's worn out her heart and head with lust and now wants to be left alone with a lifetime's worth of exhaustion.

"Don't go yet Candy. Would some conversation suit you?"

"I have to be somewhere very soon. What's it you wanna talk about?"

"Your friend Penny."

Candy says nothing for a long while, staring off into space, pondering the implications of my request.

"I'm sorry, I missed your name."

"Rosenberg."

"That's your whole name?"

"I'm hoping we could talk about Penny."

"Are you a detective? You don't seem so friendly."

"I'm Penny's latest boyfriend, lover, whatever you want to call it."

Candy lapses into silence.

More guests arrive with more booze in tow. I count at least five ethnicities, six languages, a dozen different creeds. The club's filled with surprises this morning. One woman will drown herself in the restroom trying to read a musty Thomas Pynchon short story while a sickly-looking chess player quotes at length from a Lawrence Durrell novel. So many exhausted creatures driven to physical and psychic extremity are putting in their cameos here. It's not a laughing matter, not until later this afternoon.

"What do you want to know about Penny?"

"Where does she come from?"

"That's a weird question."

"Where did she grow up, where was she born? That sort of thing. Can you tell me where you met her?"

"In Reno, Nevada. She was working at a casino, selling meth. She was a dancer I think."

"How long ago was that?"

"About three months ago."

"You've kept in touch since?"

"Off and on here in San Francisco yeah."

"You think Penny could kill someone?"

"In self defense sure."

"How about in cold blood?"

"For the hell of it?"

"Out of boredom or rage."

"I can imagine it sure. Did Penny kill someone?"

I stare at Candy over the rim of my bourbon glass. I think back to when I first met Penny at the diner where she waitresses. That first night she sat on one of the counter stools facing the entrance, those legs crossed in a mannish attitude, those arms resting on the countertop behind her, those large breasts with erect nipples jutting out like something from the wrong side of the Mediterranean. She sat there waiting to accost mostly male patrons with a menu and a wan smile. Later the same night, after I'd donned my fake beard and mustache, she dignified me with a visit in the men's room where she kindly jerked me off before heaving a great sigh of relief in the harsh fluorescent light. I remember the men's room had mirrors on three of its four walls. The ceiling was a trifle unbalanced. Penny stared at me with an open candor I found embarrassing and uncomfortable. When the two of us returned to the dining area, two idiots from the East Bay were sitting at the counter talking about NFL football, blowing cigar smoke into the harsh light. Penny smoothed out her skirt, returned to the same stool at the counter to await the arrival of more male patrons. I imagined her hands were sticky from my semen. That satisfied me. I'd left a mark, the warm white streaks of DNA. For days afterwards I was haunted more by Penny's bloodless face than by her muscular hands or those large breasts beneath the taut fabric of an ill-fitting waitressing uniform.

"Do you have any other questions officer?" Candy giggles, stands up from the table.

"Wait! I got to thinking about something. My mind wandered."

"Aren't you nostalgic."

Candy sits back down. I notice her tone's become more supportive, even seductive. I'll think about this particular moment a lot as the tale moves forward, even obsess over it. I cannot let go of the battle-axe.

"If only life were as easy as changing TV channels."

"Oh boy you are nostalgic! Is that why you're here, to reminisce about Penny the serial killer and the good old murdering days?"

"Women serial killers are very rare. I don't buy it. Listen Candy why don't we get the hell away from here right now?"

"Go where?"

"Anywhere. Get a room for the day across the street."

Candy stands up again from the table. "You're wrong. If I don't have anything better to do till evening, I'll take a rain-check on that room."

She walks toward the exit. I follow, keeping a close watch over that small tight ass. Rest assured I don't feel bad about what's about to happen. The avenger destroys the past while the citadel strives to preserve it.

I leave the club, return to the daylight. Police sirens roar past. Every voice is a scream. The rancid stench of dog shit hangs over the city's courtyards, chambers, corridors, vestibules, what have you. Breathing's difficult. My asthma's acting up.

I turn a corner into an alleyway to find broken furniture, broken toys, dirty clothes, warehouse receipts, fragments of plastered walls and rafters that make walking difficult. Dust and flakes of fire-fall drift down from archways and balconies. Curved iron railings descend along either side of the smoky huddles to where many marble statuettes rest in the back of a convoy of large open carts. Three soldiers stand at attention, their faces and uniforms streaked with blood. Nearby a fourth soldier kneels behind a pile of cobbles. He's working the bolt of a hand-operated rifle, taking aim at the boarded-up windows above him. It's a striking scene, symbolic of freedom and the spirit of the harvest. I look at what I can with a strange lack of rage or boredom. By now the general shaking of things has set up a long vibration in my head. The distant hills across the Bay are rocking to and fro. Hints of pink are there, the stench of burst intestines. A few more isolated sniper shots before another soldier falls. Never was a man so swiftly destroyed! I'm dizzy, exhausted by the throbbing in my right temple, tired of everything out here. I want to lie down.

By the time I arrive home my nerves are scorched to the flash-point. I'm in no condition to write. On the radio and TV there's enough heated rhetoric about the imperialist aggressions of the latest World-Blower-Upper to fill several dirigibles. The copper cable's disappearing. Soon the city's electricity will be cut off at fixed intervals. The leaders of our great nation remain as irresponsible as ever, flaunting expansive gestures and rhetorical flourishes, smug in their self-righteous lack of humor, rage alternating with remorse, their behavior tense, edgy, overly serious as they caustically denounce diplomatic proposals. Their answer to every question is 'no.' The local government's issued several versions of new 'candidates.' Although each is distinguishable from the other, five chimpanzees would be equally competent. No wonder I begin thinking about spreading disease and pandemics.

I walk into the kitchen.

"What the hell am I supposed to be doing here Penny?"

Penny shrugs. "You tell me."

"I think I'll go away for a few weeks to Reno. I need some time alone."

"Could you put it off till the week after next?"

"I've made up my mind. I'll be gone next week."

"How will you get there?"

"I'll drive."

"Not with my car. I need it. Take a bus."

"That's insane! You walk around everywhere like me. You're scared to drive in the city. You can't parallel park once you get to wherever you're going."

Penny shrugs. "Meaning what?"

"Meaning there's no problem with me taking your car to Reno for awhile. Too much is going on here in the city that's keeping me from writing, too many weird distractions I can't account for."

"What are you talking about?"

"There's Amber and that doll incident. There's Goldsmith's girls at the club. You know a stripper named Candy?"

"Maybe."

"I can get the Arab surrealist movement back on track if I go somewhere else for awhile. Are you familiar with the concept of anamnesis? It's the direct opposite of amnesia. What I need to do is UN-forget some things. I can't do that around here. I need to confirm that none of this is happening for the first time. I need to go back to the earliest memories of my life if that's possible and confirm what I know. Back as far as when I was born if you can believe that, back to when my twin sister and I emerged from the womb together."

"That's what the Arab surrealist movement's about?"

"That's a good part of it. The other part's delivering a shock to the system, disrupting habits and old worn-out patterns."

"Goldsmith's behind this isn't he? That conspiracy-monger!"

"He's lurking behind everything I do and write. You know that Penny. He's a cofounder of the movement. He says conspiracies are aesthetic exercises for creating novel patterns. We've been over this before. I'm the writer, the pamphleteer, the polemicist, whatever you call it. How can I do my job if I got writer's block?"

"Why Reno?"

"That's where my mother's from. That's where my sister's buried, in a cemetery there."

"I thought your family's from the East Coast."

"They moved out here many years ago. Do we have to go through this now?"

"Your mother lives in Reno?"

"No she died there a long time ago."

"You have friends and family in Reno?"

"I don't know a single person there, only passed through once on the Interstate. That's not the point. I need some time alone. Trust me I won't be here next week. End of story."

Penny shrugs, returns to washing the dishes.

Chapter 7

In a bid to take my mind off multiple social and personal distractions, Penny drags me to an open house. She wants to get some decorating ideas. By the looks of it there's been a whole mess of drinking and drama in this particular open house. Its doors and windows are wide open. Too many episodes, too little time. This is gonna be a long boring painful worthless day. Like I'm back in the military. Twenty useless rooms and counting. No rest for the wicked. Are we drowning in the same fish bowl or what? The whole place is so stupid. I'm skeptical of these nearly abandoned foreclosed homes and the immense pressure they place on my financial well-being. It's not only a California thing. My brain begins to reel, over money this time, and why did I eat that goddamned turkey sandwich for lunch? I tell the partially naked real estate broker to go blow monkey balls. Pulling black shit from the ground's not very creative either. The broker won't shut up. Penny and I are annoyed. Is there another way out of this vandalized shell of a building? The broker describes the place as 'the aesthetics of decay.' Paint-peeling walls. Asbestos-filled pipe insulation. Plenty of skeletons. Maybe we should buy the house and rent it to photographers for moderately upsetting photo shoots or to AIDS patients and recovering meth addicts or convert it to a school for the blind. Happy birthday. I'm sure we'll be glad when that's over.

Penny and I return to the sidewalk to begin our walk home. The shop windows along this boulevard are a riot of color. A five-minute car wash here, a State Farm Insurance office over there, several wild places that cater to the waterfront crowd, block after colorful block of old Victorian row-houses, the whine of tires, stereo systems cranked to the max, the everpresent burning stench. Ragged children rush into intersections to clean windshields. A young boy in Levis and cowboy boots shakes his tambourine at me. A drunken man's dragged out of a doorway by his hair. That's the way it happens around here to strangers and the like. I'm thinking Penny only wants to get home to snort a single line. She wants to become like the rest of these jerk-off pedestrians out here trapped in the debilitations of daily routine. That's burning chili right?

In the financial district we're confronted by a large multilevel powerful-looking hotel with a revolving rooftop event center, the kind of place where billion-dollar oil deals are secured. I imagine lots of photo-ops and buzzwords, fact sheets and wall charts, video teleconferencing.

"Look Penny it's the Tyrell Corporation! Nothing's more dangerous than a queer with oil money. They don't smoke cigarettes in the lavatories of a place like that." In my best advertisement voice I begin rattling off the first-class amenities. "Prime location, a complimentary gourmet breakfast, a wine list with 500 selections, starched linens, fine crystal, baths are spacious, fully tiled, the beds with handmade oak headboards."

Penny says she prefers a more informal place, something from the Spanish colonial era, standard rooms with a Mexican theme.

We're laughing it up this afternoon. I grab a rock from the sidewalk, throw it in the direction of the hotel. I misjudge the distance. The rock bounces on the pavement across the street. A filling station attendant looks in our direction, does nothing. I haven't been in a decent fistfight for years. I have it in me today, to lay some poor sucker out on the velvety San Francisco pavement.

Who's perpetuating this incredible war? A druggist no doubt or a DJ with a congested voice looking for his peak experience. Good luck asshole that's your business. Who the hell isn't maladjusted? I'd love to kick that lady's door down over there, beat on her a bit, tie her body to a telephone pole. Nothing's circumventing these forces. I don't need ninja tactics. No stripper's hustling me for drinks. I'm the world's last great freelance writer. I stand six-feet-one in my socks. I'm the middle pillar holding up the universe with no other gods before or after me. Lord Of The Heavens Ruler Of People Operation Mindfuck.

"Holy Christ Penny I'm gonna reap fantastic karmic benefits from this walking! My Mister Nice Guy routine's over and done with. No more shit-eating grin. Reno here I come!"

That comment draws a laugh from Penny.

Everywhere I look I see only sordid sex and blackmail. It's like trying to understand the lyrics of a Bob Dylan song. No denying I'm losing my grip here. It's majestic. I'm working myself into the frenzy of a manic fit of vocal scribbling.

"So much for the media fallout. I'm another column on some shithead's tally sheet, an exercise in bureaucratic flimflam."

I gesture around me to the San Francisco nightmare.

"It's a brilliant piece of silence fiction. Better yet it's the excavation of a crime scene. Mine's the performance of the autopsy!"

From our perspective it's a seven-by-seven-mile grid of pure parallel universe, good for a few laughs though nothing worth putting on your résumé. I'm waiting for the computer hackers to prove me right. My hair isn't thinning. They're the ones looking for the winning Lotto number.

"You watch Penny! We'll give them the spirochete. I'm the world's largest creature. San Fran's the pond. I'm the eight-pound snapper. These shit-heels out here are starving. They're force-fed through the narrow slit. A small piece of tentacle clings to the net!"

Across the street I see thoroughbred horseracing telecast live via satellite. We've got better things to do. I haven't watched more than ten minutes of TV in ten years. I kicked the grass decades ago, never did heroin, didn't need that distraction. Never bled from a stab wound. I only drink alcohol now. I crave unfiltered cigarettes and chocolate-covered espresso beans. Gatorade isn't too bad. Don't forget the Dew. If the authorities want to overexpose my spotless past and give it an NC13-rating I'm not stopping them. They want the details. They have to come up with something.

Off in the distance the rapid fire of an assault weapon rings out, a warning shot, a foreshadowing of tonight's explosion at the convention center.

"So much for the elected officials Penny! If you had only one Band-Aid where would you place it on a city this size?"

Penny and I make an odd entrance to our own flat. I know if we keep the door locked we'll be safe from the cops and other underpaid pedestrians. Quickly we strip each other naked. By now the reader knows I'm fascinated by Penny's body, those incredible breasts, that round ass.

You shouldn't phone me up like this, abrupt, sudden, without a bookmark, drinking so much coffee only to complain about having to take a piss later. You know there's no such thing as 'sorry' around here. The real purpose of these episodes is illustrating mutual hatred at close range. If we keep the door locked Penny and I should be safe from the cops. Nor will we have to stop screwing if the pawnbroker gets a migraine and suffocates himself out of masturbatory self-pity while listening to our shenanigans through the walls. Nor will we compete with his pathetic suffering on some absurd psychological level. You think that's impossible? Have another look. You'll see Penny's a good lay every day of the week.

"Fear And Loathing In Las Vegas has eclipsed Pineapple Express as my all-time favorite movie!"

Penny and I crush Red Bull empties after making love. I remind her to put a bullet in me if I live past seventy-five or become flatulent in Spanish. Damn this gum's delicious! They say it's a toothbrush for your tongue!

Penny's beautiful cat keeps bringing mouse toys out to the balcony along with ear mites, fleas, worms, an eye infection. I'm trying to relax out here with a beer and vodka. Penny's inside watching Jerry Maguire and drinking a pinot noir. She's got a bikini top on though we're not going to the gym today. Turns out the puppy slurped up the leftover Froot Loops milk. Now he's got the milk shits. Sure hope I don't get the liquor shits. The ceiling fan's running on high.

Soon I'll be looking around for another place to sow my literary seeds. I've been blocked for thirty minutes. Don't banks understand customer service doesn't jibe with Theremin hold-music? I'm a bit alarmist today. Our flat's so pleasant this afternoon I feel I've known the place for ages, for lifetimes. No friendly kisses ever were exchanged here. No way. Only eternal pieces of broken furniture and glass scattered about.

The scene shifts to an interior shot of an uneasy psychological alliance between coffee and booze. There I am again, the writer with his word processor and mini-cassette recorder. Again that succession of faces parades across the green fields and thick forests and endless city blocks of asphalt and concrete. Through the chiffon curtains I watch those faces, the Tenderloin's finest. A sliver of daylight barely keeps its wits on the wide white windowsill. I'm speaking the truth now, trying to write it down. Penny does some ironing in the next room pleasantly humming and singing.

Amber's mood swings have become like every other teenage girl's in any moody city in North America. One fine day the three of us will become immobilized, unable to escape from each other's obsessive clutches while Goldsmith looks on with rage. Do you love Amber like I love you two? Don't you think we should go inside now? Isn't the day coming to a close? Penny and Amber shake their heads no. Complete stupor's only a hairsbreadth away. Thank you Allah or Yahweh, what have you, thank you Goldsmith. Mirrors climb across ceilings. Ladders lift up lanterns. Feet tread heavily on stairs leading to a narrow ledge over the Machine Room Systems Gallery. Walls and turrets, rails, fittings, ceilings ground-floor to roof, a sign reading 'Access to Adam.' Veins of eyelid wild flowers, a brilliant white blaze over steel shafts, the glittering networks of the electric blue million. Dead birds hang. These eyes close at the outermost edges of sleep to allow the ancient solstice movie electrically-sex-scene to begin.

I imagine the young strippers slouching against the opposite wall whispering among themselves. A few are spellbound. Goldsmith's administered large doses of a sedative called Greenland. Where are the additional supplies for sleepwalking? I wait. I watch a small spider crawl up the nearest wall. Five minutes pass.

I can wait no longer. The ceremony must begin.

"Someone please write this down!"

Silence.

"It's about the food I wish to speak. 'Collaborating with Death' is what we'll call it. There are two reasons. First pharmaceuticals flourish in these parts. Second microorganisms survive."

The high-ceilinged room returns to silence before the windows behind me fill with bright white light. Many recollections resurface. The young girls speak among themselves. Their eyes glow with fire. Fancy phrases fill the room. I stand back, watching the scene develop. The torches lit underground are now carried into the room by three elders.

"Have compassion for your adversary. May Satan look after us all!"

Entropy becomes significant at this juncture. Its octopus tentacles warm the cockles of my heart. When Goldsmith makes a second entrance through the fire-escape window after an argument with the babysitter over communications theory, he's clutching a dying bird to his chest rather than a decaying sea creature. I didn't conjure up that idea. Its corresponding imagery occurred to me. I'm grateful for occasions like this. New ideas and images arrive Out Of Nowhere. That's an acceptable reason why I'll be clean shaven later tonight, without the fake beard and mustache. Goldsmith's suit's the wrong color, not as I imagined it. I know it must be real. It has to be real!

"What's the matter? I'm wearing a hat and tie aren't I?"

"There's nothing the matter with your hat and tie. The color of your suit bothers me."

"How can it matter what I wear? Everyone recognizes me."

"I'm sure they do. The color discrepancy forces me to respect your powers over my imagination. I don't much like that."

Goldsmith's one of the most unforgettable characters I've ever met. I can't resist measuring some of his body proportions with a tape measure. That's how distortions begin.

"You're a slob Rosenberger, a self-seeking, narrow-minded egotist. You'll never be a great surrealist. You can't tolerate me wearing a suit you never imagined."

The noise outside the windows is gaining in power and force. Grinding metal alternates with the rude sound of hammers and saws.

We're both sitting on the bed.

"What the hell do you know about surrealism Goldsmith?"

"Why are you getting so excited?"

"There's lots going on in my life with Amber and Penny. Lately I haven't had the time to write. I'm moving to Reno."

"That's what it's like in the Diaspora huh? Gambling and prostitution in Nevada."

"I'm not listening!"

"You think you've seen every way words can surprise a writer. Along comes a character you've never imagined. You can't hack it. That's what triggers writer's block. On top of that, you can't sit still long enough to put pen to paper. Your only option is speaking into that mini-cassette recorder. I'm on to something here! You can't face the dreary necessity of battling on with a plot, which leaves you the task of reconstructing a chain of chronological events. I can do that."

"What about the fact your suit's the wrong color and I won't wear a fake beard and mustache tonight? Where's the boring chronology in that?"

"Not sure I follow Rosenberger."

Chapter 8

Turns out yoga class is canceled this evening. I need to find another distraction from writing. Anything at all. Graphic design. A greenhouse. A compost heap. A Joe Satriani tribute show. I never learned to tap dance. No point learning now.

I need coffee, a glazed donut pick-me-up, and two-ply toilet paper. Dunkin Donuts clone here I come. I've forgotten how fun it is to pick out stale donuts at a bakery. Very addictive. Very challenging. The goofy cashier wishes leg hair were sexy. Size 10's not plus size though she's returned to her pre-pregnancy weight and bruise pattern. Damn I get punched harder than that in a sparring match. You call that spousal abuse? I pick some money off the floor. I cough, taste copper. Blood?

You know you've been at Dunkin Donuts too long when the resident homeless guy gets up in your grill. Pastry crumbs collect on his lap. He needs to button his fly. He says he's guilty of complicity in Abraham Lincoln's assassination.

I leave the donut shop, walk a couple blocks, open a purple-colored door, find myself facing a shoji screen that conceals a fortune teller.

I lean forward.

"When did Penny start supplying meth to you?"

Silence.

"We've got a potential problem here lady! If she gets injured in the jump we're depending on you to come up with the money. Are we together on this? Don't make me get anyone else involved. This business may end badly."

Silence.

"Where's the security director? Does anyone else have access to the Arab surrealist movement's documents vault? Anyone else call? What the hell's going on around here?"

I'm not sure if Penny's potential injury will be accidental or deliberate. I'm not about to give away surreal secrets to an enemy of the movement, one who's hiding behind a cheap shoji screen. I shake my head, nervously run a hand over my scarred abdomen. The middle of my back is wet with perspiration. Several minutes pass. The teacup contains only tea as they say.

Penny and her stripper cronies have crossed the Medicine Line. That means we got a North African fixation on our hands and many local sponsors and kickbacks. I recall a heavy glass paperweight Goldsmith used to hypnotize a parking valet. As a joke.

Not too far from here there's a pub where retired city cops trade ideas over pints of lager. Most of those guys advertise in the Gelb Pages under the Security heading though Sandblasting's more like it. A large documents vault in the pub's basement serves as an archive for thousands of hours of plane crash footage. Large portions of that footage are sold to news agencies to fill gaps in their reporting on such catastrophes.

When I return home I resume writing. It smells like a spring evening outside. The right side of my brain's experiencing a mild orgasm. Unless I strike out for Reno soon it's gonna be a long worthless week. Internet's slow. The Arab surrealist promos look like crap. I can't wait five minutes to microwave day-old lasagna before the butterflies in my tummy are eating away at the food. I wish Penny were preparing our favorite crab linguini alfredo. She's too busy buying makeup from a TV shopping network. She wants to become a working class girl. No wonder she blow-dries her hair straight. Southern hospitality at its finest. Not sure what that means, sounds kinky, a little scary. Like penne chicken pesto or salad with blue cheese or Lost Season 4 or diehard Red Sox fans or Nevada librarians.

That's what they call March Madness? I'd rather watch stuff blow up like the way they blew up the White House in Independence Day. That was a cool science project, a chain reaction in a bell jar.

I glance outside. Our puppy's eating a dead carcass on the sidewalk. How'd that happen? Penny reminds me she's resuming her Diet Dr. Pepper diet. She sleeps the rest of the evening. I insist she needs a stylist. She doesn't have a clue what to make for dinner tomorrow. The Comcast guy never arrives to troubleshoot the Internet.

Having finished off the lasagna I sit down to write about the oddly familiar Englishman I mentioned in Chapter 3. I imagine a split-level suite with a fabulous view onto a large body of water. Incense and turmeric waft from the kitchen. Masks, many brackets, plant holders, bonsai trees hang on the walls. Other things too, including a brass-handled walking stick, cast iron galleries and porticoes, antique weaponry, military artifacts. Outside, a lush garden on a terrace faces a swimming pool where a beautiful nude woman swims laps. The Englishman turns away from the pool to concentrate on the jade vases and urns on the table beside him. The wall opposite is decorated with a fiery abstract mural of horses galloping through a flaming forest. Many oddly angled mirrors throughout the room create a deep-space projection. Very high-tech. The Englishman is overwhelmed by the 19th Century ambience of vulgar Mareotic luxuries. He sits cross-legged on the floor surveying it all. Croissants, bran muffins, coffee are served to everyone present. The actors wear their theatrical makeup. Dressed to full advantage they've been performing throughout the night and will retire after breakfast. The Englishman nervously tugs at one of his shirt's French enameled buttons. The actors eat in silence. A voice from another room announces over the intercom that Tuscan-style duck and oysters Rockefeller will be served for dinner. No mere tiffen that nor tuffet of meal. These are highly successful mid-career artists who've smelled deeply of the lamp. A sense of aristocratic complacency fills the suite.

Early on, before the blood-streaked walls, before the necklaces made from beer tabs, before my arms were scarred and sores dotted my body and I pumped bullets in the general direction of the California Penal Code, I lived in New York City. I worked there in a mannequin factory. That's right I'm an original New York Jew. Don't tell Goldsmith. He may be a lapsed anti-Semite. Goldsmith doesn't exist right? Isn't he an alter ego I insert into the story like Kurt Vonnegut did with Kilgore Trout? The original idea here was the pistol goes BANG! the audience pees their pants, the story ends. I wonder if that's the proper way to go about it. You could say Better late than never.

"Which sentence is that Rosenberger?"

"'Better late than never.' My name's Rosenberg!"

"That's crazy! You're gonna leave the audience hanging like that?"

"It's beautiful in a way."

"Why not Penny turns out to be your lover and the two of you killed a babysitter last Thursday. It was in your mind? Something surreal like that?"

"You're the one who's crazy. Anyone can dream they're running around in circles with elephants and hippopotamuses teaching them to sing four-part harmony. What I want is to get the audience into my head to help me explain what's going on in there."

Goldsmith shrugs, puts down the manuscript.

"I'm thinking something more along the lines of high-ranking German officials jump out of windows to avoid getting caught by a corrupt Nazi hunter."

"You lazy bastard!"

Goldsmith laughs, shrugs again.

"No Rosenberger. The Salvation Army exists for that."

I wince in agony, groan a couple times.

Goldsmith gets up from the bed, walks over to the window. For a long while he looks down at the pedestrians below.

I can write circles around Goldsmith! He never earned a high school equivalency certificate. Luckily I have the mini-cassette recorder with me. I turn it on now. Business is business. Seems like any writer can know nothing beyond the One Word Processor God whose first words I AM are the nothing from which every story issues. That's the essence of the truthful message of Kether, to no Nothing, namely the Law through which the Empty Word gives 6 more things to the maternal side where Mother's the stern and gentle organizer of all perceptual forms. The first triad 1-2-3 follows with the appearance of the paternal aspect of the fluid wholeness indicative of 1-ness. Those two poles now so placed, there might occur the precipitation of all that ever can be. It does, on the computer screen, as the animal-triad extreme becomes a self-reflecting consciousness whose personification of eyesight's modeled on a 2-5 cross. Thus we writers create a military-type Frankenstein-living death-fruit in accordance with the sanctions of The Council of Representatives of the Twelve Tribes of Word Processing. The family-gravestone triad of 7-8-9 logically follows that infusion of self-demonstration. Humankind's uniqueness becomes undetectable to earphones and the radio. If Kether is expendable you are too kind reader. The story concludes with Sir David Hod Jimmy, father of Talmudic Law, concealing from the cosmic dancer an entire 18-minute gap entitled PersonalBoomBoom6=1+2+3.

Chapter 9

Goldsmith it's not my fault there's no story to produce tonight! I'm tired of describing Penny's naked body. I pull at her skirt to lift it up. She squeezes those thighs shut, pressing her palms down on the fabric to keep it in place. Again I see the succession of faces. Again I call out to Allah or Yahweh, what have you. Penny's large black pupils stare right through me. What's withered passion? It's a phrase I ripped off from someone else's story. A black leather sofa and a gauzy silvery-gray robe now materialize. Penny's eyes become two empty mirrors reflecting infinity. I didn't invent that phrase. Nor is there an excuse for it. The two of us enter the waters of life to listen to the sounds of waves. We're senseless with fear. I barely manage to finish reading the story before I lead Penny outside to the taxi. I sit down beside her in the backseat.

I pretend a private detective's in pursuit as we jolt over speed bumps and curbs and maneuver past many service stations. A car's trailing us, the Secret Service I imagine. I'm enraged and bored. No one tells me anything around here. The clean-cut driver says he won a free carwash today. He's quick, experienced, clever, fantastic. Next thing you know, he's nigger this, nigger that. He's become the perfect racist deep-cover agent, a triumph of literary artifice.

In Golden Gate Park Penny and I join a few other courting couples from the Arab surrealist movement who whisper among themselves in the dark bushes. Satan sets his traps everywhere out here. We're no longer in the city I once knew. Those are no longer the same pedestrians who attempt to hide their peccadilloes. A musical sadness fills the air. The botanical gardens are covered over with old World War 2 graffiti murals. The atmosphere's so reminiscent of the Congo jungles or an Eric Bogosian play. In a mid-price trench-coat I rock heel to toe on the edge of the pavement, reminding myself Thou shalt not commit adultery tonight or disrupt long-established relationships. I imagine innumerable weeping spouses, girlfriends, boyfriends, partners, lovers, wandering Jews, Israelis. I've proven to everyone commitment is the latest form of ../../../../. Arguments vanish.

Penny and I walk and walk. We walk some more. Tonight I'm heading for the overload. My arms and legs pinion like frictionless metal. My mind's become a steel trap. Genuine velocity's building here. It's plain crazy. Gimme me some Tranquility man like what they've got up on the moon. Tranquility! Gimme a tablet of Vermilion Dream! Rip a page from your Cerise Passport! In the name of utopias and the golden cup of abominations it is 'I'! Hand me that newspaper and lighter. I've got important things to do. That cop touches me I'll take a hacksaw to his grandmother. A roundhouse blow above the right ear might do him some good, knock a little sense into that bat-shit skull of his. Would the reader prefer I smash his face through a glass countertop and take sandpaper to his eyes? No denying I'm losing my grip here. It's majestic. This is where we hope the psycho murders two children after terrorizing their babysitter. Instead the so-called authorities conspire to poison our blood with a new virus and fool the scientists into looking for a cure. Not exactly Cinemascope.

By the time we reach the far side of the park where we encounter an elaborate outdoor restaurant I feel like a real Sam Spade, a blonde Satan in search of my private Maltese Falcon. I'm the devil, I'm here to do the devil's work, my love is rotten to the core. If necessary I'll die bravely for the Red Army Chief of Staff to prove I'll never transmit Goldsmith's surreal secrets again.

The beetle-browed maître d' is a very nice guy. I gotta shoot him. How generous of me. Penny and I follow the waitress to a booth dark blue and vinyl much like the waitress herself. I ask the waitress why the vases on the tables contain Flemish-style flower arrangements. It makes no sense to me. Too bad I can't work past that incomprehensible accent. I'm not about to fondle this waitress. No face-down-on-the-mattress shit or tibial restraining straps. When I realize Koreans are serving us Szechuan cuisine a chill runs up my spine. I'll order a Coca-Cola. Nor do I care their main courses are low-fat. I didn't come here to make unhealthy eating a thing of the past. Some of the Asian women in the booths are very attractive though experience reminds me their personalities go down like a cold bowl of oatmeal. Wait! Upon closer inspection those aren't Asians at all. Those are upper-middle-class white folk with serious identity issues. Like most Chinese restaurants nothing's too scandalous about the place. Plenty of polished brass and vermilions, gilt dragons on red-lacquered pillars. Not exactly balls-to-the-wall. I get the impression behind that noisy kitchen are cold suckling pigs, opium dens, lots of gambling, no running water in the bathrooms, hanging trousers, jungles and mountains, Sikh rebels, even a German beer hall.

The restless blind man who stands across the street from the restaurant knows lots of young boys with police records and Tourette's syndrome. No one knows the blind man's real name. That's tonight's first distortion. The man's droopy mustache, greasy sideburns, heavy biceps, stunted legs form the second distortion. This guy rarely mutters hello. He wears last week's socks and underwear. The skin on his bare legs is cracked and purposeful. He's a former reptile-house keeper for the city zoo. Nowadays he wanders around San Francisco decked out in dressings akin to clerical robes. He's got nothing to do with the clergy. Rage and pain are in him. He's totally incapable of charity, forcing you to be extra careful whenever you encounter him in public. Anything can happen. He keeps you on your toes, makes you appreciate the power of a screwed-up taboo. Goodwill's not a hot topic with this man. Even the local gangs leave him alone while Colombian freelancers hover in the background. His idea of a weekend getaway's a Caribbean dope run. He's not blind at all. He only behaves that way. That's the next-to-last distortion. We decide to leave him alone with his homosexual fantasies and attempt a return to the alien city streets. That decision will be the final distortion.

At one of the few remaining public payphones I touch base with Amber. "I can't talk forever Amber. I don't have that many coins. I'm at a payphone. If you need company right now, go next door. Hang out with the pawnbroker's babysitter. Penny says hi."

I hang up and hail a rare night-roaming taxi. For much of the ride I'm bothered by a Plexiglas partition that separates Penny and me from the driver. Too many traffic lights have screwed up these surface streets. The architectural firms haven't yet made their marks down here. We pass poorly decorated outdoor music stages, taco stands, sushi bars, rundown parking garages. Traffic's heavy. We make good time on the principle that three rights equal one left. Fewer and fewer vehicles are maneuvering through a traffic-light cycle these days on account of the increasing number and size of sport utility vehicles. Those lumbering monstrosities are responsible for recent increases in vehicular pollution. We know about pollution. This here's California. Gas is cheap. I bet many of those drivers have little need for the extra space. This here's California. Anything under 10,000 square ft. is unacceptable.

"What do you know about Europe Penny?"

"Very little. I was in London once. That's it."

"I've been to London. Great restaurants there. I want to see Paris and Rome. Chandi Chowk."

I bring my mouth close to Penny's for a kiss.

"Take a vacation asshole!"

I laugh. "We've gotta come up with something here. You're a pretty woman. We're alone in the back of a cab. Damn you'd look great in black lipstick and black nail polish. How about one long slow kiss?" Penny isn't buying into my comic-book tactics. I change my angle of attack. "How about a warm soapy bath in that swank motel over there? Think of it as our honeymoon cottage."

Penny's eyes read like a do-not-disturb sign. "We need to get you some food Rosenberg."

The taxi's approaching a thirty-screen cattleplex and a huge parking lot packed with Camrys and Honda Quaaludes. No curtains hang on those windows. No one seems at home there. The place could use a potted plant or two. When did they put it up? What did they tear down to make room for it?

I point. "I call that defacing public property. They've made timeless landscapes obsolete." Too bad the commercial architects forgot to bring in the feng shui experts. I predict the whole goddamned thing will be destroyed in the coming earthquake. "Those movies they're showing are for the crowds who chew sugarless gum and watch reruns of America's Funniest Home Videos."

A defaced Diet Coke billboard sets off another association-chain. "I haven't had a cream soda in years. Remember Shasta? Whatever happened to Shasta?"

Lots of teenage types are streaming from the theater now. The midnight shows are letting out. In other states they have cow-tipping. Around here it's an evening with Mom & Pop's Gold Card at Nordstrom followed by a midnight matinee. Nighttime doesn't prevent any of these dimwits from wearing designer sunglasses.

I tap on the plastic partition to get the cabbie's attention. He slides back the plastic.

"Yes sir?"

"You think there's a chance we're being followed?"

"I don't know sir. I don't think so."

"Have passengers ever asked you to follow a car?"

"Sometimes."

"Have they asked you to follow a cop car?"

"I don't believe so."

"Do you ever pretend you're being followed to make your job a little more exciting?"

"No sir."

I lean back. The driver slides the partition back in place.

"There you have it Penny. The driver never pretends."

Penny continues filing her nails.

Before exiting the taxi I ask the driver to explain his hands. He cannot.

It's a total kind of change. Tonight my favorite gentlemen's club is very crowded. Young men and women slide in and out of leather booths and peel each other off mirrored walls. Demonstrators, environmentalists, striptease artists, they're getting drunk and stoned, toggling each other's joysticks, pitching forward impatiently to make a salient point, the hypertrophied muscles of their upper bodies attempting to sweep aside all medical concerns. The scene gives an initial impression of what's the word? Socialness? Is that a useful word to coin here? Sociability?

Communal togetherness? Is that a meaningful phrase or a string of letters and white spaces I'm conditioned to pass over in the midst of a rapidly reading text? My point is these patrons are experiencing an odd form of fully functioning professionally conditioned autism, what the experts once called egotism or, in its more extreme manifestations, psychopathy. Conversations overlap and interrupt, lurching and tripping over each other's conversational tentacles worse than in a John Updike novel. Taken as a whole the voices sound like they're participating in a collective heart attack. On top of that, rather beneath it, the sounds of drums and bass guitar percuss against the walls and hardwood floors to enhance the general sense of urgency.

The voices are many and varied.

"What are you doing here?"

"You've never tasted this stuff before?"

"We can do it now if you want or after the lap dance."

"What are those attack dogs barking at outside?"

"No need to concern ourselves with that now."

"The light in here is such an imposition on our facial expressions."

"That's the asshole right there on TV!"

"What's he doing? Operating according to the laws of chance?"

"Her art's indebted to some sort of demyelinating disease."

Penny sits on a pastel-colored modular seating unit. I'm standing ramrod straight. We're waiting for Goldsmith to arrive. A draft's coming from the kitchen. I don't like it when the stench conjures dirty and disagreeable fantasies of my mother and father. I don't like how the mirror behind the bar doubles the size of the club, making it more menacing or monotonous depending on your mood.

I order a vodka and tonic. Penny orders a shot of vodka. She's sharing the modular seating unit with a young man named William Brown and his little wife who has beautifully full arms. I enjoy their company and their comparisons of restaurants in London, Toronto, New York, and Boston.

Candy's not working tonight.

First thing Goldsmith says when he walks up is "What have the two of you been doing?"

"Plotting your murder you bastard."

Goldsmith smiles.

"You'll excuse me for a moment?"

Goldsmith walks in the direction of the men's room.

"What's he doing?"

"What's it look like? He's going to the men's room."

"Let's dance!"

Penny adjusts her skirt hem. I adjust my fake beard and mustache, reminding myself every delay has its pleasures, even the climax of a Thomas Pynchon novel. I imagine Rick Moody and Pynchon sharing the same literary agent, meeting in a New York City bar to discuss something surreal from the late 1960s or early 1970s.

Goldsmith returns carrying a gin and tonic.

"Have you settled on a way to murder me yet?"

Wrong! We don't have to do anything we don't want. We'll remember this moment for the rest of our lives, the night Penny and I returned home to find everything missing including Amber. We got a kidnapping on our hands right? WRONG! Amber's downstairs hanging out with the pawnbroker and his baby daughter. She's pawned off most of our belongings and is now watching our TV in the pawnbroker's living room. Isn't TV wonderful? The stories they broadcast! Here we have a sick and dying writer in a race against time to locate his long lost daughter. How did she vanish? Is she his daughter? Are you holding? Stay tuned!

Before gathering up Amber I ask the pawnbroker to explain his hands. He cannot.

A whole week of this shit!

One of Penny's tits is hanging out of her dress. Her panties are bunched up in one hand. She's trying to prepare a late-night dinner on a food-encrusted hotplate. Enchilada soup. She's tweaking big time. Penny's been injecting meth into the iron gates of her left arm for the past week. She's on the verge of running out. Rationing threatens her with paranoia. I know she hasn't eaten real food for several days.

Purple and green become the dominant notes here tonight. That's part of the reason why the story turns more difficult. Taylor Street. Turk & Taylor?

Outside our flat's window I watch the fog roll in along with the junkies, bums, hustlers, parolees, what have you. I count them off one by one. A gangbanger over there, a gutter-punk right here. Is that one a transsexual, a transgender, or a fat girl with no boobs? They're exquisite entertainment even while I know they reek of urine and feces. Thank God I smell coffee coming from an open window next door. I watch a drunk driver sideswipe a fire hydrant and a couple parked cars, setting off a car alarm. He'll never drive without a license again at least till next weekend. I watch a hooker climb up on the hood of a parked car, pull up her blouse, press her pathetic tits against the windshield. I watch a dealer down there. I recognize her beneath the effulgent blue light of a liquor store's neon sign, a round-faced Hispanic woman with wrinkles around her mouth who's lost in an oversized puffy coat. Her lips are dry and parched. She wets them constantly with her tongue. I know she's got rocks stashed all over her, in that toothless chasm of a mouth, in those pockets, in a baggie up her vagina? No way, not till next weekend. Watching the scene develop makes me wish I had a Ph.D. in sociology. I'd write a masterpiece of a dissertation on social deviance and become a millionaire.

I can hear them screaming at me from down below.

"Kill the bloody surrealist! Don't let the miscreant get away! Lynch the murderous crank!"

Gunshots ring out in quick succession.

Too horrible to contemplate extracting those bullets.

I cackle like an insane actor.

"Lantern slides! That explains the surrealist's psychosis!"

Behind me in our dim flat Penny continues to lose control. She's in the bedroom rummaging around in a large chest of drawers. That's not mere curiosity for the absurd. Her eyes are shifting faster than normal. She tells me in a scratchy voice the railroad company's been repairing sections of track that run through a nearby vacant lot and she was scoring meth off one of the repairmen before he was murdered near a drag queen bar not far from here. He was there that night for the speed not for the cock. His coworker fled town, returned to North Carolina.

"You found what you're looking for?"

She hasn't. That's not what tweakers do. They find sores instead and speaking optimistically a scab or two to pick at in the bathroom mirror until more elaborate combinatorial-type tweaking becomes necessary and theft of useless objects kicks in. She finds a bag of Skittles to tear apart and put back together again. Her heels make businesslike clicks on the scuffed hardwood floor as she goes about her increasingly aggressive tweaker business. She says she might be able to score some shit off the neighbor's roofer friend.

I tell Penny to crash. She's earned it. Let it happen. Crash all the way down to the utter bottom.

"What are you doing? You can't vacuum a hardwood floor. It makes no sense!"

A whole week of this shit!

Both of Penny's tits are hanging out of her dress. Her panties are bunched up in a corner on the floor. She's not preparing dinner, enchilada soup or anything else. She's tweaking big time, losing control of what she doesn't own, of what she never had. Her lips are dry and parched. She wets them with her tongue. Her eyes roll with terror. For the past week she's been injecting meth into her left arm. Now she's running low and the rude clerk working behind the counter at the SRO down the street doesn't give a shit. Why should he? He hates his job. He's got a learning disability. He doesn't want to get laid. Why the hell's he wearing a tailored suit with that sleazy clip-on silk tie?

Penny starts swinging at me acrobatically with a 'Skittle stick.' She's got a strong tight little body tonight. She attacks the aquarium. Sure glad I'm not a tropical fish right about now!

I return to the window. Like me everyone around here's 'between jobs' heuristically speaking. Everyone else has got booze and drugs if they ain't got AIDS and schizophrenia. Maybe they got those too. Making fun of it all helps me make sense of it all. I should do the research, write the dissertation. Stick needles in my arms, chug Bacardi 151 straight, slam dice-cups down on bar-tops, wear an old cracked black leather jacket, die of an overdose on a Muni bus, go native, return to proclaim the end of a minor civilization. I know I'd be a millionaire.

Instead I use a Phillips screwdriver to remove four screws from the frame of a window screen. My solar plexus thrums and vibrates with anticipation. Before crawling through the opening I take a miniature digital gizmo from my pocket and press the button with an overly dramatic Brechtian flourish. Behind me I imagine a beautiful view of the theatrical fourth wall from the crest of Potrero Hill. The elevated Route 280 extension cuts south across Market to lead me back home. Early tomorrow morning I remember I'll never become a millionaire while acting like a run-of-the-mill home-breaking criminal.

Chapter 10

Next morning when Amber and I leave the car at the smog testing facility I feel like we're released from jury duty. First we stop off to buy some chips and a six-pack of Corona. We listen to a lady have a profanity-laced conversation with George Bush on the bus. I wanna buy that lady's kidney, like it's a used car lot. I wish she were unconscious. I bet her thighs are sore. That never fails to turn me on.

Wednesdays are my day off from writing, the day I embrace writer's block, the day I can shake my fists at the sky.

How bizarre that everyone in the Tenderloin will soon be silent except for me. It's bizarre. That's how life works around here. You can think of anything, anything at all. If you think about it long enough it becomes bizarre as hell and no bloody good anymore. It's sad. That's how life works around here. I should know. I'm experienced, competent, often quite bored and enraged. I've never seen so much nothing on a Wednesday morning. My eyes are dry as stones.

I feel relief and anticipation as I grapple my way up the tree branches at Powell and Market. I hold the wine bottle by the neck. I'm thirty-eight years old. I'm still revising the Richter scale. That explains the beans, the mild weather, the two pubs, the filling station across the street.

I begin screaming at the pedestrians below.

"Let the word go forth from this place and time. I'll bring modern political democracy to its highest pitch only to wipe it out!"

The morning's pulled me outside myself, made nothing impractical. I've become Basilides speaking through Carl Jung on his way to Symzonia. I could persuade every woman out here to suck a live shark. I'm not taking any more shit from this Empire of Lies. San Francisco's nothing less than a bold pen-and-ink drawing. I'm seeking out Goldsmith next. I can picture it now, him waiting for me in a sedan or better yet, a crazy drifter rushes out of the shadows and I blow him away. I behold a vast horizon of positive associations in Reno. No wonder I'm not spending any more time looking for the body of that worthless babysitter. This whole city might be demolished a year after the last photograph. I'm smiling.

My mind teeters on the edge of a soaring cliff. I await the proper shove. My identity is that of a traveler existing outside the scope of profane time yet within an imaginary circle of wood. It's been too long since those days of true sailing. No holding back now! My boat's packed to the gunwales with salmon. Yahweh or Allah, what have you, has become the Ultimate Control Point, The Master of Man, The Hub of the Wheel, The Body of the Octopus.

Amber talks me down from the tree before the cops arrive.

We resume our stroll.

Soon we're approaching an old Buick parked along the street. Its horn is blaring. When we reach the car we find a body slouched over the steering wheel.

"Son of a bitch!"

Without missing a beat I cup my hands around my mouth and yell. "Call an ambulance someone! We got a problem over here!"

You know something's up when the motor's running and the car's immobile.

"There'll be issues of probable cause on that one for sure."

Amber agrees.

Within minutes we hear sirens in the distance. It feels great initiating a new chain of events.

Everywhere we walk this morning we encounter minor catastrophe. What does it mean? Set up by Goldsmith? Another one of his over-the-top San Francisco-style pranks? A sneeze gathers in the bridge of my nose. I sneeze twice, a brilliant achievement, with broken glass and things overturned, an M7.

We're beneath a freeway overpass. The traffic's loud under here, energizing. I pick up a rock, hurl it into the darkness. "Not the ideal place for photosynthesis. The air's not honey. Where's the tulips and lutes? Gotta give the scum more room to move. It ain't easy stifling your shrieks of pleasure in the wastes beneath a freeway overpass, no lights, no action, no running commentary except my own."

Amber makes it clear I've said more than enough. Her mouth's tight as a tiny keyhole. I've struck a match on the gates of hell.

I cringe when we pass a rundown luncheonette with dull yellow walls. "That's a good place for a venereal sandwich and the house specialty Foil-Wrapped Grease Bomb."

A man wearing olive coveralls eats a burger at the counter. The way he chews and swallows looks like a dog gagging on a bone. He must be a regular. The cook pays him no heed.

Here's a church undergoing extensive remodeling.

"Ever scalped tickets?"

Amber hasn't.

Where would you stand? How would you settle on an asking price?

"That Italian deli over there looks good. Handmade Italian bread's the best!"

We walk many more blocks, miles of blocks in both space and time. I'm gonna blow out a knee.

We hit a lull. Rows of vacant weedy lots need a real hosing down here in the valley of the doll parts. Overturned roadside shopping carts. No Olympic-sized swimming pools. Even the bike paths avoid these parts. I'm expecting a maniac to turn the dogs loose on us. Not the place for elegant seaside dining. Most of the green tropical tint is gone. The palm trees look sooty. The lawns are leftovers. Studying the few billboard advertisements reminds me how much I've read over the course of my adult life, thousands of books and magazines. I own a single book, the Koran, which I stole from a mosque. I've got a wallet full of library cards. Each of my images originates from a public library somewhere in the United States, images accessible to everyone, yet only the Arab surrealist movement can do what it does best. The Zen Ring's closing. The time's Now.

I'm not one to differentiate a yard sale from a garage sale. Still, the houses around here are homemade, complete with an ironing board that folds out from the wall and a front porch that doubles as the family room. I imagine lots of spousal abuse behind those ratty-looking shades. How I yearn for a deep drag on a meth pipe to help me through this. It's tough down here. Beaten useless under Harmony by the amplifying effects of self-hangmen & rope-gangsters, Public Understanding has been dragged by its chains into the prison cell of maximum-security Helplessness. The unique human lowest self has surrendered to the Other while the lowest deadly sin transforms into a windowless booth's view onto the drunken bed-play of local government officials. Former President Dwight 'puppet-gangster-slave' Eisenhower, commander of Service Troops Divisions 4&54, instigated the turbulent animal-nature of World War 2. Afterwards he insisted no harmony-crime was brought against him. The worst criminal menace alive had injected its Gangster-impulse into others. The historians who scribble in chicken manure inform us postmodern history will cease only when a President is assassinated for life as an insane gangster. Oi vay.

Chapter 11

Is today Ash Wednesday? Go to hell dumbass! Can't you see I'm bowling with my daughter?

Amber tells me she's failing four classes, she hates life, her teachers are feeding her muscle relaxants and instructing her Canada's a city, and the goddamned Gardasil shot hurts like an asshole. God I love watching the San Francisco educational system go right down the toilet!

For lunch we eat imitation Thai food at a Denny's clone. Amber says the nightmarish voices are coming on like gangbusters, her best friend Vicki got a nose-job, a red bra's funny on a waiter. Amber's damn cute today. I know I'm required by law to say how proud I am of my daughter. She's too smart and precocious for her seventeen years. She's wearing an orange and magenta silk sundress and bright green glittery nail polish. She smells like gummy bears. She's glad I got her out of going to the Ice Crystals show with the pawnbroker. Rest assured I'm not letting him take her to Victoria Secret. That guy's bat-shit crazy and mildly retarded. Amber and I might feed him dog treats and rub chili on his face. Before the separation. Don't get me started. I lost lots of money at the Vegas black-jack tables. In the game of literary life victory does strange things to me.

The two of us are walking from the edge of North Beach to the Golden Gate Bridge. On our way we're forced to sidestep the tourists eating bacon-wrapped hotdogs. Amber's telling me about her obsession with Thai food and a random late-night baking of banana nut muffins and how she hopes to get a new job as a merch girl for a local rock band. She's painted her nails lime green. Holy Christ. Has spring arrived? Total psyche out.

The homeless guys around here are nasty pieces of work, their faces wiped out from heartburn and vehicular pollution. They're hard as rock, tough as nails, real bastards, here to stay. San Francisco's finest. Many of them are Vietnam vets caught in the line of fire, their brains one messed up mess. On the positive side where no hope exists fear's also impossible. Who can trust them? Not even the manager of a rolling-lab.

A white '88 Mercedes with heavily tinted windows slows down beside us. I stop walking, stand there undecided. The car comes to a slow rolling halt a few yards ahead. I lean against the fender of the nearest parked car, setting off its alarm. Man I go into orbit. It's an extremely loud alarm, a triple cross with five wounds. I hope its owner quickly deactivates it. Amazing how a sudden repetitive noise changes the mood of a place. My rhythm will be thrown off tomorrow. I tell Amber I gotta sit down. We find a vacant bench in the Marina.

I speak at length.

"Strip malls lack the hierarchic aspect, tending to blur into one another as you drive down the boulevards. That view is different from the sidewalk. Down here it's pure creative imagination. The higher forces are circumvented."

To prove my point I stand up, stride into a large 7-pillared video arcade, shout in a loud commanding voice. "This store closes in five minutes!"

Everyone takes note of my presence.

Five minutes later many desperate-eyed patrons are seen leaving.

Ten minutes later we strike the Comstock Lode, a 24-hour Safeway supermarket awash in glaring white light. Shopping carts are everywhere. Many vehicles maneuver in and out of angled parking spaces. Right beside the entrance stands a whole rank of colorful vending machines and rubber mats. It's a spectacle of pure chaos, the bloodless idea run amok. I love every aspect of it. We've come upon the land of the 10,000 things. Wading into the flow of customers is an intense form of S&M, exhilarating, epiphenomenal, a real panic situation. Having been unwilling to expose my skin, I never learned to swim. Here I'll take the plunge. Unfiltered Camels, chocolate-covered espresso beans, rehydrated diet soda, red paper napkins are sold inside there. The prospect of locating them in the maze of aisles sends me into mental convulsions. I scan the sales posters that cover the windows, the jagged numbers and dollar signs, the dynamic typefaces. It's not about sex here. How do the managers deal with cross-ventilation in a store this size? This is a 24-hour-a-day-7-days-a-week operation. Unbelievable! Imagine the responsibilities necessary to keep it functioning according to plan. What about the walls and floor if I set the roof on fire? I feel vulnerable and inept thinking about it. How large is the support staff? Where can I sign up for a customer identity card? Who's the brilliant mind looking down on it all? The sackers seem superior to me. I never once sacked groceries.

"How long's it been since supermarkets had hardwood floors?"

The motion of time's staggering. Amber's stunned by it as much as me. A white Cadillac limousine passes us in the parking lot. Who requested it? A woman trips on a curb-stop, spraining her ankle. I rush across the lot to help her up. She'll be fine. Some of her groceries fell onto the tarmac. I pick up two roles of paper towels, shaking them at her. "Why did you choose this brand ma'am?"

The woman's speechless for a moment. "It was on sale."

I help her into the car, a beat-up Ford Taurus. Well past the stage of low-rise hipster pantyhose, this specimen's decked out in loose-fitting sweatpants. Her buttocks sag. I zoom in on the fine hairs above her lip, hastily pull back. Her car's interior reeks of stale cigarette smoke. Stuffed animals are arranged on the back window ledge. It's another world to me, no walloping action-packed thrills here, no military coups or psychotropic revelations. If this is her life, it's theoretically interesting. As she drives away I wave her good-bye one limb at a time. Capitalism provides for everyone with or without the assistance of wall-unit furniture. Who said the laws of a nation must presuppose its economic structure?

A bit later Amber and I kill some time at a specialty store along the same street where there's a full-scale mock-up of the so-called Black Widow. I've never seen anything like it. Luminous, 14-carat, glistening. No wonder so many bored children are attracted to these barely legible headstones.

"Rats and railroad tracks. For too many years we were the victims of their narcissism. America must now recognize the dangers of constant carnival."

Later we're stranded at the Olive Garden. Bread sticks, salad, and leaky pipes in the restroom. Why am I eating this perforated cardboard? Why do eyeglasses make my daughter look and act so adult-like? Why does she fail to grasp proper apostrophe usage?

"Daddy I wish this day was one big flashback. I could set my mind off to the side."

"Off to the side like in a savings account?"

"Put it away for awhile, not be bothered by it. This humming's driving me crazy. The voices are mumbling in there."

"There are people who believe you can put your mind off to the side as you say. They're called Buddhists. They train themselves to put their minds away post-production like. They go about living as if nothing happened."

"That gets rid of the voices?"

"It gets rid of pretty much everything, everything you ever learned and believed in."

"You act like a zombie or a parking valet?"

"They call it nirvana. Life's no longer so appalling or harrowing. I recall the phrase 'extinguish the flame of suffering.' It's more like lights-camera-action! You become an actor in your own comedy. You write the lines as you go along. The main thing is you're not living a delusion."

"Am I?"

"We're deluded one way or another. When we look around ourselves, we see what we believe we ought to see. We believe what we ought to believe. Someone else taught us to believe it. What if those beliefs came from a deluded moron?"

"My life could be one big flashback?"

"If you believe it. In your psychology class did they teach you about the Rorschach inkblot test? There you go. Everything in life's a Rorschach test, a supermarket aisle, that parking lot across the street, everything. This very moment I'm seeing what I believe I ought to see. I could be deluded."

"You've thought this out."

"I'm laughing constantly. If I'm deluded I'm not to blame. The generations before me were screwed up in the head. They put their delusions in me when I was a child and screwed me up. Whole societies and communities get deluded and stay that way forever."

"Like how I thought God had a long white beard and shiny false teeth when I was a little girl. Where did I get the idea?"

"Your mom no doubt. What do you think now when you hear the word God?"

"Nothing. There can be no image that corresponds to that word."

"Damn straight! The good news is parents and teachers can stop delusion once they themselves are no longer deluded. I'm doing my goddamned best not to be deluded in this life. Repeat after me, Firm belief is a prison."

"Firm belief's a prison."

"If you believe that, you may have the one delusion that keeps you from being deluded by the other delusions out there. You're on the outside looking in. No matter what someone tells you to believe you can't be deluded by it."

"If it gets rid of the voices I'll do it."

"That belief doesn't get rid of anything. The world looks and sounds the same. The difference is you're outside looking in. When you're detached who cares about voices in this restaurant or in your head? Nothing's left except a big bag of bones, blood, the rain, and a thousand bucks' worth of X-rays."

"You want some more breadsticks?"

"Here's another example Amber. Earlier this week I was deluded into believing Penny was a murderer. I saw things like a shopping bag dripping blood, a blood-stained saw. That led me to believe she was murdering people, dismembering their bodies, burying the pieces in parks throughout the city."

"Jesus!"

"That's my point. I was deluded by the beautiful logic of the thing. I connected the dots, deluded myself. Turns out Penny's stealing cuts of meat from the diner where she waitresses. That's all."

"Isn't that illegal?"

"As I sit here I'm aware I'm laboring under other delusions. It's my job as cofounder of the Arab surrealist movement to figure out what those delusions are. For instance what's Goldsmith's gig?"

"Screwing bag ladies you told me."

"I could be deluded about that too."

We finish our meal in silence.

As we leave the restaurant Amber reminds me she's babysitting for the pawnbroker this evening. She needs to return home as soon as possible. Don't forget I'm the one babysitting Amber right now. She reminds me she wants to attend makeup and fashion school after finishing high school. Very intense stuff. Like tire changing lessons. I'm careful to remind her it's never okay to stick random things up your butt. Planning a funeral's worse than attending a wedding. Damn I've been invited to a wedding reception tonight. Amber wants nothing to do with it.

Luckily I manage to hail a rare street-roaming taxi. I open the door, push Amber inside, wave her goodbye before strolling off into the evening. It's times like these I miss the night.

Back at my favorite gentlemen's club I sit down in my customary pale green Naugahyde booth.

First thing I notice is Goldsmith's eyes are yellow.

"You sick? You don't look good Goldsmith."

"Liver problems."

"Lay off the booze."

"It's not booze-related. Bad drugs."

"Have you seen a physician about it?"

"I am a physician! I'm a busy man. I don't have time for strange doctors."

"You do have time for liver failure? Maybe enroll in a liver detox program."

"Maybe mind your own business. I thought you were supposed to be in Reno by now."

"That's your car alarm going off outside?"

"Bullshit."

"Why didn't you answer your phone earlier today?"

"You should've left a voicemail if it was urgent."

"I hate answering machines."

"I'm ordering an egg-salad sandwich on rye with a pickle on the side."

"I'll take the rice and beans."

"Keeping it simple?"

I get up from the booth, go off in search of the men's room. On my way there I encounter Santiago the bartender.

"Rosenberg haven't seen you in awhile!"

"Could you direct me to the men's room?"

"Keep going in the direction you're going. You can't miss it. Proceed with caution."

"What?"

"Just kidding. You're amazing Rosenberg. I can never figure out what category you belong in."

"I'm a writer is all. Put me in that category. A writer who's about to piss his pants."

Santiago's a martini expert. He's popular, knows lots of people, enough to form a medium-sized bowling league. He gives the impression he might've been evil in a prior earthly existence. Every woman wants to screw him.

The men's room's brighter than a goddamned flashbulb. I have to squint to take a leak. I wonder when the interrogation begins.

A man sidles up to the next urinal. He's sickly and pale, with the type of skin that bruises at the faintest touch.

He turns to me. "You're Rosenberg aren't you?"

"Why do you wear a black glove in the men's room?"

"Isn't 'glove' an amazing word? It rhymes with 'love.'"

"And 'shove.'"

"I wear the glove. My hand's badly disfigured, scarred from a burn. I don't want to make people uncomfortable."

"You're making me uncomfortable standing there. I have to pee."

"Don't let me distract you."

"I'll try not to. Can I ask you something?"

"Sure."

"Did Goldsmith do that to you? Mess up your hand."

"I'll never forgive him for it. The bastard betrayed me, sold me out to the cops. This is what I get in return."

"From Goldsmith?"

"From the cops. They're bandits motivated by greed. No justice. They might as well be smugglers."

"What's Goldsmith got to do with it?"

"He manages the club. He's responsible."

"For what?"

"For my hand!"

"You're not making any sense."

"You're drunk."

I flush the urinal and zip up.

"I'd say you and me don't stand on formality Rosenberg. Why you hang around here talking into that tape recorder? You keeping tabs on Goldsmith and Santiago? What's your gig man?"

"My gig man is I'm a writer. I'm taking notes on what I see and hear to put in my stories. Got it?"

"I take you for a nark!"

"Interesting work if it's available. Not my line."

"You're real clever Rosenberg. You're still a nark."

"You mean an undercover police informant?"

"You're a nark!"

When I return to the booth Goldsmith's vanished, leaving me alone with two vodka and tonics. He didn't order any food. I nurse the drinks for awhile, twiddle my thumbs, allow my feelings to alternate between rage and boredom. When I start to separate those two feelings they reveal the truth about my situation, about what a cold bastard I am. I start to see things in an unpleasant way. I feel embarrassed for Amber. Her father's not acting like a real father. He's acting like a rebel who thrives on hostile circumstances, like an artist who's overly concerned with how readers will remember him after he's thrown in prison and gang-raped. He's obsessed with eternity. Who can blame him? Forever's more permanent than the latest bullshit psychodrama. I look around at the club's patrons. They want their mommies? What a way to be remembered!

The club's music has a strong primal beat that reminds me of a porno movie soundtrack. Doesn't that have meaning too? I restrain myself from going up on stage and masturbating in front of everyone. I'm not a Neanderthal. I'm educated in the arts, sciences, and ethics. I own a camel skin coat. The clientele may not want to see me squirt semen across the stage. Doesn't that image have meaning for the reader? When I'm not flat broke I have my own way of imagining things.

A rail-thin miserable-looking stripper sits down across from me in the booth. She has a ruddy complexion that comes from overmedication. I recognize her. I've forgotten the name. She looks like an extraordinary mannequin. I reach for her sleeve. "I love your outfit. Is it rubber?"

"Get your hands off me you piece of shit!"

She stares straight ahead at the wall behind me like it's a beautiful TV set.

"That outfit looks good on you."

"I'm your date only till this song's over. I'm gone!"

"Where'd you read that line?"

"In your dreams."

"Don't tell me that. Pretending's contagious."

"What's your problem?"

"What's your name?"

"Sarah."

"Put your hands on the table Sarah. I said put your hands on the table."

"Why? Go to hell!"

"I wanna see your wrists and forearms. I like those gold earrings too. They're sexy."

Sarah says nothing, begins staring at the wall again.

"You're spending your paycheck on smack aren't you Sarah?"

"Eat me!"

"What do you think Goldsmith will say about that?"

"None of your goddamned business."

"I'm gonna kill you!"

Her body bolts upright.

"That got your attention. Listen closely. I know you like to live it up. That's not what's important here. What I'm talking about is a dead body, a corpse stowed away in a Tenderloin flat with a neon sign flashing across the street to give it a sleazier more romantic feel. Follow me?"

Sarah nods.

"I'm sure you know where Goldsmith fits into that scene."

She nods again.

"Also where you fit in."

She nods a third time.

"What's your T-cell count?"

She shrugs.

"What?"

"I don't know!"

"You know where to score dope. Explain that. Explain the discrepancy between drugs and disease."

She says nothing, stares down at her hideous-looking fingernails.

"The discrepancy adds more suspense, a bit more excitement to your disease-ridden life, makes it less boring, more bearable. Get the hell out of this booth before I request Goldsmith!"

The music changes to someone dragging iron furniture across the stage, reminding me of real-life bandits like Jesse James and John Dillinger. Some form of banditry must underlie the Arab surrealist movement. I get out the mini-cassette recorder.

Santiago comes over, sits down in the booth.

"Santiago who's the dimwit in the toilet with the black glove?"

"I have no idea what you're talking about."

"Count yourself lucky."

"You don't mind if I talk to you Rosenberg? You're not doing anything important."

"Nothing I can't put off till later."

"A lot of the strippers around here are scared out of their minds. Goldsmith's terrorizing the broads with threats and drugs."

"That's normal Santiago. If the girls don't like him they're free to find another line of work. Goldsmith knows what he's doing. He ratchets up the fear to help the girls keep their erotic focus. It's normal."

"Hear me out on this. Goldsmith's crossed a line that's way beyond normal."

"Super-normal, trans-normal?"

"Rosenberg I'm serious! I swear to God Goldsmith has lost it. Like he's got cabin fever."

"He feels trapped?"

"He's a caged animal. It scares me."

"I don't see it. I'm looking around myself. It's the same gentlemen's club since I started coming here."

Santiago leaves the table in time for Goldsmith to replace him.

I tell him he needs a blue sport jacket to set off that yellow complexion.

"What I need's a new watch. This one tells the correct time only twice a day."

Goldsmith's eyes are yellow, bloodshot, swollen.

"Why the hell did they move those potted palm trees into the banquet room?"

"Unlike you Rosenberger not everyone's here to knock back shots of bourbon and get a lap dance."

"Yeah there's tequila for the malfunctioning boozers and art fags jerking off under the halogen-lit palm trees. I get it. You're going for the Laguna Beach motif. Ouch that's my foot!"

"Let me buy you a drink, a strong drink that'll make you feel lucky to be alive."

"You brought your checkbook? I don't need a drink to feel lucky to be alive.."

"An espresso. A couple fish tacos. What's wrong? You're gloomy."

"It's Amber."

"Screaming at the teachers with that nasty mouth of hers?"

"She's bat-shit crazy, a total basket-case. She's complaining more and more about voices, hearing things that keep her up at night."

"Things that aren't there?"

"Imaginary things."

"That's your realm Rosenberger! She's inherited your imagination. Put that one in the plus column. You've got a young subversive on your hands."

"God forbid another expert at avoiding earthly pleasures."

Goldsmith points. "Recognize that blonde over there, the blonde with gorgeous tits?"

"She your latest mind-rape?"

"You sure I can't buy you a drink to loosen you up a little? A Seven and Seven or a Bluebird Canyon?"

"What's that?"

"A new cocktail we're serving. Let me introduce you to that blonde."

"She's not my type, too thin and drawn."

"Look at those tits, the concentric circles around the nipples!"

"Tits on a skeleton, fake mannequin tits."

"Saline or silicone, what do you do think Rosenberger?"

"Is she drunk? Look at that expression on her face."

"She's got a deviated septum that makes her a chronic mouth breather. She salivates a lot. Let me introduce you. She'll take your mind off that deranged daughter of yours."

"What's that bulge in her panties?"

"She's a transsexual."

"You bastard! You got the wrong guy in the wrong century! Don't do this Goldsmith!"

"Sometimes the desperate have no choice. Okay, tell me how you plan to deal with Amber. What's Penny think?"

"Amber hates me.

"Let her hate you. She's grown up. She's doing her own thing now."

"I need to be alone. I don't know why I'm here. I need to be alone to figure out what to do with Amber."

"Put her in the prayer line at one of those tent revivals in the Central Valley. Bang her head against the wall several times. That'll jar loose the dark forces. I can hear it now. My name is legion – we are one!"

"You're a real master of the Yiddish language Goldsmith. How dare you mock me! This is more than tradition. This is blood."

"You're paranoid. You think your daughter's got a crack in the head. It's only growing pains, a passing phase. The experts have a million words for what she's going through. You should've been a Christian like me before you became a Muslim. You wouldn't be so paranoid."

I avert my face, clasp my hands to my ears. I can't make the data stand still. The surroundings hardly inspire confidence. It's as if I we're discussing the fate of twenty thousand dollars of stolen money. I realize Amber's got zero choice in the matter of her deluded mind. Despite her precocity she's far too young to have any standard by which to judge her distance from the Straight & Narrow. The voices must stop. They're an abomination to the idea of an intact soul. Amber's mom's not Jewish by blood or by choice. I'm the closest thing Amber's got to the Jews if you believe in religious blood ties. If you don't? I haven't told Amber. This ain't Israel yet. The Arab surrealist movement's more than a mere slip of the tongue. Is there a punch-line or am I supposed to provide that too? I imagine a white marble archway in Tel Aviv and a path through it leading to a large lawn demarcated by an Oriental screen.

Chapter 12

Events are coming full circle though I suspect the arcs won't exactly meet, which means we're talking about a spiral here not the closure of a circumference. I can imagine Penny strapping Amber's body across the trunk of our old Buick and me holding each garment up remembering how Amber looked wearing it.

I begin Wednesday evening bored off my ass in an old-fashioned telephone booth. The door's stuck. My cellphone's dead. I lost the charger. I taste copper when I need the feel of clay. Maybe I'm not turning the handle hard enough. Plenty of hiking trails in here. The hot tub and sauna call out to me. I start mulling over Oscar red carpet predictions. Anyone leaving the city for the East Bay? I need a lift! Can anyone give me a ride as far as Emeryville? I need a lift to Reno!

Easter's only three weeks away. Four more days before I'm off to London! The small joys of life eh? Forgot my passport and debit card. I'd like to purchase a Bluetooth too. God I hate yelling into the payphone at Penny. I sent Amber home in a taxi – trust me! Please tell the pawnbroker she might be late. We got lost in the marina! I need to step out of these super tight cycling shorts. Pedestrians are frowning at my crotch. Are my glands swollen? Trust me I'm no hypochondriac. I enjoy the sunshine even while organizing my week. God! I want to hitch a ride to Reno before the Arab surrealist movement takes another turn for WHAT? Perhaps I'll star in a spaghetti western. Life's dull in a phone booth without vodka and painkillers. I miss drinking Absolut straight from the bottle. Things are fine otherwise. Except some dude is firing a handgun in the parking lot across the street. I hope he's got enough sense to aim at the ground. Why don't local liquor stores carry my favorite brand of vodka? Why do college kids love St. Patrick's Day? One thing I learned from the military is how to drink vodka while dressed up as a clown.

Later I'm traveling through the empty center of the city, directing a cabdriver to take the shortest way. Nothing works. He's not listening. The asshole doesn't speak English or any other language known to man. He's wearing a Harley-Davidson T-shirt. His cab smells like a goddamned locker room. The backseat's stained with dog piss. I'm appalled. Am I in San Francisco or Managua, Nicaragua?

"Hey man we have to hustle. The florist closes early. We got a wide open lane there. You could speed up a little?"

Nothing changes absolutely nothing.

"Hey man I have a loaded gun aimed at your head. You better speed it up. Now!"

If anything he slows down a bit.

"I'm gonna fuck your mother and feed her tits to the alligators!"

He mumbles something. I get no other response.

"You motherfucking worthless cocksucker!"

The cabdriver turns around and smiles. Unbelievable!

"Anybody ever tell you your mouth looks like a diseased vagina?"

He turns around again, laughing this time.

I throw up my hands in exasperation.

The florist is not much of an improvement over the cabdriver. She manages to smile yet appear on the brink of vomiting.

When I'm in a hurry why do I forget to feel sorry for incompetent people?

"Smell the bamboo in here sir? Can you smell the bamboo in here?"

"Is that what it is? Yes I can smell it. I'd like to purchase one hundred dollars of your freshest most exotic flowers."

"Big occasion sir?"

"I can't reveal my motives. Let's try to be quick about it. I have a plane to catch."

"Very well sir."

She disappears for more than ten minutes. I feel like I'm trapped under a box. My asthma worsens. The succession of faces returns.

"How's it going back there? Got those wrapped up and ready to go?"

The woman reappears empty-handed. "My assistant's working on it sir."

"Chop-chop!"

She smiles. "You have a plane to catch."

"Goddamn right I do."

"Big occasion?"

"It's business lady! I work for a petroleum company. If it weren't for me you'd be unable to deliver your flowers and go out of business. Got it?"

She disappears again. When she returns she doesn't have the flowers. She's holding a stack of snapshots.

"These are my daughter's wedding in Vietnam. You want to see?"

"I want the flowers!"

"Soon sir very soon."

"Christ!"

"See they had a beautiful wedding."

"I'm sure that wasn't the last time your daughter will commit adultery. Forget it. Answer me this lady! Why do incompetent and lazy people turn me into a bigot? Is it my fault I'm the bad guy here?"

As if by magic the florist's assistant appears with the flowers. I pay. I'm off.

Later I'm seated at a table in a revolving rooftop gentlemen's club thinking Taco Bell would do this body some good, as would a Reno titty bar road-trip. I stop sipping bourbon long enough to shake my booty. I'm so restless I can only watch the woman at the next table eat a five-dollar foot-long. She needs a burst of energy. Goodness gracious sex is easy around here! BDSM is a necessary skill in any Nazi fascist nightclub. I watch the revolution begin beside a portrait of a late-18th Century military figure and a high school Muslim cheerleader dancing in uniform on a stripper pole. Some dance to remember, some dance to forget.

The Bedouin bouncer's dressing up for a celebrity death-match. I feel like I'm preparing for jury duty. The house band's amazing. The songs are amazing. I'm losing my voice from singing too loud, and my stomach's making weird noises. The chick next to me must think I'm farting.

A fight breaks out. Hell yeah! I could punch the bouncer in the throat right about now. The gentlemen's club rule is you never get physical until they touch you or your girl. You break their jaw. A bouncer must handle whatever situations arise to protect the clientele he's charged with protecting. What's it like to be a space shuttle pilot, a brain surgeon, a criminal? How would you go about killing someone you love or mutilating yourself? The mechanics of it, the minutiae of it. I've forgotten how hard it is to make that stuff happen even with pillowcase creases across my face from a rough night's sleep. I exit the club's fire exit, barricade it, dash through the courtyard to Van Ness where I parked the Buick. Am I forgetting something? On the way to the wedding reception I stop for coffee, donuts, poached eggs, hash browns.

Chapter 13

Night begins when I need to pee from that coffee and I realize I left the
exotic flowers back at the club with the exotic Muslim dancers.

God I hate being the awkward one at a wedding reception! Failing to
make eye contact? Check. Looking aimlessly out the window? Check.
Staring at the ceiling? Check. It's my American Idol look. Nothing fancy
here. The caterers are offering vegan pizza, cupcakes, Tylenol PM,
Smirnoff Ice 40s. My hand's tired. The off-duty stripper's not done yet. It's
creepy. Am I revisiting my Jewish roots? Has the world gone mental?
Stuttering hippie strippers are not very sexy even in San Francisco and
Rotterdam. What's the collective noun here? Big things, little things, other
things not worth mentioning. The world monetary system crashing last
October. Full Metal Jacket. Related Ponzi schemes. Why do snack food
prices go up every single year? Oh sweet Jesus you and your random
iPhone upgrades. I can't wait to order a French vanilla iced coffee at
Barnes & Noble tomorrow.

Favorite thing about late-night wedding receptions? Open bar.
Weirdest thing about late-night wedding receptions? Buddhist monks
lifting their robes to take a leak. A surreal light's shimmering outside.
Yellow becomes the new black. I look at the horizon, at the stars, whatever
the light source is at night. That light appeals to my sense of history and
drama. I take a hit and hear ice-cream truck music. Smoking meth's like an
Olympic sport in an Olympic-sized swimming pool. You might as well fire
the starter's pistol. Happiness squared.

We've got a beautiful little late-night party here on the front porch,
with barbeque, strawberry pineapple smoothies, acoustic guitar jams, lots
of booty-shaking, spin the bottle, beer pong. This fast-forward shit's crazy
as hell. Moments later we're drunk at Mel's Drive-In on Geary. Fast
forward again to Costco, to Petco, to a second dance club. More virtual
followers please! I don't care who's dying of tuberculosis. Stop texting me
about it! A shitty opening band can ruin the entire evening. Too many red-
headed sluts are moving around the dance floor like battleships. Their
high-pitched whining's not a good sign nor is the world exploding into
normalcy.

I hear the Central Valley's super-exciting this time of year. I can't
quite fathom it. Patience is not one of my many virtues. I have baroque
obsessions. I'm the last in a long line of inbred psychopathic aristocrats
who hear aristocratic voices in their heads. I used to claim I'm 100%
Jewish. I'm in awe of accidental double exposures.

The reception becomes a late-night argument above a garage. We're
yelling our asses off at a poodle with a Mohawk and a guy with a

Superman logo tattooed on his chest. He lubes up his cock with lotion, starts jerking off in front of the poodle. I'm alternately enraged and bored. I feel like I'm on a game show. A chick starts playing an electronic keyboard. Tonight's shaping up to be a real cloak-and-dagger act. IMAX is not the experience. When did you first meet Osama Bin Laden? Who's the kitten? Who's the infrared?

I imagine a retarded Arab boy in cut-off jeans committing perverse acts on a stage at a late-night wedding reception in Reno. We call him Rockerboy. He's an Arab boy with a finger up his ass and electrodes on those freshly shaven Muslim balls. His mandibles are soft, translucent. He's drenched in pure virgin olive oil, drowning in sweet red wine. Rockerboy was shot down over the Iraqi desert breathing oil smoke. He never fumes airborne toxins. Nothing's swollen. He never associates with the diseased, never wears ripped pink stockings over his left thigh.

When I awaken I have a crick in my neck. My left eye's twitching. Everyone at the table's acting stoned. Can they detect I'm horny? The club's crowded with more than 100 witnesses, including unwed gold-digging female opportunists flashing their boobs. You can't hear dick. Everyone's talking and texting. Turn off that white music! Get your Arab asses back to bed! Christ! Outside, people are lining up to purchase $45 concert T-shirts, $8 chicken sandwiches, $5 el cheapo cans of Tecate beer. At twelve ounces per can times 18 cans that's 216 ounces of flat beer for $90. God bless those bare titties. One chord's fine, two's pushing it into blues, at three we've hit jazz. Here's a free copy of the Koran.

Wrong! I don't have to do anything I don't wanna. I'll remember this moment for the rest my life, the night I return home to find everything gone including Penny and Amber. We got a missing persons situation on our hands. Not exactly. Penny's waitressing. Amber's downstairs babysitting for the pawnbroker. Remember? I open the door. There's Amber in the pawnbroker's living room watching TV while the invisible infant sleeps in the next room. Ain't TV wonderful? The stories they broadcast! Here we got a sick and tired writer in a race against time to locate and murder his psychotic daughter. How did she vanish? Is she his daughter? Are you holding? Stay tuned!

I watch Amber rock back and forth on the pawnbroker's sofa. She's got her hands between her thighs pressing one hand against the other while squeezing her legs shut. Her eyes are closed. Her face is tilted toward the ceiling. Her hair's the wrong color. She's wearing a wig. She can't know I'm here standing right behind her. Look at that mouth, those delicate lips! Look at those dainty earrings, that quaint little tattoo on the nape of her neck! Her rocking increases in intensity. An occasional moan issues from her quivering mouth. That's too much for me to bear. I understand no rules exist against her playing games with the pawnbroker. I doubt the pawnbroker put her up to this charade. Yet she's trying rather hard to be enticing isn't she? I have a right to be angry with her for not finding it unpleasant to be exposed and stared at. The pawnbroker's a heavy-set man, big in the belly. He drinks heavily. I imagine he winces a lot when the sciatica's acting up.

I back away from the sofa, step over to the mantelpiece. Here's a little brass Jesus, a crucifix un-nailed from the wall. I walk into the master bedroom. There's the king size bed with the two-year-old infant asleep on wrinkled sheets and stained pillowcases. I walk over to the sleeping baby, stare down it. A standard baby. No unusual markings, no unusual mechanisms or limb movements. I follow the outline of its face with my index finger. Any buyers? I smile, reminding myself it's illegal to pawn off infants. My feet are sore. I turn around, return to the living room.

Amber's startled to see me.

"How long have you been here Daddy?"

"Long enough to get a hang of the place. When's the pawnbroker return?"

"Anytime now. Did you see the baby?"

"The baby's sleeping. What have you been doing? I'm not supposed to be here am I?"

"He won't care."

"Can I sit down on the sofa beside you? My feet are sore."

"Sure. It's gonna be cramped."

"That feels good!" I stretch out my legs, wiggle my toes.

"Daddy why are you down here?"

"I can't find the right frame of mind to write tonight. I'm not in the mood to do my usual wandering. I've done far too much wandering the past few days. My feet are sore and swollen."

"Where's Penny?"

"Waitressing at the diner. Did I ever tell you about the time I worked in a mannequin factory in New York City?"

"In New York?"

"I thought you knew I lived in New York for several years after I dropped out of med school. I worked at a mannequin factory. The upper floors of the place were abandoned. They were infested with pigeons. I used to go up there and eat my lunch and feed the pigeons. I took smoke breaks up there too. Sometimes I drank a little. I liked the place. It was quiet. I was alone. I was careful never to tell any of my coworkers about it. They had no reason to suspect."

"You used to smoke?"

"Pall Malls, a pack a day. I still do when I'm nervous or get a strong craving."

"Did you drink bourbon?"

"I did and one day I drank too much. I passed out. When I woke up I was still up there with the pigeons. It was way past dark. I couldn't risk getting caught. The company would fire my ass. I had no choice except to sneak downstairs and out the building. That involved walking through three floors of mannequins in near total darkness. It freaked me out. I can't explain why. I imagined they were alive, watching and grabbing at me."

"That sounds stupid."

"It didn't feel that way at the time. To calm myself I lit up a smoke. Problem is, and I'd find this out the next day, I must not have extinguished the match. The next morning the entire building was gutted. The whole place burned down. It took the firemen most of the night to put the blaze out. With nothing holding me in New York, I got in my old Buick and drove west, finding my way here to San Francisco."

"The end."

"Sort of."

I lean back further into the deep sofa, move my right hand to Amber's collar. That's the tricky part. Amber responds by raising her own hands to her chin. She's trying to find an answer to this odd familial puzzle. I hope she finds a solution before it's lost forever. Where? She's pretty much given up. I have to slap her hard across the face twice three times four!

"That's the way it'll be goddammit! I'll have sexual problems with your mommy if I want. I'll make your mommy scared of this rubber penis! Penny means so much to me. I've got chronic writer's block. The pawnbroker wants to stick his tongue down your glistening throat!"

Amber can't understand the sharpened yellow editing pencil. Before she screams she'll clutch those knobby little knees to those pointy little tits. I'll carve out the permutations and combinations.

Penny used to glance at me. Amber used to laugh at me. Goldsmith insisted he would have nothing more to do with me. Famous movie stars rode bicycles along a highway in the stifling sun. Stories never ended so terribly. Writers knew how to prevent the Supreme Court from suing them out of their future royalties and stopping stranger things from happening in their literary worlds. A young girl was struck below the cheekbone by a stick her father yanked off a cherry tree precisely when a famous movie star was bludgeoned to death near a California Interstate. That bore some resemblance to what happened to Amber. That's what happens between every father and daughter.

Look at how these fingers flex!

On I-80 East the magician begins to die. The night brings unbearable suffering, minimal acquaintance, armed robbery. The magician's dying inside me. Penny and Amber will soon be gone. I'll arrive in Reno. There's nothing anyone else can do about that. I gamble before taking on the great tasks of a surgeon. Who's there? Tonight the whore I hired. What does she tell me? Yes her. She says out-of-town customers don't matter. She listens to me listen to myself. There isn't anything anyone else can do about that. I gamble, gamble some more while the magician dies inside me.

Look at how these fingers flex!

Thank God there's nothing anyone else can do about the morning light roaring through the motel room's flimsy gray curtains. Rest assured the whore lying on the bed will have fair warning. Trust me on that. Streaming, pouring, flooding from her gaping mouth. A sad yet exhilarating occasion. That's what happened to me last spring when I gambled.

PART 2 Reshad

Chapter 14

It's dawn, the air's cool, I'm shivering outside an old synagogue or mosque. The only audible sound is the hissing of rain.

I should sense something's gone horribly wrong.

Through the night my mind's unloaded its blackness. I now want to sit for the rest of my life staring at cinderblock walls rather than traipsing through set-pieces. I want existence by deprivation of logic. I want the handle of a bladed weapon. I decide to depart. After a half hour of agony I'm dead with the handle of a bowie-knife protruding from my throat. There my powers of discernment end. The cassette tape runs out. Perhaps my wooden head struck the pavement outside I'll never know fallen right into the gutter or risen skyward with the elephant-colored pollution of burning leaves.

Surrealistic mosques and tropical beaches rise up in the distance. I see nationwide flag-burnings, raw hamburger patties, spectacular views of electronic keyboards. I haven't stepped into the Literary Void since Tuesday. I need this experience to boost my energy and erase last night's final distortion. 'The natural forces of nature' is what I call the Literary Void, 'steam rising from a saucepan.' Such calamity, as if new dawns were seeking distance and space for their unfolding. The gold chariots and courtiers are gone forever, reduced to ragged shreds of newsprint and damp heaps of bills. We got left only science for the sake of science, the fleshless constriction of surfaces, the zap! of a 12-volt car battery. In the Literary Void shapes are slightly different every fraction of a second, up and up forever, deeper and deeper into darkness.

I could relate some real horror stories from down here. I've been manhandled, roughed up, plagued by deficits. Last week I nearly drowned in a can of dog food. I've learned that only a vast dream of creative evolution can topple government buildings. The first step in that direction is envisioning a network of points and lines called the Arab surrealist movement.

Operation Melancholy Stupor begins with the ripping out of friends and family and the changing of colored forms. The Indigo Entelechy serves as radio-conjunct between the $9+1+1+0+1=12$ Shock Planes of Particularization. The laws of the USA are grounded on orders from the V-S-C Zoom Zoom. Soft tones vibrate into three hallucinogenic pillars that whirl form, number, and sound over an interval of Maria Virgo's isolated space. Among the diversity are a grassy park beside a fire station, a giant-size cheetah, Virgil's quotes on the one-dollar bill, 52 cycles of influenza pandemic killing over 1 billion, the revolting graveyards of jealous beggars, auspicious volcanic activity, huge rocks from the California hills rolling into sea-boulders, the chromatic display of Soviet Bloc incendiaries, the vacant streets of Tribeca, stink-bombs set off at a public meeting place, 77,000 tons of nuclear reactor waste, the Jellyfish Control Act, Barry Bonds' elbow pad, Al Pacino acting like an insomniac cop, two former UN weapons inspectors, three potential suicide bombers.

What kind of breakfast joint runs out of porridge by 10am? Where's my Jamba juice? Hah. Blackberry cobbler and coffee are a good way to enjoy a Thursday morning. Vitamin Water, Marlboro Lights, Daft Punk are also the shit, as are homeless meth addicts. Two peas in a pod. The purple didn't work again. Sorry that makes no sense. The waitress put too much Splenda in my coffee and now thinks I'm invisible.

I look up from the table, glance out the window at the diner's parking lot. Some asshole with a leaf-blower shows up, sending the audio right down the tubes. The camera picks up the vibrations. Soon the scene is too sickening to imagine. When I pick up the signal again another movie has replaced the previous one. Now it's the murder of a Jewish writer's daughter, with a pointless subplot involving two unemployed wanderers. The movie's only attitude and posturing, inferior material. Tremendously moving? Hardly. There's no logic or depth to the faceless thousands driving around in the background, shopping at strip-malls, acting like morphine addicts, while the three of us are held hostage by a knife-wielding maniac in a Nevada ghost town. A pall hangs over the entire set. The only thing missing is a yellow-and-red billboard advertising $200 cesspools.

I say Let X equal X. The torch that was passed to a new generation of Americans sixty years ago has burned out. No one left cares to keep the flame a-goin'. According to the morning paper this suburb's career opportunities consist of specialists, managers, supervisors, coordinators, stylists, consultants, and analysts who assist others in finding employment. They could use a thrust alignment. Lots of irrelevant and gratuitous washed-out stock footage too.

How long's it been since I blew my nose into a real newspaper with real newsprint? Look at those inky headlines!

"Bounty hunter's boy murdered."

"Psychotherapist who raped psychotherapist wife allegedly schoolmate of Goebbels."

"Plane crashes caused by coincidental mishaps in cockpit."

"Shortage of Roman Catholic priests in Costa Rica."

Another ass braying about the middle class.

Ads for life insurance and children's toys.

"No interest till the year 2050."

"30% off discontinued golf bags."

"Better auto service, lower prices."

"Coupons must be presented on first visit."

"We accept competitors coupons."

Far too much emphasis on financial uncertainty, automobiles, laser vision-correction, and weight-loss. Who cares if that woman favors a sports bra over a fuller figure comfort bra, if she uses Lady Speed Stick, if she spends hours picking through rug assortments at Wal-Mart and makes a big issue of shopping for bedding separates? Her daily routine's an ice ballet. Her entire life's conveniently tucked away in a two-drawer filing cabinet. Uninvolved with gangster-run gentlemen's clubs, she's another white-bellied female who's dying for a smoke.

I feel safe and protected here in the diner's booth. I'm hungry, very hungry. Look at how my fingers flex! They flex and flex again. For the first time in several days I feel the compulsion to write, to get it down in writing rather than speak into a recorder. I remove the sharpened yellow editing pencil from my pocket, pull several napkins from the dispenser, begin writing a goddamned poem, a prose poem, something like things tarnish, carpets fray, moldings crack, mantelpieces lose their sharp edges. Human contact wears things out, makes them gray and musty smelling.

Little by little I sink into the booth as the diner turns quieter, more peaceful. I'm a man like every other man around here. Human contact wears me out, makes me bored and enraged. I have few complicated desires. Nothing's striking about my appearance, not this morning, except for the huge spinning globe in my hands and the bullets I fire into it.

The waitress joins me outside for a smoke.

I tell her I rarely smoke.

"Me too. These cigarettes are heavy little bastards."

"What if you had a full empty?"

"A full empty?"

"Imagine your whatchamacallit had some blue stuff inside."

"We gotta follow health regulations around here."

I give a short laugh, shrug my shoulders. She's trying to humor me. I imagine we could run away, the two of us, everything hunky-dory, no one suspecting anything. Her eyes have the right mix of courage and confusion.

I ask her what her name is.

"Guta."

"What kind of name is that?"

"It's what people call me."

"Keep plugging away. They'll make you a manager. How long have you been working here?"

"Two years starting my third."

"I love diners. I've spent a good portion of my life in diners and gentlemen's clubs. You got family?"

"No I'm alone."

"Up to your old tricks again?"

Guta frowns, stabs her cigarette into the ashtray.

"Where are you from Guta?"

"Reno."

"That's a coincidence. I'm on my way there now."

"Today?"

"Tomorrow. I hope to find some new material there without arousing any suspicions."

Guta frowns again, says nothing.

"Don't get me wrong. You're free to come with me if you like."

"I can't leave here at the drop of a hat. I got responsibilities."

"Can't you see you're not behaving like a human being right now? You're a machine. You're someone else's steering wheel."

"You shut up! With you it's high speed forward. We get your type in here on the nightshift."

"Thank God I'm not the only one around here who knows how to run off at the mouth.

"Has something happened? You're nervous and preoccupied."

"Something's happened! Yesterday I did something you might not understand."

"Skip it."

"I murdered someone."

"Only in the movies."

"Watch this closely." I remove the revolver from my pocket, jam its barrel into my mouth.

Guta stares at me.

I stand like that for awhile, long enough for several patrons to exit the diner and take note of me. None of them seems alarmed. Such spectacles are commonplace nowadays.

I remove the revolver, wipe the spit off its barrel, return it to my pocket.

"Did you see that?"

Guta stares at me intently.

I frown. "What's the matter? Why are you standing there?"

"What did you say your name was?"

"Rosenberg."

"You're a lucky man Rosenberg."

"That sounds authoritative and overly dramatic. Next time remind me to bring along Bertolt Brecht. How much did you say a full empty costs around here?"

"I have to get back to work."

"I have to get an oil change."

"Godspeed you."

"You keep plugging away Guta. You'll be a manager."

Guta walks back inside. I return to the Buick. I sit there for a long while watching my fingers flex again and again on the steering wheel. I feel safe and protected in the car.

I need to get going. I can't be around here much longer.

Chapter 15

I hate driving to Silicon Valley any day of the week including Thursdays. It's utterly, utterly pointless. I'm stuck in an asphalt loop with no motivation to describe things. Since when does the wind blow out of the north? Bay Area filling stations are super boring. It's like sitting on the toilet for two hours straight.

I'll give my liver the day off. Getting interviewed in the ICU would suck. I don't want to compare that to anything else. I know Penny's Buick's a piece of crap that's failed its inspection twice and deserves more than a stupid oil change. I don't care. Fresh oil should get me as far as Reno where I'll refuse to sell out even in the noisiest gentlemen's clubs. God I hope this sweater never smells like cigar smoke again!

Earlier this afternoon I had a good time at the shopping mall. I'll summarize it as 'Huevos rancheros with Candy at the Cheesecake Factory.' Candy tells me she's selling Mary Kay not wearing a bra. I feel like I'm cradling a shotgun in my lap. She has a love-hate relationship with crazy glue. She keeps finding viruses on her new computer. She has no idea why that orchid's still growing. She stopped watering it two months ago. You have a dead father right? We know he killed himself in the basement.

You look hungry! Why don't you have a Twinkie?

"Go home you worthless Jew! Leave me alone!"

It's crunch time baby, tubas and hooting beavers. I'm making a quick stop at the Stanford computer lab this afternoon. Break out the sweatshirts and fake IDs. Don't be afraid to let your light shine!

I discovered his MySpace page on Valentine's Day. A Japanese shut-in or hikikomori. He says he types slow ever since he got headaches after falling off a motorbike. Damn what's the point of that Hitler-like mustache? It don't make no sense to me. He says pepperoni and toothpaste are a weird combination. I crack my knuckles, walk away from the computer. I've done far too much Internet surfing this afternoon. I ransacked the Apple Store, booked a flight to Portugal for $5, hacked an EBay auction, bought three books on urban vegetable gardening, applied for a job at Starbucks. Now my emails keep bouncing. Was that a job offer? Time to buy a new suit. European cut.

Screw the problem statement. Let's hit the Internet again. I'm too busy to take one hand off the keyboard. I change my career choice again and again. I wanna touch her inappropriately before advertisers convince me to buy Penny's birthday presents a month early to get 10% off. Godiva chocolate with her name written on the wrapper, fudge pops, pizza roles, the latest A.C. Newman CD. Penny's crazy cousins who live in Indiana or Iowa have been faxing our phone line this morning. They're shameless. There's nothing else to do except screen-shop. It's like summer camp with fewer rules. Hooray for barely readable sentences minus the morbidly awesome vampire parts. So many shitty paragraphs, so little time. Dear tech support you suck! A $308 bar tab is why they call it happy hour. Here's the Trader Joe's web site. Epic weirdness. Cheese and vodka anyone? I imagine Penny waking-and-baking while she watches a politician get his chest waxed online. Blatant lies everywhere! Pink dolphins. Gloves at Target cheap as shit. A tiresome black suit. I love celebrities who constantly Tweet. They make me feel like I have a life. Otherwise I get bored filling out Starbucks online job applications. Why's no one else around here wearing green? My scary head nearly explodes. I hate overproduced hair salon music and renting movies for my iPod when I'm on the road.

Driving to Reno turns out to be more annoying than morons who forget to use the Reply button in emails instead of Reply To All. Jerry Seinfeld can go to hell. Yahoo email sucks balls. If you're the guy in the next lane with the new iPhone, congrats man, I hope it doesn't kill you or your marriage. Nothing pisses me off more than getting blown off by a travel agent who solicits magic-lantern puppet dramas to spread lewdness, corrupt society and drive our citizenry away from religion and corpse-burning. Here we have Syria's answer to the Barbie doll without a head-cover and hideous makeup. What else is so ghastly? A Mel Gibson movie? A shitty little dust-jacket photo of Goldsmith and his flip-flop blister.

T minus 48 seconds.

It takes a traffic jam to teach me I'm dyslexic. I'll vomit. Nothing physical. I hope I make it through California Customs unmolested. I tell the customs officials to slap me if I ask silly questions about Middle Eastern and Slavic terrorists. Logic or gut feeling? Those guys need more punk rock in their lives. Yawns are contagious. It's not groundbreaking news the Russian mafia aren't hijacking commercial airliners anymore. Oh the joys of car-lag. I'm stuck in another asphalt loop. How will I survive the next few days? This cannot be happening right now. My toe's a bloody mess. I need to poop!

Fire alarms, fire trucks, mandatory evacuation. Another exciting evening in the Sierra Nevada Mountains. Go to hell California. The Internet was made for porn. I'm panning for gold in my best ballet slippers. As if I need another reason to lose weight around here. Carrying a drunken Englishman on your back ain't easy. Goldsmith owes me a burrito too. Trust me I haven't touched the sauce in years honest to God Diet Dr. Pepper. People are annoying. I don't care what state they're from.

I couldn't sleep last night, kept having the same nightmare over and over again. I took four showers in three hours. I felt squeaky clean. Now the sunlight hurts my eyes. No one cares. What goes well with pizza apart from garlic bread? Cheese puffs and wine. Did I mention the high cost of dry-cleaning leather and Father's private burial in Rotterdam?

The doctor's tests are drawing blanks.

The doctor reads out the roll-call sheets as skinny rotting prisoners and mutated children are herded into the room and laid out across the checkerboard marble floor in sharp silver rings and glossy plastic. Bad health is the status quo around here. The nurses wear gloved eyeliner and smeared dark red lipstick. They smother themselves in painkillers. The larvae awaken at 9:00 under the watchful eye of the doctor. He wears iron-straight pants with green metal cuts and thick black slashes. He's an island of dignity inside a hive tiger, or a cat that sleeps in the sun.

Goodnight cruel world. I lie back on the hospital-like bed, look up at the ceiling, consider my options. I stand up again. I'll never do anything as messy or inconsiderate as shoot myself in the head or slit these wrists. I'm a grown-up. I drink vodka right out of the bottle. Florida might be a nice get-away. Or Broadway.

This is the worst goddamned motel I've ever stayed in. Beyond the smudged window a pinkish sun sets beneath a neon motel sign. A few dusty dented cars move along the boulevard. I imagine Penny removing her bikini and vaguely rubbing her breasts as she stares off into the distance. She's tight-lipped, has dark rings around her eyes, wears an elastic bandage on her left leg. The bleak evening light makes her look like she's aged twenty years in twenty minutes. Standing at the window I begin tossing the motel key up in the air. I know I'm being pulled into a forbidden place deep within myself. I'm reluctant to use the word 'problem' if 'problem' means 'drama.' I'm beset by intense visions of railway platforms. I've badly neglected Amber. Very badly.

I open the door, walk outside. A helicopter circles overhead in the darkening sky. Amber was very pretty. Right now she might be reclining on a poolside chaise longue while Penny swims naked in the motel swimming pool. I walk across the dusty parking lot in their direction. I'll tell you again this evening's dreary, with the wind blowing less violently than before. Why the hell did we come here? Penny and Amber look pale. My asthma's acting up, coming in little spasms at regular intervals, a sensation so familiar I'm disgusted by it. Across the street a car swerves into the plate-glass window of a roadside diner. Very weird. A line of sweat breaks out on my forehead. I feel weak. Everything begins to spin. I collapse to my knees in an empty parking space, surrendering to that weakness. Isn't it enough I'm the one who's sick here? Tears well up in my eyes. I gasp for breath. I weep a long time without trying to stop. When I manage to stand up again and resume walking, I'm aware this scene has a pleasant Brechtian theatricality about it. First I was a broken-down alcoholic poet. Now I'm a shipwrecked sailor catching first sight of land. Twice death has brushed me with its wing. Sirens approach from the palm trees and desert off in the distance.

When I join Penny and Amber at the pool I realize I'll make the fist thrilling discovery of my life right here in Reno. How pretty they look! Pretty and sickly. I shuffle out to the end of the diving board, sit down, let my bare feet dangle over the chlorinated water. Penny languidly swims laps in the pool. I watch the last line of shadow move toward me from the shallow to the deep end of the pool. I'm very weak, have difficulty breathing. Everything I see weighs on my eyes, tires me immensely. Penny rises up out of the pool, revealing her delicate shoulders, her round naked bottom. She joins Amber in the adjacent chaise langue. Together they give the impression of sunbathing even while the sun's setting. Penny draws her legs to her chest. Amber stares at me with huge silent eyes. She smiles to show off those brilliant white teeth. The health of her little body is breathtaking. I feel bored and hideous. What am I waiting for? Reno's a drag. Reno's so messed up I have to remind myself it's a bunch of pictures and sounds. The place is far too depleted. I don't own this time or place. I can no longer see or hear to write words. I have no special thoughts. I notice two firemen pulling a hose through the shattered window of the diner. Flames eat away at the back of the building. Thick clouds of smoke rise into the sky. I imagine the customers are in shock. Penny returns to the pool. I lie back on the diving board exhausted and stare up at the darkening sky.

Chapter 16

"What are you talking about?"

I smile. "You're funny, bright, interesting to talk to. You give me pleasure. I trust you."

"Will you let me blindfold you?

"Right now? You have the blindfold with you?"

Outside the uncurtained windows the sun is bright, the blue sky gleams. It's cool inside here. I'm squinting. I lost my sunglasses along the way to Nevada. A blindfold shouldn't make much difference.

"Swallow this pill."

"That pill is the blindfold? Give it to me."

I'm sitting on one of those orange-colored fiberglass hospital waiting room chairs. I'm not in the ideal frame of mind when the male nurse puts the pill on my tongue. I chase it back with a couple gulps of water from a small paper cup. Nothing happens for a long while. I look down at the jagged black scuff marks on the floor where someone was dragged against their will. I look up at the paint-peeling ceiling. I look to my left at an end-table covered with piles of magazines missing their covers. I glance to my right at a framed black-and-white photograph of Amber that hangs on the wall for some mysterious reason. I look down again, this time at the palms of my trembling hands.

"You have no reason to worry Rosenberg. You won't feel a thing."

"Nothing's happened yet. My mouth feels dry."

"That sounds unpleasant. To take your mind off it think about blueberries. Don't you love picking and eating blueberries? Think of something pleasant anything at all."

The only thing that comes to mind is burning the American flag.

"Hold that image in your mind's eye. Got it?"

"I think so."

"Now put this in your mouth and bite down hard. Don't swallow. Just like that."

Later I wake up alone lying on a bed in a grubby-looking motel room with puke-green cinderblock walls and harsh fluorescent lighting.

"Anyone here?"

Silence.

"Penny you there? Goldsmith?"

Silence.

My jaw and limbs ache. My toes are curled. The skin over my abdomen feels like it's divided into distinct segments that have each received a different kind of massage. The bed's sheets are unusually stiff. When I rise I'm a little unsteady on my feet. The pressure in my head's vanished. I assume that's the way things work around here. Things, patients mostly, disappear into the night. Those of us left behind meet their departure with a dull kind of acceptance. No one asks any questions though some of the patients make outrageous paranoid claims. The print on the pages of books and newspapers injure one patient like sharp objects. When you hand him the morning paper he twists his face in agony. His voice squeaks like air through the pinched off neck of a balloon. As for me I still can't get the image of stabbing pencils out of my head. Part of the problem may be the doctors are taking patients off lithium and putting them on a new type of mood stabilizer. I'm sure that'll be fun to watch.

My doctor's initials are E.C.T. I shit you not.

The male nurse is a short stocky black man with a shaved head and bulging biceps. He wears a dark blue T-shirt, jeans, and a black nylon jacket. Right now he tells me to take off my shirt and lie on my stomach across the bed. His hands, huge, warm and slick with oil, work their way up from my waist to my shoulders. My calves are next, my feet. As his hands move over me, my jaw and limbs turn limp. I'm no longer confused. Everything's circulating, every blockage removed. I experience an epiphany the likes of which drove James Joyce to suicide. I realize the guilt I've experienced over writer's block has blocked up the rest of my bodily and mental functions. For that reason alone I'm a sick and malfunctioning individual. The nurse turns me over. The treatment process reverses itself up the front of my body with care taken to bypass the genitals. I groan blissfully. Everything's circulating again. It's like rapidly flipping through TV channels with the remote, what they used to call channel surfing. I experience secondary and tertiary epiphanies. If you can't unscramble an egg, you can unscramble a brain.

A few hours later the lights go out for the mandatory afternoon nap. I have trouble falling asleep. My ears are ringing. Something's ringing somewhere. When I do fall asleep I dream I'm lying naked on a stainless steel gurney. I hear the hissing sound a nylon sleeve makes when the male nurse pushes his arm through it. He wheels me into a mosque. A refrigerator door slams shut. For awhile a team of doctors mumble among themselves. I hear the sudden crack of a sheet shaken free of its creases. I feel cool cotton glide over my legs. I awaken. Penny's pinching my arm.

"Hey there! How are you feeling?"

"Not too bad."

"I don't like the looks of your nurse, the black man with the big muscles. He looks and acts more like a bodybuilder than a physician's assistant if you ask me."

"He takes good care of me."

"You think these treatments will help destroy the writer's block?"

"Hard to say. It's too early to tell. One thing I notice is my thoughts are moving more freely now if less rapidly."

"Want me to kiss you?"

Chapter 17

This evening I loiter awhile in the third-floor entranceway before unhooking a role from the Truth Receptacle and placing it in the doctor's satchel. Later I'll watch the middle innings of a Red Sox game. Satan sets his traps everywhere around here. My collection of denials occupies a whole wall of filing cabinets overflowing with newsprint and videotape. Those represent my poetic impairment and the flat as I left it. No wonder I get trapped in these bizarre domestic situations. Literary security's not the name of the game around here.

   Doctor, that wasn't a home invasion. It was a more fully developed sense of self. Back in my cell I lie down on the cot. My body relaxes. I unclasp my hands to reveal the male nurse's clandestine message.

   I remember cops surrounded the motel. A lieutenant spoke urgently into a headset. I know what he said word for word so help me God. That's exactly what he said. I better pay closer attention. The memory disperses, crumbling, disintegrating, what have you, with less pandemonium than I expected. No one attempts to hide his or her peccadilloes around here. The air stinks of Xerox fluid.

   I cudgel my brains to make sense of everything absent the aid of a mini-cassette recorder. Fatigue distracts my eyes with dark nightmare landscapes of memory, fragments from an ancient life touched upon again and again and interleaved with strata of unintelligible voices. A pea-field in a handkerchief, the swish of passing train cars, the large dome of a mosque, barges on a river, the mild comforts of air-conditioning and weak American coffee, a radio reporting the completion of another sale of F16s to the Imperial Air Force as preparation for a war not yet glimpsed or guessed at though strenuous efforts are under way.

   I imagine the cops moved out early that morning when the Governor announced a challenge to every surreal terrorist not yet ready. Nothing else he could say about Islamic servitude submachine-gunning Jesus Christ in Uncle Tom's Cabin over a piece of stale religious bread. Followed by another eleven-minute infomercial on the proper use of the New Testament and life-sized stoned elephants. Sea World is beside the point you chicken-ass shits! Take that piece of the Dead Sea back to your own worthless country. Reclaim these bourgeois baby blankets for the executives to scream in. Rioters haul your raw materials to the pineal gland. Public joy through spirit-possession! 19th-century street events! Candle-lit reality! Dashing onto running-boards! Gelatinous balls of salamander eggs! Girls singing ecology, reclaiming the territory at sundown! The Governor murdered at breakfast! Cops, parades, bank robberies, fires. You want

California eradicated from the map? How much modern-day urban traffic sewage would confront 400 liberated beings? Dreams of democracy shot from the barrel of a gun. Those banners announcing my capture are burned down again while this criminal's attempted assault is rephrased to selfless murder in the name of capital letters. Oh how valid murder of a single one is the most difficult criminal case!

I suspect the circuits in my head are being messed with.

A latticework of searchlights blazes into my eyes. Many doctors and therapists roam about the wards, repeating odd phrases.

"They're such a sick a lot."

"That's a nebulous state that can as easily lead to sleep as to awakening."

"Proves yet again you can't have love and long-term marriage."

My latest doctor's a dramatically handsome man with a pirate-like swagger. He points in my direction, strides across the ward to stand right in front of me.

"Trust in Allah. Tether your camel first Rosenberg!"

The burly black nurse steps between us.

"Doctor if you could try not to shout so much and approach the patients with a little more calm."

"I'm not his mother!"

"Perhaps try to be his friend."

"Nor am I his friend Reshad!"

Thus I learn the black nurse's name is Reshad.

"He needs help doctor professional help."

"Shut up Reshad. They all need professional help. They wouldn't be here otherwise. Where did you say you studied medicine?"

"Johns Hopkins sir."

"I pity you."

Reshad steps back a few paces, keeps quiet. I struggle to maintain my composure. The doctor's nose is within an inch of mine.

"Your dinner will be served a little late today Rosenberg. I've got a very important assignment."

I nod.

"First let me remind you there's a saying in the Koran. 'We will try them until we know.' It should be obvious that 'we' are the doctors here."

I nod again.

"Tell me what you're thinking Rosenberg."

"I'm thinking I can get through this disagreeable stage and have pleasant relationships again. It'll require lots of goodwill and honesty on my part."

The doctor raises his eyebrows, laughs. "What a lot of horseshit! Get undressed Rosenberg!"

"Right here?"

"Right here and now! You're a smooth talker, making parodies of the real things in life. Get undressed! Let's take a look at your goodwill and honesty."

Reshad turns to the doctor. "Sir you'll be late for your train if you keep on with this."

"I'm treating a patient. You're talking about trains!"

"In all fairness asking a patient to remove his clothes at the drop of a hat for no apparent reason is not professional."

"I'll decide what's professional around here! Drop your pants Rosenberg!"

Once it's clear the nurse will not intercede on my behalf I begin disrobing. Other patients milling about the ward stop to watch.

"Tell me what you're thinking Rosenberg."

"I need to get undressed."

"That's all? They tell me you're a writer. Why don't you write what you want and let me read it sometime? When something can be misinterpreted it inevitably is. That's an unfortunate fact of life. Seems to me you lack suspicions of your present predicament. Take a look around. Tell me what you see!"

"The ward."

"What's happened to your powers of perception? Henry James once told an aspiring writer to become someone on whom nothing is lost. If you're a writer take a look around the ward. Enumerate what you see."

"Patients, furniture, tables and chairs, windows with bars."

The doctor lifts up a hand. "Stop right there Rosenberg."

One of my feet is raised from the floor as I try to pull off a pant leg. I wobble for a moment before falling down. Reshad reaches out for me.

"What are you doing? Let him be. Let the man fall. That next-to-last sentence is one of the great secrets of the world."

I look up at the doctor, say nothing.

"Your assignment's to write that sentence over and over again. It might do you some good."

"Write what and where doctor?"

"On the walls of your cell. Be neat about it too, with a flawless white space between each sentence. I want you to write Let Him be, Let Him be, Let Him be, over and over again. That's with an upper-case 'H.' Reshad will give you the chalk and markers won't you Reshad?"

Reshad nods.

"Have we squared the circle? Your assignment is to understand the omnipotence of Allah or Yahweh, what have you. Once you've done that the real treatment begins. Cheers! I have a train to catch."

I turn around, head for the corridor.

I come to a cell with its door ajar. I crane my neck to look inside. A grossly overweight female patient hoists up her nightgown and mime masturbation before grabbing a doctor by the scrotum and squeezing like a vice.

"Arghhhh!!!"

Her eyes are fixed on his. Green vomit and menstrual blood cover her nightgown. She laughs full and mockingly. She keeps squeezing.

She mocks him. "Arghhhh!!!"

He responds. "Arghhhh!!!"

They're speaking an ancient language I've never known or studied. I stand still watching the scene develop. Nothing I might do could make things any worse for the doctor. I step inside the cell, make a quick scan of the premises. The walls are adorned with satanic symbols including a pentagram and an inverted cross. There's even a framed certificate confirming the patient's membership in the Church of Satan. She's lost her mind, her temporal lobe's not all there. Tattoos and lesions cover her body. Those are fresh cuts on her face. Maybe it's a coincidence.

The patient continues to squeeze. "What would you like to drink doctor?"

"Arghhhh!!!"

"I beg your pardon?"

"Arghhhh!!!"

"Shut up you're in Dubrovnik I don't hear you!"

"Arghhhh!!!"

She's squeezes still harder. The doctor's face is turning an odd shade of purple. "You're gonna die up there doctor you and your bloody testicles!"

"Arghhhh!!!"

"Captain Howdy says that's not very nice!"

"Arghhhh!!!"

I can watch no longer. I'm tormented by a desire for drink.

I find my way back to the cell to discover I've been supplied with all manner of writing instruments. Here I come face to face with a brand new form of writer's block. I realize you can't dictate style in such a confined space. Without a mini-cassette recorder how can you settle on a correct style? Perhaps mental gymnastics is the way to go. Send my mind off on autopilot while my hands do the more repetitive stuff. Back in the mechanical era they called it automatic writing, an avant-garde hotrod form of spirit possession. I get most of my kicks from setting up and knocking down oppositions. Blending the poles. That's been a fundamental message of the Arab surrealist movement over the years. I make a habit of cutting against reality's grain. I'm a swordsman ripping through the carpet. I'm one of the top five best-dressed patients. The doctor said he had a train to catch. What else am I supposed to imagine about that train? Who dictates its schedule?

I begin writing Let Him be on the walls of my cell. Let Him be Let Him be Let Him be. My hands take over. My mind goes on autopilot. I find myself sitting at a wobbly table in the breakfast nook. Amber sits across from me. She's using her right pinkie to stir the ice cubes in a Diet Coke. The overall effect is hypnotic. I'm reminded that a reliable way of mixing virtue and vice is to dirty the sacred and cleanse the profane. That's the way they did it in the Exorcist. That's not the way Rimbaud and Henry Miller did it. My approach here is more along the lines of the Exorcist. An unruly teenage daughter in a plaid skirt and knee socks was supposed to be the focus of Part 1. This is Part 2.

Chapter 18

What do I witness later tonight? Let's say it's a mass of data awaiting the correct interpretation of an emerging mental illness.

Lights burning in the next ward reveal a fantastically amusing scene that includes scores of children, mostly nude boys whose eyes are mirrors reflecting infinity. I didn't invent that phrase. The memories are razor-sharp. I remember them from the darkness of Hell. They're messenger boys! In the bathroom mirror my eyes are red-rimmed and rheumy. I shake my head again, this time imagining I'm stuck between the second and third floors listening to a telephone ring several times more. The air is thick with dampness and drug-assisted hypnosis. Having made it past the night guards I ride the elevator down to the basement accompanied by the pest control staff who smell of cheap perfume and cigarettes. We enjoy a smoke in the service corridor, milling about, discussing the events of the day. We agree those are serious young boys upstairs, bouncing their basketballs with overly serious babysitters in tow. I imagine each one of them is a strategic military or naval target with a coded trigger-phrase buried deep in his mind. They're ready to surrender on their birthdays to the child rapists and kidnappers who spring the traps to get their bait, the opposite of what criminals once did here in North America.

Let's say one those nude boys is a bit too horny for his age. Let's say he's cursed with a precocious penis. Try to follow me here. He's a Korean boy with a thing for little white girls, an unhealthy thing involving tennis racket grips and clothesline. One day on the playground he approaches Amber out in the open, so as not to arouse suspicion or fear. He's nude. That does create some concern. He has an enormous erection long straight glistening with Vaseline in the hot afternoon sun. The tennis racket grips come later. Right now he wants to crush the opposition, Amber's tight little twat. Amber approaches him warily. The young boy has North Korea written across his back. She doesn't want to reward his belligerence and provocation too quickly. She's deployed her guided missile destroyer.

I want the reader to imagine that scene in great detail without feeling discomfort or revulsion. If you find genuine humor in it, good for you. I digress. None of what I describe in the last paragraph happened outside the reader's imagination. The doctor assures me the description serves a specific therapeutic purpose and should not be expunged from the record.

Amber's prolonged immobility's torturing the muscles in her back. Her lovely mouth distorts with contempt as the priestly doctor in those priestly robes lifts her prosthetic limbs to demonstrate how they work. A fifth at most. Next thing you know Amber adopts lascivious poses, making inarticulate noises and strings of incoherent phrases.

I imagine Amber plummeting right through the floor of the examination room. She's yelling all the way down into some sort of bottomless pit where they've lost the rusty keys.

"Daddy this isn't Hell is it?"

"No Amber in Hell the demons leave the women and children behind. That's not what's going on here. I'm bringing you along with me. We're off to the races!"

Let's say Amber loathes me. I know we've become strangers to one another. It's more than that. She can't stand the fact her life's become a bizarre form of hysteria. Forcing water into her mouth and eyes might flush out those demons. Breaking her ribs would be doing her a favor. Grabbing her by the neck and strangling her would put her into a more remarkable world, a model world social and simple with no sleeping around or seizures and vomiting in the media portrayals.

I must have a demonic look on my face. Amber begins to pout. I've never seen her pout like that before.

"Daddy it's dark down here. I think I've torn my skirt!"

"For your sake Amber I'm pleased if that's the worst of your problems. You'll get used to the dark. Trust me."

What else do I witness tonight? The community demonologist informs me a dark force snapped my daughter's neck last Thursday. A week later I'm at an absolute loss. I'm dizzy. The harsh fluorescent lights dazzle my eyes. Beaten useless under Harmony by the amplifying effects of self-hangmen & rope-gangsters, Writer's Block struggles to chain and drag me into the prison cell of maximum-security Helplessness. My unique human lowest self becomes lost to the Other Side, the lowest deadly sin, transformed into a windowless booth's view onto the drunken bed-play of jaded hospital officials. Hospital president puppet-gangster-slave Eisenhower, commander of Nursing Troops Divisions 4 & 54, instigated the turbulent animal-nature of World War 2. "We're committing no harmony-crime against our patients! We're preventing the worst criminal menace alive from injecting its Nazi impulse into the less fortunate!" The experts smelling of chicken manure inform us history will cease when a hospital president's assassinated for saving the lives of insane gangsters. Oi vay.

Can I blow my nose now doctor?

I remember walking over to the wobbly table in the breakfast nook to get a yellow-colored editing pencil. I had a great deal of unscheduled material on paper I wanted to pare down, whole paragraphs, blocks of text I needed to reduce or remove as by cutting and slicing to prepare for a secondary reassembly of those pieces into a less convoluted narrative. 'Polishing' is another word that comes to mind. At that moment I was in a frantic state of mind. I feared I was bogging down, disappearing into my own methods, locutions, and literary mannerisms. I was losing hope in the English language. Nothing worse can happen to a writer than losing faith in his own language.

When I left our flat to visit Amber downstairs in the pawnshop where she was babysitting I was carrying that yellow editing pencil.

I remember thinking. Not in your wildest dreams.

Not in your wildest dreams.

To this day I believe the English alphabet is a great one, an imaginary world whether or not we're here to take the oath yet much more than a mere industrial hunger fragment. Inside its grammar forgetfulness is more luminous than a Titian painting. Even a block of stone knows how to recall that evolved silence. The Indian treaties are also important. By the way nice brocade there doctor. No more of that industrial scum and treacherous cruising! Get it the hell away from here! Would you ask for the constant? It's time for overboard research, the only choice we got.

From the hospital ground's immense elevation, the long striking distance becomes a piece of bad looking, a religious story recast to calm my hunger and blame my digestive system for not connecting to my throat more cleanly. To the pedestrians crowding the streets below we patients are the outsiders, the unexpected human beings with a more primitive logic and a free-stream creation. Much like squirrels going white before a hard winter we obey the call that refuses these vestigial times of contraction. Yearning for a larger stomach of hunger is as unnecessary as goldfish though yearning remains a part of great literature, the cedar of abundance as it were. Non-artists continue to mess up the music and movies with baskets of flimflam. The Interstates this year, with more checkpoints in the evenings. Cops searching out that sexy ideal our stomachs have chosen for us. Taste's on our side of life, not the one the officers stand on. Whichever corporation achieves the highest brain penetration wins out. A few months after birth each newborn's equipped with a socket-mount beneath its scalp allowing for complete control of the infant's perceptual environment. No one ever told you that? Rest assured doctor no discomfort's involved.

Chapter 19

The sun's up. My ass ain't fallen asleep yet. Not exactly a beer garden or a weekly column in Maxim. Trust me I won't start acting like a madman yet. That's for later. Let's think up ways to rearrange the furniture in this cell.

The doctors lock you in a room and throw away the rusty key, leaving you with little else to do except exercise your imagination. If that's not a blessing in disguise I don't know what is. I see pile-warts, yellow-hammers, flickering disco balls. I hear thunder. I imagine Penny's in the next room fondling the laundry. She watches the latest movie about a horny Thai hairdresser who lives and works in Holland and collects penguin bones. The critics say it's the greatest drama ever. They should know. They've seen every movie in existence.

I think about lots of weird things early in the morning. I think about pubic hair. I think about Penny and me in Reno wearing matching wedding bands. That's not what I call creepy. I imagine last night when Penny climbed onto the hood of our car a cop appeared around the corner. Penny's a brave woman, decisive, with a great many baroque obsessions. She's the last in a long line of inbred psychopathic aristocrats. She hears voices. This morning she's passed out. Penny has bronchitis I imagine not food poisoning. It's a virus or bacteria or my dick in a box. I'm such a sweet boyfriend.

I dreamed of robots last night. To hell with evolution right? Why should I evolve from monkey stock? Later I'll imagine the 2010 World Series of Poker and blow up marshmallow Peeps in an imaginary microwave. Interstate-80 has my full support. Can I see those Reno pics? What's the vibe out there? Last night I had an epic emotional breakdown in the shower. I became destroyer of worlds. I felt productive for once. Hooray for the Rolling Stones. Now it's up to the doctors to determine if I can be a better husband and father starting today. What was bad about yesterday? I gave up drinking. Damn I'm sore. These feet are not made for slippers.

Five cups of coffee. I'm tired.

Rather than hit the snooze button a third time I walk out of my cell into the Back Ward. Reshad's sleeping in one of those orange-colored fiberglass hospital waiting room chairs. I yell at him with my favorite demon voice. No response. He mumbles in his sleep something about women being disgusting and why don't they put only two servings in a vodka bottle. I can't believe Reshad's snoring. How rude. Where's the nursing care in that? Real men don't hit retarded girls. Ever watch The Shining? That man was a genius. Too bad you can't get paid for coming up with shit like that off the screen. Drugs screwed up his career.

Busy morning. I scrounge around the ward for breakfast. I feel like shit, all kinds of shit. My tummy makes funny sounds. I can't find the Advil. On TV I find Jesus and Oprah and a new show called Crime & Punishment Las Vegas. Here's a patient's shampoo horde. Conundrums. Intuition or gut feeling? Let's escape to Japan for the vernal equinox. I need six hours of procrastination to help celebrate Albert Einstein's birthday. Your cancer relapsed? Solution? A drunken bike ride.

I find my way to the chapel, walk up to the altar, begin praying to Allah or Yahweh, what have you. A hand on my shoulder interrupts me. I turn around to find Reshad.

"You're Rosenberg one of our recent admissions right?"

"That's me. We've been introduced I think."

"Sort of yeah. Some of the doctors around here are jerks. You get used to it. I've been assigned to your daily care. It's part of the protocol. You look good. You're lean. You have a nice firm body. Where did you say you grew up?"

"In Massachusetts on Martha's Vineyard."

"Where did you go to school?"

"At a university in the Boston area."

"You're a long way from home. I've never been outside California. Let me correct that. I was born in Indonesia. Less than a week later my parents moved to the U.S., to California. I haven't left since. I now have a slight California accent."

"Are you married? You have a large family?"

"No on both counts. Mine's another calling. I take it you're a religious man. What denomination?"

"Islamic surrealist."

"Both of my parents were Muslims. Indonesia is the largest Muslim nation in the world. What makes an Islamic surrealist fundamentally different from other kinds of Muslims?"

"It's not what you think. Let not the harlot tempt thee to excess in her delights."

"That's intense! Have the doctors supplied you with a Koran? We have some copies floating around here. Given your devoutness it's only right you should have a Koran as part of the healing process."

"When does the healing begin?"

"It has. It did the moment you were admitted. Everyday you're getting better in very subtle ways."

"Forgive me for asking such an odd question. Why am I in here exactly?"

"You walked into this room of your own free will."

"I mean why am I in this hospital?"

"The answer to that is not so straightforward. The doctors and nurses are working it out. The healing process is a work in progress."

"Have I done something bad enough to warrant this type of confinement?"

"That's the crux of the matter Rosenberg."

"I don't recall anything bad or much worse. Can't you take my word I didn't intend any harm to anyone or anything?"

"We cannot. There's a likelihood you're making that claim in a deluded state of mind."

"I know about delusion."

"You may not know what you're talking about."

"You and the doctors do? You're NOT deluded? You know me better than I know myself?"

"It's a solid blow to your ego. Once you're able to live comfortably with that notion, you'll have completed at least two-thirds of the healing process."

"The notion that other people know me better than I know myself? Strange. I never learned that particular delusion from my parents and teachers."

"Let's take this up later. It's a huge topic, too large to deal with in a single conversation. I have to make my rounds. We'll continue tomorrow morning."

Reshad leaves me standing alone in the chapel.

Let me get this straight. I'm supposed to play along and acknowledge I've forgotten I once lost control of myself? For that reason alone these doctors want to make a freak out of me? I got arrested? When I gaze up at the Crucifix I'm reminded of an old Mel Gibson movie. That's supposed to be me up there? The bleeding guy with the fake mustache and beard suffering from post-traumatic stress disorder.

I can hear the pedestrians outside screaming The guilt of the survivors! The guilt of the survivors! The guilt of the survivors!

Off in the distance a telephone starts ringing. No one's picking up.

I swear I'm a calm man not given to outbursts of impulsiveness. I'm fond of dogs, dried fruit, and swimming. Taking orders and assassinating people are not two of the things I do best. Nor can I crack safes or break codes or seduce secretaries in foreign governments. I'm fairly anonymous, a man of slightly above-average height with curly brown hair, otherwise unremarkable, blessed with the single name Rosenberg, a useful and interchangeable name among the Jews. I do own a revolver, an antique 9-millimeter Walther P-38 I use to scare away writer's block.

The telephone continues to ring making it very hard for me to concentrate on prayer. My knees hurt from kneeling. I move to a pew. I'm stranded in a house of worship that fails to relate to the dictates of my own religion. Frustration builds up inside me until I start kicking at the pew. I kick and kick until my feet are throbbing. The results are impressive. When I rise to leave, the pain of standing sends me collapsing to the floor.

Later I awaken in my cell. A nurse has packed ice around my feet and elevated them.

A beautiful young woman approaches the bed with the assured manner of an airline stewardess.

"Who are you and what are you doing here ma'am?"

"Can you hear me Rosenberg?"

"I can hear you fine. Could I see some identification? A driver's license, what have you."

"Can't you recognize me? It's Penny. I don't have my wallet. I lost my purse. That's the truth."

"Did you arrive by limousine?"

"No."

"You're loitering."

"I came to visit, to see how the healing process is coming along."

"You're loitering. You have no ID. That makes you a vagrant in the state of Nevada."

"What are you talking about?"

"How much money do you have?"

"Fifty cents."

"Let's see it."

She removes two quarters from her jeans, holding them up.

"You're not from this part of the country yet you expect me to recognize you? We've had lots of breaking and entering lately."

"I haven't done anything wrong. Why are you acting like this?"

"Please don't stand in the light!"

She moves to the left, says nothing.

"You're not from around here. You come here to observe me. I tell you I'm fine. Still you loiter! You don't belong in this place. Watch out for the other patients. Don't step on them. Some are quite belligerent and easy to piss off."

"You're the one I came to see."

"Some of the patients will join us shortly. That's par for the course. You stick close to me. I'll take care of you. I can't be responsible for your physical well-being. You don't belong here. You say your name's Penny?"

"I haven't done anything wrong!"

"You're a vagrant in the state of Nevada. If that's not wrong it's not exactly right. I'll summon Reshad to see what he's got to say about that."

I press the button.

Reshad appears.

"Do you know this woman Reshad?"

"She's your friend Rosenberg."

Penny turns to Reshad. "Why's he acting so weird?"

"Don't you recognize this woman? She's your girlfriend Penny. You told me yourself you lived with her."

"All I recognize is vagrancy. I recognize someone who doesn't belong here and has nowhere to go. She's got fifty cents to her name, says she hasn't done anything wrong. She's a vagrant. Come back and see us you hear?"

"Cut the shit Rosenberg!"

"I've never seen him act like this before."

"He's a strung out on painkillers. Earlier he tried to destroy his own feet. He took out his frustration on Christianity, smashed up some pews in the chapel, got blood all over the floor and altar."

"He's out of his mind!"

"That's a reasonable explanation right Rosenberg?"

"I suppose that's reasonable. They say a double-minded man is unstable in his ways. "

"Should I come back later?"

"That would be best. The medications will wear off in a few hours."

The woman leaves my cell.

"Rosenberg you can go back to sleep."

"Thank you Reshad. In spite of having to twist myself into an 'S' to lie down on this cot I slept well yesterday and last night."

"We can get you a different bed."

"Where's my sleeping bag?"

"We can't hand those out."

"Oh yeah I'm on suicide watch."

"Call it what you want. It's protocol. Zippered enclosures are not allowed."

"How far away are the mountains? Where do they extend?"

"I'm leaving Rosenberg. I'll see you in a few hours. Sweet dreams."

When the beautiful young woman returns without an escort less than ten minutes later I lunge at her with an editing pencil.

Chapter 20

Is this traveling in style or what? After what I did to Penny they're never gonna unbuckle this goddamned straitjacket. They call that 'acting out'? Translate my behavior into real money please. This ain't no worthless stage people!

The doctors are reducing me to a novel form of stillness to accelerate this memory into motion and force me to recollect some ugly things I did. I'm familiar with those tactics. I'm a writer. I'm on intimate terms with memories and imagination. Most people are scared of their own imaginations, incapable of writing a story filled with oddball jerks doing weird shit with pussies and guns. Our collective imagination's the great mixing bowl of the higher realms. That's a grand thing I tell you.

I must be endowed with X-ray vision. I glimpse a door at the back of my cell. When I open it I step into a McDonald's. Something important must be going on here. I'm the only customer in the place. The beds are unmade. I don't want their free food. I prefer old pork and stale bread.

I wet my lips.

WAIT! My eyes need more time to adjust. Turns out this ain't a McDonald's at all. It's a harshly lit service corridor smelling of oil, fresh paint, and cinderblocks. Behind me a toilet flushes. A telephone starts ringing. I'm supposed to walk to the far end, to those swinging doors down there?

I wave my fists at the ceiling.

"How long are you gonna leave me in here?"

Silence.

When I arrive at the doors they swing open to reveal Goldsmith. He's wearing overalls and a San Francisco Giants baseball cap. He's carrying a toolbox and a clipboard.

"Why the sulky face cub scout?"

"Go to hell Goldsmith!"

"They caught you huh? That seems rather careless. You do have the fatal flaw of trusting people."

"Have you seen Reshad around here? The black male nurse Reshad, the guy who delivers my meds and writing instruments."

"Don't know him. I'm on the outside remember? I'm on the outside looking in."

"You have lots of nerve to show up like this unannounced and awful smelling. You wanna get the shit kicked out of you?"

"We're both busy people Rosenberg. Let's cut the small talk. I'm here in Reno to learn if you were in an incapacitated frame of mind when you murdered your daughter."

"You've become a detective? I never killed anyone."

"You don't remember killing anyone. I'm telling you right now you're gonna give me the information I want."

"Where's Reshad? He'll manhandle your ass."

"It's only the two of us Rosenberg. That's what it's gonna be until we get to the bottom of this sticky situation."

"That cheap cologne you're wearing hardly conceals your need for a bath."

"Please don't make me threaten you."

"With what?"

"With federal prison."

"Not Luke Skywalker or Vincent Van Gogh or Dr. Malkuth?"

"Don't make me threaten you!"

"Ancillary authorization required! State your name and business! What's the name of your company Goldsmith the name of your employer?"

"That shit won't work with me. You know me well enough to know that."

"Your access code is invalid!"

"How long will you keep up this predictable charade?"

"Level eighty-one is long!"

Goldsmith stares at me with awed obedience.

"Roman Castevet is Steven Marcato rearranged!"

"Rosemary's Baby?"

A very Brechtian theatrical pause. I hope it tickles his Tanis root. It sure tickles mine. As usual Goldsmith's failed to see the funny side of things. He thinks this nonsense has gone too far. It's only begun. My imagination's the great mixing bowl. From it I create an endless series of permutations, combinations, juxtapositions. Why should I waste my time sorting that stuff into ethical categories like good and evil? I can't touch or taste those two words.

I pretend to lose my cool by staring at the ceiling for awhile. I'm faking boredom which is not as easy as it sounds.

Goldsmith stares at me in awed silence.

I grow impatient until I'm forced to imagine two married psychotherapists of different theatrical persuasions. They're paid to relate important stories about war and peace. On weekends they volunteer as counselors on a suicide hotline. The city government sets it up, lays it out for my description while the local taxpayer foots the bills. I admire this therapist couple. They respect me and Penny.

I imagine a casually corrupt atmosphere. The two therapists are lounging on an antique canopy bed in the middle of a spacious bedroom eating a bread pudding bathed in Irish whiskey. The bedroom's window is open to the scents of a lush Edenic garden and the sounds of a tale called *Before Kabbalistic.* A long time ago when real estate was at a premium the ultimate nuclear chaos in the center of infinity where the Ternary conducts its force to the Septenary was occupied by a hermaphroditic fertility deity once called Crawling Chaos of Iniquity, later All in One-One in All Christmas. With a strong mechanical pressure and a heat of some 600 degrees centigrade, that deity established the limits of the Knowable. Random bumps became little eyes. Faces crawled upon the Skagit Flats. The dark embrace of gaining a will and the lust for panoramic vistas created a total elevation gain of 1000 ft. Eagles and osprey soared overhead transcending socioeconomic boundaries. The protoplasmic decad-body of Christ struck a pose in two three four abridged or reduced forms of the Host after which the Mint Cross issued forth the 10,000 goat-forms of Duality. The common formulas for notation existed in those forms including the twenty-first letter of the Roman alphabet, the blood of Dick Clark, carnivorous plants, an old man on a porch smoking a glass pipe and reading an oversized cellophane-wrapped copy of the Tibetan Book of the Dead, an umbrella-man, a grassy knoll, a woman in a polka-dotted dress, a curbside epileptic, a congressman with a pot-leaf belt buckle, and the extension of the Quaternary into every 7-11. Nothing was formed by the 4 straight lines on the Straight & Narrow path of the Magus, no fire sprinklers or multiple exits. Yet between madness, suicide, and pointed noses the nightmare of infinite contractions gave birth to our society when Fiber Woods fled into Saks the 5th time on Sothoth Avenue.

When I awaken, the straitjacket's gone. I'm sitting down. Standing right before me are Reshad and Penny.

"Expect a visit from one of the staff therapists later this evening Rosenberg."

"Save the taxpayer's money. I'm in a most normal frame of mind right. I'm blooming even while the doctors have prohibited it."

"You have no say in the matter. It's protocol."

"Do you know Indonesia's national motto?"

"We learn it in school. In English I believe it's 'unity in diversity' or 'unity through diversity,' something like that."

"I experienced that state in a dream, unity through diversity. I concentrated hundreds of different functions into a single spherical plastic apparatus. Allah assigned me the noble task of learning how to operate it properly. The great mixing bowl."

Reshad scuffs his feet on the floor.

"Do you recognize this woman with me?"

"Penny!"

"Earlier you didn't recognize me Rosenberg. You called me a vagrant. You lashed out at me with a pencil, tried to stab me with it. That's when they put you in the straitjacket."

Penny reaches out to touch my shoulder.

"How much earlier was that?"

"You were tranquilized out of your mind."

"Believe me Penny it's the same story everywhere in this ward. Soiled clothing, television, death. They're devouring us like food. Their mouths water when they see us disgrace ourselves."

Reshad shakes his head.

Penny reaches out to touch my shoulder. "I'm sorry Rosenberg. I wish they didn't have to dope you up on meds. It's part of the healing process."

"I'm not much of a believer in the meds myself, not the purple-colored ones. Ever since arriving I ingest them to keep these hands and feet from harming myself and others right Reshad?"

"It's protocol."

"For the benefit of the gullible taxpaying tourists right? The crazy white foreigners and the blue-eyed legal freaks who want me to learn there are no harmless motives before subjecting me to that irrevocable deathlike experience."

I bang on the table for a moment. A rather witty gesture, Brechtian enough for the reader's expectations to get lost in it I hope.

"I don't give a shit if it is your protocol Reshad. This place cuts the vitality right out of my lungs. It's a wasteland, a brutal and triumphant occupation of the mind, a grotesque instrument of human torture, intolerable, utterly intolerable."

Penny bursts out laughing. "You're not representing Amnesty International are you?"

I bang on the table again. I feel like I can blow up mountains. I've corrupted the machine, disgraced the machine, the marvelous machine, that vulgar sentimental scoundrel. Observe my friends! Observe!

"You tell me to expect a visit from a staff therapist. That's part of the protocol too. How about imagining a young man in a British naval uniform instead or a stripper named Candy with a lethal red fingernail or a fat Englishman at a diner who's got an artificial limb and wears sweat-damp clothes?"

I continue banging on the table louder and louder. Why hurry the healing process? I might have time to plant a poison dart in Reshad's tattooed Indonesian back.

"The great mixing bowl. A dog, a bird, a flower. Horrifying isn't it? Disgusting intolerable odors of dog shit and diesel. One thing after another, different flavors, different anatomy. My daughter who was killed in her sleep by the pawnbroker while I sat at the keyboard editing a story and drinking straight from a Johnnie Walker whiskey bottle. How's that for the big showdown? You getting this down on your notepad Reshad?"

"Save it for the therapist."

"What's the point if a therapist's job is to sit there and listen? A counterman at the local diner once helped me play cop. A bartender named Santiago served me drinks and saved my life. You were there Penny. You jerked me off in the men's room."

Penny reaches out to touch my shoulder. I brush her away.

"Don't tell me you're trying to wring a confession from me!"

"Rosenberg she's here to support you during the healing process."

"Break out the Band-Aids!"

I start kicking at the nearest chair. "Get away you little brats! Get out of here! You're the worst of the worst!"

It's like shooing flies off bloody cuts of meat. In an instant the two of them are back on me.

Penny shakes her head. "What's happening to him? "

"He's going through the healing process."

I fling my arms out. "A maze of distorting mirrors inside a greenish cube Reshad!" I kick and kick and kick at the chair and the wall. It's wonderful how badly my toes hurt. Who keeps whistling?

"You're getting damn close to bringing out the straitjacket again Rosenberg!"

Abruptly I become immobile absolutely immobile cadaver-like. The transition is so sudden that Penny is stunned. Reshad can't hide his astonishment.

I find myself in the most normal of states again.

I clear my throat.

Penny clears her throat.

Reshad shakes his head.

I massage my sore and bloody toes. "I get it Reshad. There's no reason to play the fool here. Not every place on the planet can be run like Hollywood."

Reshad shakes his head.

Penny wipes her nose on the back of her hand.

"Hear me out on this. The great mixing bowl."

"Later Rosenberg. Visiting hours are up. I have to show Penny to the exit."

"Another mirage for a lonely traveler?"

The two of them leave my cell, making everything simple again, leaving me to pinch myself and remind the pale green cinderblock walls that nothing matters more than drug-assisted hypnosis.

Chapter 21

This evening the power's gone out in our ward. I've conformed to the darkness by bringing out the tubas and hooting beavers. I catch glimpses of patients in candlelit windows. What strange tiny rooms! I adore the abandoned buildings across the street, with their beautiful little meth addicts. Why the hell are our patients worried about losing their meds? Everything's legal in here so long as there's no open containers. We'll emerge unscathed. You watch. What could be more life-affirming than a skeleton key and a paper cup of meds?

That guy in the clown suit does look creepy. He may have a captive or two in the basement. The future fluctuates forcing the doctors to change up the ward every weekend. Something gets unplugged or damaged. Though they don't like that and they don't want that, it's not a negative thing. This evening they'll cook a fancy dinner for the well-behaved patients, whole-wheat spaghetti with veggies and pesto and shit. Afterwards if the power returns we'll watch Wall-E and Finding Nemo and hammer back shots of tranquilizers.

Pics of Reshad's new female assistant appear in the dictionary under 'trailer trash.' She's proud of her bitch status. She can get away with it too. Aren't you a shallow piece of shit! Here's an amusing little game we play before we murder each other over a sausage roll. We have one piece of cellophane to share. An amusing little problem. Good Friday's no excuse for bad prison sex. Reshad's assistant can barely stand the sight of my cock. She stuffs it in her mouth and ass every chance we get. She's fondling her breasts right now. She's fifty kinds of screwed. I screwed her twice already. If she's got a nosebleed, vodka and pride are what I got left. The musculature of her ass for instance. That hat's awesome. Time to order Chinese take-out! Time to roll out the duct tape! It's gonna be a busy night tonight in the Back Ward. I'm on top of my shit. I love the newly installed Egyptian ornamentation. A building with history is so hard to find in Nevada.

Back in San Francisco Penny's preparing matzah ball soup, fried chicken, corn beef with coleslaw, Russian dressing on rye, gumbo.

Everything's finished for the day. Her evening now depends on the night. No more mustache rides. She broke out the Nair.

I've begun hoarding stuff under my cot, cans of cream soda, odd letters I've received from Goldsmith. He writes he's shutting down my favorite gentlemen's club, turning our strippers out onto the streets of the Tenderloin where they're raped or die of a drug overdose. It's true if you wanna know yourself you gotta be constantly on the edge, a hairsbreadth away from total psychotic collapse, strung out to the utmost limits like a first-person narrator in a Knut Hamsun novel, like Nutzach Nietzsche in the last months of his sanity keeping it out there long enough to finish Ecce Homo. I know what's happening here.

"Rosenberg you think killing someone's more exciting than screwing someone? You think it's more stimulating?"

"Never thought about comparing the two."

"Were you ever wealthy, a man of money?"

"No."

"Where did you grow up here in Reno?"

"In Massachusetts."

"Your parents were poor?"

"They were wealthy."

"Ran a business?"

"Worked for city government both of them. In Boston. They're dead now. They didn't include me in the will. We had a falling out many years before over my dropping out of med school and converting to Islam."

"They're not religious?"

"That's the point. They never set foot in a synagogue. They were atheists yet they called themselves Jewish. It was idiotic if you ask me. They wanted to be part of a religious culture without practicing the religion. That's stupid, intellectually dishonest."

"For that reason you converted to Islam?"

"We gotta talk about this now?

"Let me get this straight Rosenberg. You're an educated man. You have a bachelor's degree in philosophy. You dropped out of med school for God's sake. Now you barely make ends meet in one of the worst neighborhoods of San Francisco. You're a struggling writer with no gainful employment."

"There used to be the gentlemen's clubs."

"You weren't earning money there. You were a client."

"I earned some money running errands for Goldsmith."

"My point is that may be par for the course in San Francisco. Where I lose track of the thread is when you murder your own daughter. Why do you think you did it?"

"I had a kink in my neck. Muscular atrophy. Something like that."

"You were in pain?"

"I got it! Writer's block! Why not? The voice of God told me to."

"You killed your daughter out of frustration over your own writing?"

"If you like sure. As many reasons as you want I got 'em, reasons that set parts of my body in motion, reasons with a will behind them. Isn't that what you want? Drama and suspense are fine and dandy so long as we keep the explanations simple. Tell me I'm right!"

"I want you to explain how one minute you're dining with your daughter at a restaurant eating breadsticks and pasta. The next you're strangling her on the neighbor's sofa."

"You wanna know what happened in between right? There's Zeno's paradox. You wanna know what happened in between. What can I say? Things change. Life doesn't have to make sense. Cars disappear."

"Including the suspension?"

"The suspension, the engine, the transmission, the rear end, the drive train, the electrical system. I'm glad you appreciate my position. I wonder how many narks you know. What's a nark look like doctor?"

"A nark looks like an imposter."

"What's an imposter look like?"

"Rosenberg do you think you're mad?"

"I wasn't until you called me a murderer. Man that hurts."

"Mad as in crazy, insane. Do you think you're insane? Does that word make sense to you?"

"I'm not sure I can answer that. I don't think I'm hallucinating or hearing voices."

"How can you be certain? It's a rhetorical question. Let's not go there. Getting back to the issue at hand, do you believe killing someone's more exciting than screwing them?"

"It's apples and oranges."

"You believe there's no basis for comparison?"

"Right."

"At the least they're two forms of human behavior."

"Okay I agree with you. I don't see the basis for comparison."

"If you were insane would that make you special or unique in the eyes of Yahweh or Allah?"

"There's lots of insane people in the Back Ward not to mention the rest of the hospital."

"You believe you're in a hospital?"

"Yes."

"You could be suffering from a delusion."

"I monitor my mind for delusions."

"Do you think you're being held against your will?"

"That's my impression with the locks and keys I see everywhere."

"That could be a delusion right? This hospital and every worthless thing in it could be a delusion or an illusion. You never know. You have no basis for comparison right? My point is if we're honest with ourselves, genuinely honest, which I know is rare, we must admit we can never know whether or not our subjective realities are delusions. We have no basis for comparison. We can't surmount our own perspective."

"You're telling me what I already know."

"We have to be agnostics about everything in our lives, God, everything. We can never know with certainty we're not deluded."

"Okay I follow."

"What's holding you in this hospital?"

"A delusion of imprisonment or an illusion. I'm not sure what the difference is. I never learned to use the word 'illusion.'"

"Let's say a delusion happens in the patient's mind while an illusion happens in the mind of God. That could be the basic difference. What's holding you here?"

"I answered delusion. I've deluded myself into believing I'm captive. Isn't that what you want me to answer?"

"You're missing the point. If you're deluded why do you persist in that state? What's keeping you stuck in that state?"

"I don't know I'm stuck?"

"Unawareness or ignorance is what's holding you here in this hospital?"

"Okay."

"Okay what? That was a question! Now if you're ignorant or unaware you're deluded how can you overcome or escape from that delusion?"

"By becoming aware of that fact."

"We've arrived at our first important conclusion! If deluded people are deluded, they don't know they're deluded. So it seems at first. We've left something out. A second party, an outside agency, someone who doesn't share the patient's delusion. That someone is the doctor or therapist."

"You're not deluded?"

"I'm likely deluded. The point is I don't share your particular delusion, the one that's responsible for holding you captive and limiting your options. I can inform you of your delusion. That removes your ignorance. Secondly I can show you a way out of your delusion. That removes your powerlessness. When you regain knowledge and power you're cured of that particular delusion and the healing process nears completion."

"That'll cure me of every delusion?"

"Impossible. We have no basis for comparison. We can never know if we're absolutely free of all delusions. That's not the goal. Our goal's to shed a particular delusion once it becomes a burden and holds us captive. Therapists are trained to point out the patient's ignorance of his deluded state and pave the way for change. Damn I should write a book on this stuff. I know it'd sell!"

"You're deluded into believing you're not a good writer. You can't write a book that sells."

"That's why I go to my own therapist. You're picking up on this stuff fast! It explains every blockage Rosenberg. It explains the state of the world we live in, why things are slow and reluctant to change. We need outside experts to point out our delusions. Yet our pride prevents us from following their advice. As a result we remain mired in the same delusions throughout our lives. Pride supports ignorance. Ignorance supports delusion. That's the fundamental law of our reality. Perhaps."

Any wonder after that session I feel like throwing up all over myself? I'll get even with the bastard. You watch.

I walk over to the ward's single TV set, place my face against its sides to feel the vibrations. Something like ZZZZZZZZ. If you've ever been to a Methodist church service you know what I'm talking about. A voice on the TV makes an announcement.

"One giant step for mankind!"

I look up to see Reshad striding across the ward toward me.

"Rosenberg how's it going?"

"Not well. I got the third degree from a staff therapist. Dr. Brenschluss."

"Muttonchops and a receding chin right?"

"And a trancelike voice."

"He's doing his job. Why don't you go back to your cell and write in your journal for awhile? You look edgy. You need to settle down."

"Give me one of your crappy tranquilizers."

"Not before dinner."

Up on the TV a Gestapo interrogator begins beating his next victim with a hose. I use the remote to change the channel. The next image is of a woman hanging her nightgown on the back of a bedroom door. I change the channel again. Static.

"Rosenberg are you familiar with African green monkey traps? They're set up so a monkey can reach into a cage to grab the food without being able to remove its hands unless it drops the food it so badly wants to eat. Get my drift?"

I inspect the structure of my hand, look up to find Reshad staring intently at me.

"Did you know my daddy was a locksmith?"

"Why the hell would I know that?"

"He taught me how locks work, how to pick them, how to be good with electronics and mechanical things. He taught me how to escape from a locked room."

I begin inspecting my hand again.

"Don't stand there like a moron!"

"What do you want me to do?"

"I've got something planned for later tonight. I'm inviting you to take part."

"More self-improvement?"

"You'll find out later. I can't risk talking about it too much before it happens otherwise the doctors will get wind of it and clamp down on the Back Ward. You play chess Rosenberg?"

"Knight to queen's bishop three."

"Indian defense. You're good, very good."

Reshad tells me the Back Ward's a gruesome place in the winter. Many of the patients become excessively poly-ideational, retreating into imaginary miniature worlds of tiny porcelain dolls and see-through robot men. Complexions turn pale and gray. Anger mounts. Nightmarish convictions reawaken. The doctors can bow their heads sheepishly.

"Clowns to the left of us, jokers to the right."

"Patrick Bateman's more like it."

I hear the Brechtian strains of an orchestra fiddling away in an orchestra pit. A nurse pounds on a bathroom door.

I bite my lower lip before biting into the glazed chocolate-filled donut. I taste chocolate and cinnamon. Reshad bites into another piece of take-out sushi He sips from a can of Diet Coke. For the first time I notice one of his eyebrows is higher than the other. His mouth's twisted. He grins crookedly. He mutters through yellow nicotine-stained teeth. He has a tattoo on his bicep that reads THE KINGDOM OF TRUTH WILL COME.

Forgive my importunity. Are you paying attention to the havoc I'm wreaking here?

Sweat collects on Reshad's forehead. Sweat runs down his arms. Sweat collects everywhere. Sweat interferes with your vision. Sweat runs down the cinderblock walls. The Back Ward isn't air-conditioned in the summer. This could be Leavenworth.

I stagger over to the cage-like windows where the scratched glass breaks up the fading sunlight. What's outside those windows at this very moment? A scrappy little boy walking down the street with Rollerblades slung over his shoulder. What's the story with his ripped pants?

A two-door Toyota pulls up to the boy. The backdoor opens. A beefy-looking arm jerks the boy inside.

I burst out laughing.

Was that his sweat-drenched father?

I wipe the sweat from my eyes, biting down hard on my lower lip as if to puncture and deflate the tissue.

This cannot be happening.

Memories of Amber are returning. A snow-white robe levitating behind the windshield of a car parked in a fire-lane that encircles a windowless supermarket. Big raindrops beating down on a sidewalk.

"What's out there Rosenberg?"

"I thought I saw something strange. It was a memory blip. You smell that burning?"

"Not going full-blown epileptic on us are you? What's up with your project? Never hear you talk about it anymore."

"The Arab surrealist movement?"

"Yeah."

"Medication's destroyed it, doctor's orders, something like that."

Reshad smirks. "What'd you say the purpose of the movement was? What are you trying to accomplish?"

"I remember it well. I started welcoming all-comers into the movement when the writer's block took hold and didn't let go. That night, those nights I couldn't sit still long enough to write anything down. My mind raced. When my mind races, my feet and legs do too. I went for long walks through the city. Rather than write down words I spoke into a mini-cassette recorder."

"That was the Arab surrealist movement? Wandering around talking to yourself?"

"I let my mind race, gave free reign to my imagination."

"I don't see the Arab or surrealist aspect."

"When I worked myself into a frenzy of vocal scribbling, fantasy outcompeted reality. That's the state I called looking out my backdoor."

"You're a compulsive daydreamer. Big deal. Lots of patients in the Back Ward are. Most of them can't switch it off."

"Do they want to?"

"They can't even ask themselves that question. That's what sets you apart Rosenberg. You fascinate the doctors."

"I never wanted the movement to be a private affair. I didn't want to be a bored and angry anonymous man. I wanted publicity and to recruit followers."

"Recruit people to wander around daydreaming and talking to themselves? You think healthy adults want that?"

"I didn't it either until the writer's block hit. Something happened. If I'm basically a good person I'm still an outsider. That means I help people in nonstandard ways."

"You'll either drive them mad or kill them."

"Paradoxical isn't it? You're a doctor. You know how hard it is to help people who don't want to be helped or don't realize they need help."

"Help them die?"

"They shoot horses don't they?"

"You've taken it upon yourself to put people out of their misery? What the hell were you writing when you got writer's block in the first place?"

"Short stories and outlines for novels and screenplays about the lives of imaginary characters. Fiction. I forced my imagination down in print, in lines of written words. I didn't realize it. I was like a horse wearing blinders."

"You're using lots of horse metaphors. Do you know how you got writer's block in the first place?"

"Stress. My wife had moved out, leaving me alone to take care of our daughter. I don't know if that caused the writer's block. It sure disrupted my writing routine."

"You alone were responsible for looking after your daughter?"

"That's right."

"You'd been married long?"

"Sixteen years. We married right after my wife got pregnant. We hadn't been 'living together' for several years."

"What pushed her to move out and leave the kid behind?"

"The usual stuff that breaks up marriages. Compulsive overeating, drug abuse on her part, compulsive sex on mine. We weren't seeing eye-to-eye on anything. By the end, the only thing holding us together was our daughter. I went to the gentlemen's clubs everyday. I'm not sure where my wife went."

"Who looked after your daughter when you were at the clubs?"

"When Amber wasn't at school she hung out with our neighbor, a man who ran a pawnshop downstairs. She babysat for him. It turned out to be a very bad idea. It was a stressful time for her too. Her mother leaving us caused the psychological problems and suffering that pushed Amber over the edge."

"Meaning what?"

"Meaning Amber had to be relieved of her suffering."

"That's where the Arab surrealist movement stepped in? I don't see where you get the phrase 'Arab surrealist movement.'"

"It's a work of the imagination. I'm mixing fantasy and reality."

"What about Arab? Why not Muslim surrealist movement?"

"It is what it is! Why do you keep giving me the third degree? I don't like explaining things. Every explanation's a cover-up, a lie. Let me gather my thoughts." I give a nice long Brechtian pause. "When you tap into your imagination the way the movement does, with such intensity, you get input for things like poetry, as well as mystical input from something higher. Yahweh, Allah, what have you. You're pulling down religious symbols and images. You're like a conduit between God and humanity."

"You've thought this stuff out."

"Isn't that proof enough I'm not irrational the way the rest of these patients are? I've got no choice in the matter. I'm the instrument of something else. I gotta accept my fate."

"Why would God choose you?"

"Why not? He chooses everyone else. They don't 'hear' Him."

"This conversation's going nowhere. You can't 'hear' yourself."

"Look Reshad help get me out of here. That's the main thing! You admit I'm different from the rest of these patients. I don't belong here. The only contribution I can make is out there helping bring humanity closer to God."

I point through the windows.

"That sounds incredibly idiotic coming from someone who murdered his own daughter."

"I relieved her of suffering. I can do the same for lots of other people."

"Doesn't it occur to you I have personal and professional ethics?"

"I wouldn't want you to do anything illegal. You can quote me on that. I'm sure you can figure out something a bit more legal than illegal. Use your imagination."

Reshad smirks, gets down on his knees.

This cannot be happening.

Reshad's grabbing my ass so hard I can't pry his hands loose.

I bite down hard on my lower lip.

All I can think about is cigarettes and cigarette smoke and an American in London stepping off the curb looking the wrong way who's struck and killed by a lorry.

"Jesus Reshad where did you learn to give head like that?"

He yanks my dick out of his mouth.

"I practiced on bullies in the bathroom at the White Castle."

"You naughty boy."

"It takes two to be naughty you naughty boy!"

Reshad doesn't realize I'm imagining his mouth is Penny's mouth. I'm the only boy in the Back Ward tonight.

"You gave head to bullies every day?"

"I was the crew boss."

"Two bullies at once? They ever hit you over the head with a brick?"
"Stop talking!"

Reshad rests his eyes on my ample member. He's imagining I'm one of those bullies, the bully with the big bad leg who immigrated from Rotterdam.

My legs are trembling. "Can't we do this sitting down? My legs are devastated from standing so long."

"I want you towering over me."

"It's an S&M thing for sure."

"One-hundred-percent."

"What an absurd way of putting it!"

Reshad clears his throat, resumes deep-throating.

I resume sweating, biting down hard on my lower lip.

This time I leave Penny out of the fantasy, imagining instead Reshad's amazing mouth is a jagged hole through his throat and my cock's filling up the emptiness inside him. Through the hole I glimpse an entire metallurgical lab awaiting delivery of copious spurts of protoplasm.

I grip Reshad's gleaming scalp, focus on the ward's ancient checkerboard marble floor. I try not to let my pulse interfere with the naughty sounds I'm hearing. At once I imagine dropping a brick on Reshad's head. A smashing success warm, wet, sticky.

Chapter 22

Doctors and therapists keep files on everything.

Reshad promises me that tonight's literary hijinks will have bug-like qualities including a burglar-alarm panel and a Ziploc bag of cold fingertips.

What do you wanna imagine next kind reader? The cheap and deadly meth I heard about in Guatemala? A package of frozen chicken wings from Costco? A timeless love story by William C. Shakespeare? Masses of metal trapping bunches of kids in overweight vehicles? How the media hates engineers' bodies dumped on the Stanford campus? Get your channels changed! You're overdue a truth session! I warned you at the beginning my real name's Rosenberg. I gladly risk the scorn of being considered unpatriotic.

I need to get out of the way before the edge of the Literary Void starts bleeding like an open wound. So many dead things down there, how familiar, one and all incorruptible, bone for bone, concept for concept, image for image. Where have I seen them before?

Tonight I'll apologize to Reshad for not making Part 1 a bit cleaner and sufficiently entertaining. It does surpass everything clinical and anything less astonishing is my editor's fault. A blue color? That's for Part 3 when I write about travel disorders. For now let's describe the sleeping ward ganging up become chucked in hunger. I'll add an element of excrement in there. That's when cosmetic dissolution becomes celibate organ addiction. Take a sad song. If they're horrifying what becomes of those military experiments? Ditch the law you stupid Jesuit! Smell the limes on the brisk wind as we bury our government! The enemy at this earlier date is pulling the universe away from us. The blue eye has tracked in too closely. Next time there'll be proximity if we gotta burn it out of them. Too many of us in here are overdramatic and defunct. Take the nurses in one ward running hot enough to warp a goddamned spaceship. The many subconscious manic mood men out on the ace of spades. We gotta burn it right outta them! Better yet pour gallons of mouthwash into their eyes to clear up that vision a bit. Let's let 'in general' become the first place without that which is general.

The material in Part 1 continues to unfold even while we're occupied with editing Part 2. Train wreck in Maine. Brakes failed to work. Arkansas jeweler hanged. Man's head blown off at a prayer meeting in Alabama. Infection from cattle. Ghastly joke in Jersey. Frightful collision of two high-speed trains on a Colorado mountain curve. Two lives crushed out. Bodies frightfully mangled. Three passengers missing. Fire followed the crash. Yellow fever spreading. General stoppage of travel.

The experiment of destroying a human body with potash was carried out today in the Back Ward. A cadaver was cut up, placed in a solution, and a fire ignited. Within minutes the flesh dissolved. At the end of two hours only a few splinters and a small amount of fluid remained.

Lots more horror tales around here, lots of metal floors, fire-hammered railings. You can see it in the patients' eyes. Incumbent on everything send the schizophrenics to hell! Fifteen spade nurses come at us. We shoot their assistants first. The many young women in white pajamas working to protect their own asses when the helicopters arrive are appetizing to me. I'm one slick guy. The black market's door gunners get a big body count tonight. The crushed remains of men, sudden fits of vanity, get a weekend pass to Da Nang, else get blown away. Such a beautiful life.

Morphine's for the pain, gooks kill you screaming, slipping us pain in a world of suffering, stoned every night, unconsciousness, stoned, a brief time to stay, do, fighting with the grunts refusing to leave their units like a law unto nature. Off we fly, our injuries full of holes, getting fixed up a bit in Japan, pressing my own business, searching for tranquilizers, moods varying, shooting up, chills, apprehension on lay-over in Okinawa, seven-hour flight to Honolulu, pains, extreme chills, shooting two vials a day. Hooked I shoot it. Nurses in town can get it. Everybody does it. Worst before leaving Saigon in my joints my legs. Lemonade airplane the whole goddamned trip, pounding headaches of nervous energy. I shoot it.

Back home conditions of desperation evolve among the soldiers in the rehab units where uprooted means of destruction haunt them. A heavy thing. You gotta stay high to deal with it. I obey the law of seven months in-country before seven years of bad dreams back home. I turn freaky over the Army's goodwill, firing fifty rounds from the edge of my bed. So loud. Those are our guns. Could be VC or NVA up there! Pouring out fire support to protect our men! Push come to shove I open up on anybody. I scatter medical supplies around the ward to be sure. Seven months later back home I crouch on the edge of my bed, blades spinning in dreams, two doors sliding open onto a landing strip in-country, giant double blades of Chinooks bringing in transport, mail bags, food supplies. Go up for awhile, come back down at a support base. Sandbagging bunkers. Dirt roads. Stuck filling sandbags for three weeks. Officers walking around in fatigues. Relax, head low, run like hell if you're under fire hit the dirt soldier!

Not the kind of place you'd visit on Christmas morning is it? The harsh fluorescent light turns every patch of skin sickly and purple giving the patients an unearthly pallor. We are unhealthy. We spend most of the daylight hours immersed in morbid and clinical obsessions. We don't have regular work to give meaning to our unhappiness. We've been deemed incompetent, ineligible for work. That leaves boredom and rage. Later on TV a murdered polar bear. No wonder I'm prone to flare up at trifling misunderstandings. No wonder I have to keep going to the bathroom. I don't understand why the doctors despise me.

I spend most of my days alone in the cell dreaming about Penny, writing this story. At the end of every day nothing's accomplished. Did you know Reshad enjoyed dressing up in girls' clothes as a kid? That's his business. I don't care much for girls' clothes unless they're on girls. I find them too tight and constrictive and gaudy. You might say they pinch me below the prostate.

I admire Reshad. We share the same blood and memories. We're prone to making the same mistakes. When he plays with my genitals I fantasize about Penny. I forget Reshad's in the room. He gives a firm hand-job and an above average blowjob. The only weird thing is he likes me to put strange things up his butt. I can't mention what. I assure you he enjoys it. As a result of those shenanigans I've begun to have the first homosexual dreams of my life. Thank God is what I say when I wake up. Where's a yummy snatch?

It's dark around here tonight! Did they cut off the power again?

"Reshad?"

"What?"

"I'm hungry. Why's the ward dark?"

"Listen Rosenberg there are specific ways of escaping from this godforsaken place. There's a methodology, like positioning yourself for a quick move to the right or left depending on what happens."

"You mean luck? Blind chance?"

"I mean intuition. The actual process is like intuition. It's impossible to find a flaw in it."

"Who taught you that? Your medical school professors? Is that the purpose of medical training? To teach you to look for an escape route in paradoxes."

"It's my job to take note of contradictions and help people escape from their delusions by way of those contradictions."

"You're starting to sound like Dr. Brenschluss."

"Can't you see we're on the same side here? We're both inside when we ought to be outside, out there in the real world."

"Think we ought to go back and wake the rest of patients before we escape?"

"The hell with them. They're too far gone. You and me, we still have a chance. Before this, four years in a federal prison. I'm not going back. Four years is a long time when you're taking it one day at a time. Four long years before they're convinced I'm not a criminal. I'm not in control of myself or responsible for my actions. I'm leaving this place. I'm inviting you to come along. It boils down to whether or not you trust me."

"I trust you up to a point. Where would you be heading once you get out?"

"I'll worry about a destination later when I'm on the outside."

"You're gonna help me start up the movement again?"

"Listen Rosenberg there's lots we can do out there. The Arab surrealist movement is an excellent example. Can't you remember it? What happened to the Arab surrealist movement you spoke about when they first put you in here?"

"That's where we'll start? Like that?"

"Pull yourself together! You're so strung out on meds you've forgotten your purpose in life. You're tired. I know the feeling. I don't care to stay in here any longer. Nor do I want to go back to prison. Four years. No way. Not again."

"It'll rain any day now."

"What are you smiling about?"

"Martha's Vineyard where I grew up. I never took responsibility for my childhood. That makes me less of a criminal and more of a madman."

"Here's the deal Rosenberg. I've watched the nurses and doctors use a particular door everyday for the last year. You gotta follow close behind, don't look around or act surprised, keep your face hidden."

"Tell me about your mother."

"Stop talking nonsense. Take this beard and mustache. Paste them on your face. We'll turn around and walk out the way we came in."

I follow Reshad's instructions. That's what he wants. I trust him. We may have more in common than a fox and a buffalo, or a fax and a buffalo. We're two peas in a pod, pursing our lips, smoking our cigarettes, hearts swelling beneath our lungs, behaving like we're stranded in a Chuck Palahniuk novel. A couple days ago the doctors declared us 'biochemical enigmas.' The varieties of available behavior are infinite. Why not pretend exhaustion and lay our faces in our hands? Goddammit we'll turn around and walk out the way we came in if that's what Reshad wants. We're not crazy or irresponsible. We're emissaries from another galaxy. We're on the side of bank robbers, draft dodgers, and smugglers who hijack the U.S. postal system for their own seditious and obscene needs.

"I can't wait to get back out there Rosenberg to see what kind of scene they're making these days. C'mon follow me. Don't look around too much and cause a stir."

"Who's making what scene?"

"The passengers man, the movers, the pedestrians, the bystanders, the hangers-on, the outsiders with uncombed hair and battered leather suitcases, the types that populate your short stories. I know. I've read them. Stay close!"

I stub out my cigarette, adjust my mouthpiece, lean forward against Reshad's back. We begin shuffling forward in the darkness. Our conversation becomes a whisper.

"I've counted them a hundred times or more. Fifteen hundred and eighty-seven paces."

"You're very fast with the figures Reshad."

"I'm Muslim's why. We invented algebra and trigonometry."

"That's handy. What about the Christians?"

"Carpentry mostly."

"Building a roof?"

"Building stuff out of wood. That's carpentry. You use the best wood available. There's still the likelihood of termites and warping from damp and humidity."

"The Arabs and Muslims do it different?"

"They build things from stone over there. Wood's not right for the desert in a place like Yemen."

"I have my doubts about that. I recall tents in the desert, tents made from cloth."

"It depends. Desert versus city."

"People rarely notice that difference."

"I'll notice that difference when I get out of here. That's part of my religious training, taking note of differences, discriminating. Keep your head down and your hard-on. We're passing the first checkpoint. We don't wanna set off any alarms and awaken the night guard."

There ain't nothing I wouldn't do for Reshad. I place my right hand on his shoulder to better support myself. The fog of medication is lifting, rolling back out to sea. For a fleeting moment I wonder about Penny. Is she still working at a diner in the Tenderloin? I imagine her sitting on a stool at the counter turned to face the entrance of mostly male patrons who sport jagged hard-ons in their ancient Aztec blue jeans. Her large breasts jut outward, nipples erect. They're like cups or vessels. She directs a corrupt private detective into the lady's room, a mean-faced bozo who's embarrassed by the intensity of his own feelings. After she draws the shades he'll ask her to be rough with him. He's never done this before. Done what? This is the Tenderloin for God's sake, a worthless diner in the Tenderloin. What haven't they done there?

"Isn't this exciting? Don't you feel the beauty in it? Pay attention man!"

"You're hypnotized Reshad. Why do you think you'll get away with this?"

"What are you talking about? We've fooled them all."

"Strange I can't recall anyone by that name."

"That's the craziest thing I ever heard. Don't you get it? We're gonna be outside, out there man. There'll be real money, real robbers, real police, real bullets. Lots of company too, deviant professors in semen-stained overcoats, clerks opening cash registers at gunpoint, columns of names and numbers ripe for the picking. I'm telling you what you know. You're not in room 303 anymore. Can't you see that?"

"There'll be scotch, bourbon, and rye?"

"Vodka Rosenberg your favorite! Vodka and tonics at your favorite gentlemen's club! We ought to get into the liquor business."

"Or tobacco. Cigars. Cigarettes, pipes, and cigars."

"We'll need a humidor for that. Easy does it. Watch your step. Keep your hands on my shoulders."

"Isn't that a champagne cork on the floor?"

"Looks like the doctors were celebrating tonight. You've got your mouthpiece in?"

"Yeah."

"Champagne's a woman's drink right Rosenberg?"

Places, places, more places. That's what I'm thinking about right now. Waving down a cab, looking out a different window every half hour, glancing at my watch, wondering if Reshad saw the same things I did in that dusty rack of girlie magazines. Where to Reshad? How much time we got left? They don't call it a 'movement' for nothing you know. Women too, lots of women in dreary places, several booths for patrons, a long Formica counter with swivel stools, empty Styrofoam coffee cups, old balding men in shabby clothes sitting at a counter ordering hamburgers and coffee. Girls yeah girls is more like it. They're never women no matter how old they get. They're beautiful girls with long straight hair, wide sensitive eyes. They barely speak. Reshad knows I've got classified information on those girls. He's a sick young man himself. He knows about keeping records on secrets. He's full of surprises. On the outside they'll call him a quiet handsome type. In here he's a pathetic liar. That's the function of his special genius.

"Tell me more about what we'll have out there on the outside."

"Shhhh keep your voice down! We'll have six miles of inaccessible cliff and a roomy little cottage for you and your girls and me and my handsome quiet types. We'll wake up at eight every morning. We won't panic. We'll look bored enough to have lived there our entire lives."

"Okay I believe you. Our work? Will our jobs pay by the yard, bushel, or hour?"

"You're funny Rosenberg."

"Could you give me an example of a job with a name? I could sell women's shoes at Macy's. I could be a counterman in a diner and serve bland sandwiches with pale tomatoes, wilted lettuce, and stale mustard. I could listen to the patrons at the counter talk 49ers football and clean up their coffee spills. I could impersonate a private detective without a license!"

"Shhhh! You could do that. Why do any of it when you only gotta open your eyes to see that greater things are bound to happen. Ours will be the most important movement of the past ten or twenty years. It'll be like boom! boom! boom! big assholes all the way up to the moon!"

"Reshad the hell with a job. We don't need the money. We've had it worse. The streets and highways will be an endless supply of source material. That'll suit the purpose of the movement. By now the disarray is universal out there. Everything's broken, every city's a junk heap. You only gotta open your eyes to see it."

"I'll be damned. They changed the locks on this door."

"That's to keep the tourists out, the old balding men in shabby clothes and the waitresses on leave from out-of-business diners."

"C'mon Rosenberg we gotta turn around and go back where we came. We're gonna have to resort to Plan B. No whiskey till the job's over as my daddy used to say. Be quiet, turn around, follow me."

I remember a previous time sipping white wine while looking out a plate-glass window. Penny sits across from me. A bit later we leave our drinks on the table to make love in the back seat of an old Buick parked in the hotel's underground parking garage. It's Monday afternoon, the first time Penny gives me head. She's wearing a wedding band. We're not married.

I bite my lip. I'm sweating.

"We have to be careful Rosenberg. You daydreaming again? Open your mouth. Say the first that comes into your head."

"Lung cancer."

"You sure you're okay? Don't be pompous. Look at the bright side. We couldn't have chosen a better time of year to make an escape. The height of summer. I can picture the shirt-sleeved men and women with flowers in their hair walking along streets and boulevards thumbing for rides. There's a whole generation with a new explanation. Many people in motion."

"Don't be ridiculous Reshad. What's Plan B?"

"Stay close. Take very small steps like in the ballet. We don't wanna wake the night guard. What are you doing? You can't hang back like that. Get closer!"

"If I were any closer I'd be on the other side of you."

"Groucho Marx?"

Off in the distance buried in the darkness a telephone starts ringing.

"That's no good Rosenberg. One of the guards will have to answer it. That means they might make their rounds. That's no good."

"Intolerable, intolerable. They told me you were decorated for bravery in the war."

"Cut it out! You can be so heavy-handed, so Germanic. I'm going as fast as I can."

"Loose bowels?"

"Shhhh!"

The phone stops ringing.

"Most of the guards around here are deaf Reshad. What's it matter? The way I see it, noise won't get us caught. When the lights come up we're screwed. No two ways about it."

"What's that?"

"Sounds like a TV. The phone woke up one of the guards. He's watching TV. What's Plan B? You never filled me in. Those are minor details Reshad. Window latches, door handles, wainscot."

"Stand still! Someone's coming!"

I do my best to stand still. I'm looking out at the black scenery. I see pinpricks of light in the darkness. Reshad is torturing me to death. He doesn't know the way out. He never did. He's never short on hypotheses. Those aren't keys that turn tumblers in locks are they?

The dark presence passes. Reshad relaxes his stance.

"We're good to go. Shake it out Rosenberg shake it out. Relax."

"You're pulling my leg aren't you? The whole thing's a farce. There isn't any escape route. There's nothing outside these walls right?"

"Don't be ridiculous!"

"I'm trying to be realistic is all."

"Plan B is to go through the laundry room. I'm not pulling your leg. You know the one-eyed orderly who pushes around the white cart? He told me about the laundry room. It's in the basement. They never lock the door leading from the service corridor to the outside. That's where the cleaners pick up and drop off laundry."

"A one-eyed orderly?"

"That bearded guy who lost his left eye to a flying piece of metal. He looks like an out-of-work Santa Claus."

"You mean the existence of God?"

"Go to hell Rosenberg! You know who I'm talking about. His name's Tariq."

"Don't know him. I'd remember a name like that. How can I know for certain you haven't been lying to me Reshad? I'm trying to be realistic. You take advantage of my deluded state of mind to get me to share in your own delusion. You're that lonely huh?"

Silence.

"Cat got your tongue?"

Silence.

Oh dear he can't bear disagreement can he?

I grope along the nearest wall until I find a light switch.

"This ought to clear things up once and for all!"

A harsh fluorescent light flickers on.

Reshad's vanished.

The door stands open before me.

Good God!

Outside it's hot. Beautiful. The view is splendid. The summery nighttime, the clear night sky, the full moon, the poorly lit hospital grounds, the sounds of the night, of cars passing on gravel roads, of Arab-looking dogs yelping like jackals. Everything's up for grabs. Who's the dead guy in the gutter? It's the Big Smash-Up!

I imagine a dry sirocco wind blows right down my throat. A taste of perspiration clings to my lips. The hot air is something I dive into, swim through as much as in hell as in heaven.

How well I remember that final night leaving the Back Ward!

I take my right hand, I remember, my right hand in my left. I lift both hands to my face. A shudder runs through me. I feel intense heart palpitations. I step over the threshold. I imagine behind me mobs of patients and night-guards fast asleep with their groans and their arms outstretched as if on a thousand rows of crosses. I can't go back inside even if Reshad were to call out to me immobilized forever in his Biblical psychosis.

I've changed. There's no time to reflect. I touch my forehead and eyelids. As I lean forward I feel the faint vertigo of falling before walking becomes easier, less tentative. I stride out to the road that runs by the hospital. Right there idles a rare night-roaming taxi with an Arab-looking driver sitting behind the wheel sipping coffee and reading an Arab-language newspaper. When he sees me he laughs, invites me inside. I take a seat in the front. I notice a caged white rabbit on the backseat.

"Hello sir I'm Bachir! Don't mind the rabbit. It's not hunting season yet."

"My name's Rosenberg."

"Where to sir?"

"A hotel I guess or a motel, someplace to spend the night."

"Not a problem. There are many nearby. It's a beautiful Nevada summer night. We're off!"

Bachir has a long narrow nose, a long narrow face, strange staring eyes. He must sense my disorientation and appreciate my tendency to crane my neck at everything we pass. I have to check the agonizing impulse to blurt out questions summoned by every nighttime object and mountainous landscape I glimpse through the impeccably polished windshield.

I pick up the Arab language newspaper on the seat between us.

Bachir turns to me. "You had a try at reading Arabic sir?"

"English is more than enough for me right now."

Bachir laughs.

I realize I've got no money to pay Bachir. I become nervous.

"I'm short on cash this evening. I'll be honest with you. I have no money at all, not a single cent to my name."

"Not a problem. I'll give you my business card. You can mail me a check when you start earning money again."

I cannot believe what I'm hearing. I'm amazed.

"You trust me enough to do that?"

"I do sir. Here's some cash to help ease your transition."

Bachir hands me a pile of crisp twenty dollar bills.

Again I'm stunned. "What did you mean by 'ease my transition'?"

"A gesture of generosity nothing more." Bachir sniggers under his breath.

I'm becoming paranoid. Does this man know me from somewhere? Why was he waiting for me at the curb? Reshad summoned him? Perhaps he works for the hospital and he's taking me right back to where I came from. He knows perfectly well what's going on.

"Do you think we're being followed?"

Bachir glances in the rearview mirror. "I don't believe so sir. Is anyone expecting you? Is there someone you're scheduled to meet?"

"Mostly people I want to avoid. You can never be too careful about those things."

"What things?"

"Pursuit and persecution."

"Paranoia sir."

"I'm paranoid? That doesn't mean we're not being followed. If you don't mind Bachir I'd like to find a hotel out on the Interstate far away from Reno."

"You're the master here. We'll do whatever you please."

I'm beginning to think Bachir's tricking me. This is too easy. None of this seems to be happening for the very first time. It's been thoroughly rehearsed, one big lie set up to dash my expectations of eternal escape. I don't want to spoil my luck. I do my best to project nonchalance.

"What did you say you're doing with the rabbit in the back?"

"I'm taking care of it for my nephew while he visits his parents in Beirut."

"I thought you said something about hunting season."

"I was joking."

"You're from Beirut?"

"No one knows where I'm from. Both my parents died when I saw very young, killed by the Israeli army. My certificate of birth perished in the fires of war."

"You were an infant when it happened?"

"I managed to get healthy by myself."

"You came to America?"

"Something like that. The phlebitis set in. Now I worry about blood clots."

Bachir laughs.

"You speak English without an accent. If it weren't for your Arab-looking headgear and those Middle Eastern-style slippers I'd assume you were American."

"Thank you. I want to be considered American. They're happy over here. They have excellent doctors. Do you like to gamble sir?"

"Gamble?"

"Yes casinos. That one over there's open twenty-four hours and includes a strip show. Would you like to try your luck with the tables and the ladies?"

"I told you I have no money left to lose. I lost it when I hit a difficult patch in my life."

Bachir laughs, pats himself on the side. "Have you thought about writing your memoirs? You've lived a rich and varied life."

"I keep a regular journal. That's a head-start."

"You carry it with you wherever you go?"

"Damn! I realized I left it back there."

"Shall we return?"

"No way. I'll have to reconstruct those episodes from memory."

"You must have a very good memory sir."

"I once relies on a mini-cassette recorder I carried around with me. The doctors took that away. That's how they cured me of writer's block. Do you know about hypergraphia Bachir? It's the compulsive need to write on any and every scrap of paper within reach. They put you in a cell with pens and pencils and pads of paper. Soon enough you get hypergraphia."

"Look sir! Another casino that's open twenty-four-seven. Look at those blinking lights! You could play the slots and enjoy a glass of curaçao or vermouth with your cigar in there. My friend Moktir works there as a pit boss. You should see how long he lets his hair grow."

Bachir laughs.

I feel words of contempt freeze on my lips. Bachir's remarks seem idiotic to me. I'm embarrassed that only a few minutes earlier I felt threatened by the apparent mystery of a man with such a narrow look on his face. I must check the violent urge to push Bachir right out the driver-side door before he shoots off his mouth again about varicose veins or some such stillborn topic. What airs he puts on. What sketchy comparisons!

"Earlier you said I lived a 'rich and varied life.' Where did you learn that phrase? What did you mean by 'living'? That's what I want to know."

Bachir coughs, clears his throat, ignores the question. "What are your plans after tonight sir?"

"My plans are to take up things precisely where I left off. I'm gonna scare the crap out of everybody. The train leaves at midnight as we used to say."

Bachir laughs, not letting me finish. He's lost his sense of self-respect. I ought to box his ears.

"How's that?"

"Want me to make a diagram for you? Good God! I'm not drunk, I never drink anything. There's no surviving your hopeless racket Bachir! Why don't you mind your own business for awhile and safely drive me to the nearest hotel?"

Bachir doesn't laugh or cough this time. He doesn't exist. He's properly nonplussed.

The rapid-fire nature of the evening's events is testing my patience. I've not escaped more than an hour. I feel tremendous pressure and expectations impinging on me. Everything's become fire, thunder, and lightning once again. Everything yields and drifts, carrying me off in dazed whirls of panic and blinding white confusion. I'm skeptical about what's going on out here. The Cult of Blood! The Cult of the Dead! High and Low! Left and Right! You understand me? Their heaven's a disgusting brothel. Their hell's a banker's catastrophe. Good lord it's happening at the same time on fifty different channels!

I turn off the TV with the remote and look about myself for the first time. The bright, modestly furnished motel room strikes me as an extravagance. I'm seized by a furious panic to push everything out of the room into the hallway, furniture, fabrics, engravings, each object of highly questionable value and metaphysical worth. I must look idiotic. I sure feel idiotic rushing about the room in such headlong abandon.

I lie down on the floor, stare up at the ceiling trying to calm down. As I lie there I realize I've got much better things to do than move furniture around a hotel room. I've got an artistic movement to attend to. I need to get my shit together if I stand a chance of ever realizing that movement.

Hours later when I rise to my feet the morning sun's shining through the window. I can hardly believe it. Outside, Bachir's cab sits idling on the tarmac waiting for its newly appointed driver. Bachir's vanished.

It's time to move.

I drive off in the cab.

PART 3 McKillen

Chapter 23

Tense silence.
A slight breeze.
Faint illumination.
Power at seventy-five-point-five percent.
One moment please.
Aligning and focusing beams. Strapping myself in.
Ladies and gentlemen gather round the flat-panel screen. I have an announcement to make.
Welcome again to the Arab surrealist movement.
"You hear that Goldsmith?"
Silence.
"Goldsmith you hear me? I'll win yet! You watch me speak into this microphone at the side of my mouth!"
The screech of tires ends further communication, sending me on my way.

My new home becomes the interior of Bachir's cab, a glassy more portable version of the cinderblock cell that once attempted to confine my body and startle my imagination.

After false starts in Parts 1 and 2, the Arab surrealist movement is under way again. I can see the progress. I've described Penny, Amber, Goldsmith, Reshad. I've described San Francisco and Reno. I've thumb-tacked pieces of scrap paper over the plot holes. Every time I think I'm done I need to add a little more on. I purposely miscalculate. That's the purpose of the Arab surrealist movement. Surprise. Disruption. It's dialectical too, as the purpose of the bayonet is to kill. Please don't ask me what the hell that means. I can look out the windshield at the sky until I realize it's almost break-time. I do that anyway. I've paid my dues. The preparatory legwork is done.

I've heard it said there's only two good days on a job, the first and last. If your job is to incite revolution, what matters is everything in between. A revolution's not finished till the day it's performed. If that day's the last day, the last day may in fact be the best day of that job. I'm distributing pamphlets and tracts for the Arab surrealist movement faster than I can rewrite and publish them. The installments are getting shorter and shorter. It's as if I were starting a chain reaction. Hello there! Are you from the Nobel Committee? I didn't think so. I'm a storyteller. I should continue telling stories right? I'm a spokesperson. I'm holding down two jobs at once. What do YOU do for a living? My name's Rosenberg. That's German not Hebrew, German for 'rose mountain,' German as in 'Wolfgang Amadeus Mozart.' Don't ask me what his name means. Nationality? No preference. I don't know what a Jew is anymore.

The reader believes I was institutionalized once. I wasn't crazy, I was unethical, immoral, what have you. I suffered from a moral failing similar to an alcoholic or a fornicator except I was a murderer. Most of the other patients were crazy and more interesting to watch than most of the crap on late-night TV. The doctors weren't stuffy or pedantic. To prove it they later destroyed my records. Every action and every word spoken in that institution one way or another implied sex and violence. The doctors and patients were equally complicit in sex and violence. Each group used different words in a different grammar to discuss sex and violence, yet every discussion without fail found its way back to sex and violence if it ever left there in the first place.

However:

Things change. Sometimes when things change things get weirder and weirder.

I'm now far enough away from the subject matter to stop any reader dead in his tracks. I might haul him off to Hell the way the infernal forces did to Amber on that singular night.

Will anyone in the audience call my bluff?

You reply that everyone should have a hobby, even a writer. What anybody does about his drinking is his own goddamned business. Nor am I paranoid so long as I never set foot in Nevada again. I'm super careful too. I have everything I need including frozen orange juice concentrate. When I go for a drive I might see an avocado on the side of the road, I might hear strains of the Star Spangled Banner from an open window, I might get bored and decide to abandon the car and hitchhike to Tallahassee. You get what you pay for. You can't truly own anything or put up a fence around anything in this world. That ain't socialism, that's common sense.

Let's pick up the action at the first time I ever used a mobile phone, the first time I saw seagulls in flight, the last time I visited that screened-in porch overlooking the hideous Atlantic Ocean.

Chapter 24

Before dawn a strange dream awakens me to the sound of rain driving hard against the windows of the hostel. How much time has elapsed? Minutes? Hours? On the bottom bunk across from mine a wizened old man plays solitaire on his bedcovers. Deep lines run from his nose to his mouth. His dull eyes reflect immaculate medication. This man might have an unexplained illness. He might not. Either way the caregivers will soon be shoving a spoonful of Cornflakes into his mouth at the request of a wealthy grandson.

Here we have the resumption of a movement. This time I feel it in my bones. How thrilling to experience an occult adventure, to sit behind a steering wheel with the windows rolled down enjoying the wind and the movement of the road, watching the lights of the last freeway exit retreat into darkness. Travel becomes more than theoretically possible. Travel becomes a lie. The reader cannot know the terrible meaning of 'far.' I drive two or three hundred miles in one day to spread the printed word of the Arab surrealist movement. Hardcopies jerk-wad! Spam filters can go straight to hell. So many miles so many years. Where's the local chapter of the Temple of Venus?

At eighty-plus miles per hour the golden pastures zoom by in a golden blur. The landscape never changes except to get hotter and hotter and increasingly more monotonous and beleaguered. I'm going somewhere very fast, somewhere older than mankind itself where the local police force is stretched to the breaking point. An ancient way!

I'm systematically drunk on top-shelf liquors. I'm getting my thoughts together, keeping these hands locked on the cab's steering wheel. What else can I do? Let me guess. The drivers out here on the Interstate despise me. I'm underemployed right? Pathetic swine. The reader tells me those are depressed drivers. I don't know if they're taking the proper medication for God's sake. Vagrants on wheels are the order of the day, their eyes more glassy than plastic, with little razor cuts for mouths and skin burnished down to the inflamed layer of veins and arteries. Vagrants moving like panicked machines if that's imaginable without microchips. Why not? Imagine those same machines feeling immense pain over their entire bodies.

Hey machines get moving! Try showing some humor!

Alas they can't hear me. They're mechanically afraid of the Big Bad Wolf trampling their flower-carpeted earth.

I reach into the glove compartment for the Indonesian fez cap Reshad gave me to wear the night I escaped from the institution. It's called a songkok. Cool eh?

At this speed the dusty grass on the side of the road is no longer a thing on the horizon. Roads branch off and vanish into smaller signless road-like isometries. At the end of one of those roads stands a Hungarian caretaker dressed head to toe in black who receives everyone in silence. Damn there's too many things I don't know about these roads! Gold and green begin to alternate faster and faster. One moment the fields are deep in verdure, the next more golden than gold itself. I hear roaring sounds in my ears. I see very dusty roads encompass the fresh air and broad skies and a million acres of wilderness frozen in midair. This is occult country. I'm having an occult adventure. The roaring grows louder. What's that weird sulfur smell? I watch artificial THINGS become aware of their environment. They're conscious in a highly artificial way. I feel positive. I know how the mind of a detective works.

A split second later the roaring subsides when I hit the high-rise district. A strange feeling of contrast sets my nerves on edge. The broad skies have narrowed, almost vanished. The box has a lid on it now. The narrow streets and high gray walls give the traffic a processional aspect, reminiscent of the phrase 'soldiers of industry.' I park the car, get out, and boldly penetrate the pink shadowy light of the congested lanes of the eastern quarter of the city. I'm restless again, very prickly. How much time has elapsed? Minutes? Hours? Here the vagrants no longer sacrifice farm animals. The pedestrians are more fidgety than a sandpaper undershirt. Their clothes are filthy, very sloppy too. I imagine a love for rain is what's wrong with those godawful galoshes. I hear half-starved pedestrians exchanging stories about unemployment, exploitation, and an enormous cataclysm scheduled to occur later this summer. That's what my editors call the Apparition of God? A commercial city without glamour? Bizarre domestic arrangements? I watch the Persian dockworkers. I listen to their velvety inflections. I watch the Russian porters with their blank expressions and extraordinary pallor. I watch them bear their burdens from warehouse to ship. I watch the extraordinarily young beggars in rags argue among themselves outside a mosque. I watch a drunkard try to put on a T-shirt by putting one leg through the neck and the other through one of the arm holes. I watch him rip the shirt beyond repair. Here's a man on his knees sucking another man's glass dick. Gobs of spit dribble freely. Little's changed around here except the bad lute-playing. Everything's poorer. I can't get over how much one beggar looks like my dying grandmother. That's what I said. My nerves are on edge. The reader cannot know the terrible meaning of 'far.' Where's the local chapter of the Temple of Venus Vaginal Canal?

When I return to the rural roads, first thing comes to mind is Penny's head bent over Amber's stooped shoulders. I feel a sudden surge of protectiveness as I recall the harsh fluorescent lighting, the cinderblock cubicles, the footsteps ricocheting into darkness. Along both sides of the highway set well back from the road are Iowa-like farmhouses, large white frame structures set up on sturdy concrete blocks. A long narrow lane bordered by trees links each house to the highway. Tall silos tower beside barns. Scattered about here and there are feedlots, fenced gardens, sheds for chickens and hogs. Fence posts painted a particular color indicate what insurance company a farm belongs to. Many of the farmhouses are freshly painted while others are neglected shacks. Billboards advertise a local cornhusking contest. I stop the car, look out over the mile-long rows of corn. Here it is, the golden buckle on the Corn Belt.

I get back in the car to discover the CD player's not working. I'll have to hum if I want music.

A bit later I stop at a 7-Eleven.

"What do you want?"

I ask the grumpy-looking Pakistani gentleman behind the counter for the key to the restroom. He wears baggy gray sweatpants and no shirt. His torso is covered with a thick growth of hair. Rather than providing a key he snaps me an angry look.

"I can't walk in there can I?"

He takes several deep breaths, rubs his stomach as if it hurts. "Across the street there's a funeral home. Use their restroom."

I frown, point off to my left at a Test-Your-Blood-Pressure machine and a door displaying the international male symbol.

"I see the men's room right over there. I know you have one."

"We don't. Try across the street at the funeral home."

"Who the hell are you?"

"I'm the supervisor."

"Ah fuck this thing. It's fucked. You're fucked! Yeah you. You're the one who needs supervision."

I roll my eyes.

He rubs a grubby hand down his face, squinting at me.

I grab my crotch.

He glances down into a Styrofoam coffee cup.

I return to the parking lot and look longingly across the street at the funeral home. Maybe I should go over there after all.

I'm certain to screech the tires when I exit the 7-Eleven's parking lot.

The funeral home's front door stands wide open. I walk inside. A service is under way for a middle-aged man who died from an AIDS-related brain tumor. I linger for a moment at the casket before setting off in search of the men's room.

Early the next morning I awaken on the debris-littered floor of an embalming room. Rain is driving hard against the window. A slight stench of decomposition hangs in the cold air. How much time has elapsed? Minutes? Hours? I've got a terrible hangover from systematic drinking. What's going on? I hear sobs coming from the chapel further down the secret passageway. I curse the Hungarian caretaker under my breath. He's a lackey, a stable boy, a neurasthenic bachelor. His name's Kalman. He's supposed to be asleep not making love to his son's preschool graduation portrait. What now? The barber arrives tomorrow to trim the cadaver's hair. Rumor has it the barber's got a pierced cock.

I peek into the chapel. The caretaker makes the sign of the cross over a closed casket. I walk over to the caretaker. He's wearing baggy yellow pants and a green T-shirt.

"Unable to sleep tonight?"

"I keep thinking about Adony."

"I heard yesterday about the demise of your little son. That must've been awful. I can't imagine him burning up in a fire."

"Smoke inhalation killed him."

"His body's intact?"

"Yes. Rather than try to escape from the fire Adony crawled deeper and deeper into the house hoping to find shelter in his favorite little cubbyhole. That was where the firefighters found his lifeless body."

"Before the flames reached it? Do you know what caused the fire?"

"The investigators said it was caused by an overturned hotplate. It's unclear WHO overturned it."

"You mean it could be arson? Was the hotplate deliberately overturned?"

"You're not from around here are you?"

"No I'm not."

"The questions you ask. They're very hypothetical."

"I'm trying to make sense of what happened."

Kalman runs his hand over his hair.

I say nothing, letting him take his own time as he looks down at his son's memory picture.

"I'm not ashamed or angry. That's what makes it so horrible."

"Kalman what were you feeling when you overturned the hotplate? What were you thinking?"

"I felt so ashamed I can hardly explain it now. Wouldn't it be better if we kept this under wraps?"

"Risk creating a scandal? For God's sake don't pretend none of this happened. Your little son's dead. There's the proof!" I tap the closed lid of the casket.

"You're underestimating the harm it would do this community. To think that I, the upright caretaker, murdered my own son out of petty fear and cowardice. Imagine the outcry."

"You plan to live the rest of your life carrying around this dreadful secret?"

"It's not a secret. I can tell you I was in the kitchen that afternoon when I felt the overwhelming urge to overturn the hotplate. The tablecloth caught fire, the curtains. That's when I ran out the door to the front yard."

"You forgot about your son's safety? You took off running down the middle of the street?"

"Down the sidewalk."

"You were screaming for help?"

"I said nothing at all, ran as fast as I could away from the burning house. At that point I wanted nothing to do with my house or anything in it."

"That wasn't very sensible Kalman. Sounds like you were living out a weird sort of escape fantasy."

"The further I ran the more miserable and uncertain I felt. I ended up here at the funeral home. I heard sirens in the distance. I could picture it so clearly."

"Your son dying?"

"The house burning down. Only later that night did I awaken with a start to realize my son had been in the house. I forgot about Adony until I woke up later that night. I knew he died in the fire."

"Could we perhaps be more open about this? What are you trying to tell me?"

"I forgot about my own son! My forgetfulness killed my son!"

"Nonsense. You DID remember your son. You didn't turn around to retrieve him or let him cross your mind till you remembered him eight hours later. That's not absentmindedness or forgetfulness. That's intentional Kalman. You're a murderer plain and simple. If you let the fire do the killing, that doesn't mean you're not a killer. You could have beaten him to death with a metal pipe, strangled him."

Silence.

"I gotta get back on the road Kalman. You've been most hospitable to me. I appreciate that. Goodbye."

"What did you say your name is?"

"Rosenberg."

I drive back across the street to the 7-Eleven. The Pakistani supervisor behind the counter recognizes me.

"You found the men's room?"

"That was yesterday. I also found a place to crash for the night. What's that loud whining noise?"

"Wait a minute."

The Pakistani bends down below the counter to make an adjustment, stands back up. The noise continues, coming from everywhere and nowhere at once, louder than everything else in the world, louder than the monolith in 2001. I'm forced to imagine an energy density unseen in the universe since the Big Bang.

"I said what's that loud whining noise I hear coming from the back?"

"It's a boat, a boat engine up on blocks my brother's working on."

I imagine the propeller spinning hard trying in vain to move the engine forward when it breaks free and slices into human flesh.

"You sure that's not a jet engine? Is it safe running a boat engine on land?"

"It's no big deal. My brother knows what he's doing. He outfits antique wooden boats for clients."

"I hope he has a couple beers in him and good earplugs."

"My brother doesn't drink. Wait a minute." The Pakistani bends down, stands back up.

"What are you doing down there?"

"Nothing. How can I help you?"

"Do you sell toy guns and water pistols?"

"You'll have to look at the far end of that aisle over there next to the magazines and that rack of sunglasses."

I find two pink plastic water pistols and one green-colored plastic gun that shoots plastic disks. I find four different plastic Halloween masks and two rubber Halloween masks. I go over to the cooler and find six plastic bottles of drinking water. I take that plastic and rubber stuff up to the counter.

"You think he could cut that engine? I feel like I'm losing my hearing."

"That'll be all for you? Twenty dollars even."

I pay with a twenty-dollar bill and quickly leave. I don't feel like driving. I've got no choice.

I turn back around, return to the 7-Eleven.

The noise has subsided.

"Can you tell me how far the desert is from here?"

The Pakistani rubs his stomach, wincing. "Not far if you take the road. Two hours. There are some Navajo towns near the base of those tablelands out there." He points over my shoulder, wincing again. It's a reflex.

"A place to stay the night? A public parking lot?"

"I've heard the government's converting the old coal mine shafts in those cliffs to underground bunkers and tunnels. Contractors and engineers live in those towns."

"What are the Navajo doing about it?"

"There's no question of their loyalty. They speak Navajo."

"Sounds like the Manhattan Project."

"I've never been back east."

"What's your involvement? Where do you fit in?"

"I supervise this store. The workers and psychologists come in here to load up on perishable goods."

"Psychologists?"

"They're doing what they're told."

"What are they told?"

"As I understand it there's one psychologist for each engineer and contractor to make sure nobody goes nuts out there."

"Going nuts doing what?"

"You mean right now?"

"What's going on out there?"

He pauses, staring blankly out the windows. "Whatever it is they're burning up a hell of a lot of electricity according to my friend at the local power company."

A look of amusement dances in the Pakistani's eyes. He nervously caresses a turquoise pebble that hangs around his neck.

"What's that?"

"My lucky stone."

"May I see it?"

He reluctantly shows it to me, turning it over to reveal an inscription embedded on the reverse side.

"Any special meaning?"

"I think of it as a transmitter that's wired with DNA circuitry."

"It's only a stone right? You're not a person with psychic powers."

He doesn't respond, flashing me a ferocious-looking grin. I wonder if this guy isn't a bit autistic. He doesn't seem interested in taking me seriously. He's acting like he's smarter than everyone else. He owns a talisman and knows about government contractors mucking about on computers in a cave.

His voice becomes a throaty whisper. "You didn't come here on your own did you?"

"Like I'm stupid, like I don't understand. Is that the point you're trying to make? No one else knows what you know. That makes you special. Is that it?"

The Pakistani lifts his hand. "Don't for any more details."

"Good God don't be ridiculous! You don't have any friends out here do you? My curiosity's piqued. I'll have to check it out for myself."

His eyes narrow. "Whatever you do don't get caught."

"Isn't that what they told Jesus at the Last Supper?"

His eyes narrow further.

Silence.

"I'm willing to take that chance." I snicker and leave the 7-Elven again, reminding myself that denial is the second rule after 'don't get caught.' Beyond denial there's spontaneous human combustion.

I drive off. That's right. A very bizarre situation indicates a very bizarre motive. For that reason alone I'll explore the Utah desert. Let's imagine I'm a mullah reciting prayers to the heavens. I'm mujahedeen studying the Koran and learning how to dodge automatic weapons fire. Shit imagine whatever you want. It's your imagination. If I can't find shelter among the mansions of the rich I'll try for the abandoned villages of the very poor. That will feel like progress.

Am I immortal? I'm bored. I have to move. The hour-and-thirty-minute drive from the 7-Eleven to the area of the underground caverns is a true test of my patience. At the first desert village, I park the car and get out. Business must be slow around here even if a network of tunnels runa beneath the ground. I shade my eyes, peering off into the distance. Isn't it philosophical how the suffocating heat creates an unrelenting surrealistic nightmare?

A lone sign welcomes me to PEKINGVILLE. If this ain't the Middle East, it ought to be. Feral dogs starving to death roam dusty streets, feeding off the rotting corpses of soldiers. As dead people go these soldiers don't smell that bad. Machine gun ammo belts filled with live cartridges are draped over fences and exposed pieces of wall. I stare at a pile of blackened shriveled hands wondering if perhaps I value my own hands a bit too much. I go off in search of that magnificent pile of golden teeth. Am I in danger? Yes your majesty. Much like a marine who lives in constant expectation of dying in combat, I've crossed over into Fatalism Mode. I consider myself dead rather than in danger of a sudden maiming or mutilation. My hair's a thick sweaty matted mess. My dungaree jacket's torn and sweaty. My dungaree trousers are ragged, sweaty, and ripped at the knees.

I have yet to see a single living soul out here. I wipe the sweat off my face, take a swig from the water bottle, start walking down the village's dusty main street. I move gracefully I imagine, gliding across the ground the way Jesus did back in the desert villages of Galilee, villages like Nazareth and Capernaum. I recall that Nazareth is exclusively Palestinian, which answers the eternal theological question of whether anything good can come of Nazareth. I don't let the thought distract me. I keep a sharp eye out for any signs of life. Most of the windows around here are intact though much of the paint is peeling. What's missing is people and other familiar sights like dogs chasing cars and men chasing women. This place must be old. I see a lace curtain fall back into place in an upper-story window. I could be imagining it. I'm feeling more and more like an intruder here. I pick up the pace to accelerate the overall experience and improve my chances of reaching a subsequent episode.

There it is, a small tan-colored chapel plain-looking enough, yet something's fishy about it. Nearby a piebald horse with inflamed eyelids and restless hooves is tethered to a scrubby-looking oak tree. I begin making a slow circle of the building when the backdoor flies open and an old wizened hag in a cornflower-blue dress dashes outside screaming at the top of her lungs in a foreign language. Spittle flies from chapped and bleeding lips. She starts lunging at my face with a rusty butcher knife intent on disfiguring me. I back off to assess the situation and notice she's missing her two front teeth and her head's wrapped in bloodstained linen cloth. I imagine she's a lapsed Mormon fed up with the ways of the Creator. She's taking it out on me rather than on a meth pipe. She reeks of sweat and urine, reminding me of something else entirely. This arrangement's not easy for either one of us. I'm as pissed off as she is. I pick the nearest wrench up off the ground. With one mighty blow I smash her skull in, killing her on the spot. Whew! Though justified in defending myself from an ill-tempered woman, I don't feel happy about murdering her so effortlessly. As I walk around the body I'm careful to avoid the growing pool of blood.

I remember entering that tan-colored chapel, which was a bit more ramshackle than rickety or dilapidated. I remember the inconceivably bad lighting, the old cassette player blaring tinny music, the odors of old clothes and dried apples, the two-headed dwarf chained to the altar. I remember that dwarf like it was yesterday. Christ was she legit! The red hair, the straight nose with those finely arched nostrils, the full lips forming an O when she modestly averted her eyes to the floor, the bellybutton bejeweled with a flashy stud. What the hell was her eye color? Damn my cock's swollen! To this day I've thought day and night over that encounter. I still can't grasp what the rope, those handcuffs, and the flag-draped coffin meant.

Before I maneuver the cab back onto the highway I pull a rubber Halloween mask over my face. I look like a troll with his elbow hanging out the window. I smell like Old Spice. I'm starting to feel legendary again.

I need an accomplice to truly feel legendary. Fact is I can't complete the Arab surrealist movement relying solely on myself. The movement requires accomplices, collaborators. At the moment Goldsmith's out of the question. My calculations might be wrong. My calculations are never wrong! I know I need an accomplice, a thin Jewish asshole similar to myself who behaves like he's thoroughly exasperated. I wonder if I shouldn't have died the moment I was born, strung up by an umbilical cord. Out here I never feel pain, fear, or loneliness. I never belong anywhere for very long. The eyes don't close in death by strangulation, looking more horrific than five million dollars of non-sequential bills.

I swerve into a rest area built over a large dry lake-bed. I park, remove the rubber mask, leave the car to stretch out my legs for awhile and take a toilet break.

Who's that man over there sitting on the bench, the guy with the artificial limb and legs crossed at the knees? His sensors are deployed. He seems oblivious to it all. I guarantee he's got layered systems. He's one scary-looking bastard. As he rotates his head back and forth he looks more like a drug addict than a brilliant software engineer. The muscles in his neck contract with each bite of the thick sandwich dripping mayonnaise.

I walk over to the bench, sit down.

The man remains silent.

I lean towards him. "Good place to take a rest huh?"

"I'm thinking and eating."

"I let myself drift off into thoughts."

I point across the way to another man who's chasing a little girl in a dress around a swing set.

"You think that's his daughter?"

"Only one way to find out."

"It's her and him. Must be tempting."

"She's a bitch. You better go talk some sense into her."

I laugh.

The man clears his throat. "Let's dispense with the usual American formalities. I'm McKillen."

"I'm Rosenberg. You hitchhiking? Can I offer you a ride? The destination and timing's up to you. That's my car over there."

"You a cabdriver?"

"No. I drive a cab."

McKillen smiles. "A stolen cab's fine by me. I spent several months in a monastery. I escaped."

"Impressive."

"You could call it that. It wasn't a cakewalk. I thought about sex every waking minute. After I'd tortured myself long enough I decided to leave, walked out the door in broad daylight. No one stopped me. Yourself?"

"Committed to the Arab surrealist movement."

"Never heard of it."

"You don't sound too sure."

"It sounds familiar. If I once knew about it I've long since forgotten."

"It's about disturbing social and psychological patterns."

"Sounds intense, maybe criminal. Reminds me of the lyric 'My name is called Disturbance.'"

"Sympathy for the Devil?"

"Street Fighting Man. I bet it's pretty low-rent do-it-yourself type stuff right?"

"It's cheap compared to lots of other things. It still costs money, which I'm getting very low on by the way."

"At loose ends?"

"Cops are a potential problem. They've got to learn they're dealing with a staunch character here."

"I got money, lots of cash I stole from a safe before I left the monastery."

"You stole money from a monastery?"

"Money and valuables. I had no choice if I wanted to survive after leaving. That vow of poverty left me with nothing."

"What sorts of valuables?"

"Jewelry mostly. I took the money to help me survive, not to get rich. If you want some you can have it."

"The movement's budget's pretty basic. Gas and meals are the main things and copy shops where I print out and photocopy the movement's pamphlets."

"Where are you staying?"

"I pull off the road or find a parking lot and sleep in the car. Once in awhile I'll stay at a motel for a shower and a bed."

"Damn that IS cheap. Take whatever cash you need. I got no plans. The only thing I ask is you let me tag along for awhile. That'll keep me occupied till I make up my own mind about things."

"Great. It's a deal." I reach out my hand.

McKillen tenses up. "When you get to know me better we'll shake hands. Right now it's strictly business."

"Suit yourself."

"Did you say the cops are on your tail? I'm not surprised. Sounds like you're practicing disorderly conduct and inciting riots."

"What's important is I feel like I'm being followed even if a person's not back there. That feeling forces me to be vigilant and live in the present."

"You're paranoid."

"If I am paranoid it doesn't mean I'm not being followed. Being hyper-aware makes the days go by very fast. Events and episodes fly right on by. I imagine life's divided up into a series of paragraphs and chapters. Every indent or spacing on the page marks where the past ends and the present begins."

"Must be difficult maintaining that line between the past and present without going nuts."

"That's how things are for me. I go from this place and person to that place and person. No regrets. Everything's good that I never did. I once tried to record everything on tape. Now I memorize everything photographically. Later I'll write it down in storybook form."

"You're on permanent vacation."

"Not at all. This is the hardest kind of work imaginable, no salary, no job security, no recognition except from the authorities who criminalize what I do. That's not a vacation at all. That's a calling. That's a vocation if you ask me."

"Man you've thought this through."

"I've got no choice. The moment I leave anything to chance I'm done. Tragedy's a funny thing that way."

"It sounds intense and philosophical, like an ad for an amusement park."

"I imagine the movement more as a series of increasingly vacant rooms. Whenever I lose something I can't find it again, it drops to the bottom of the world where I'm glad to leave it. Ask my ex-wife. A Libra husband's not an easy man to please when he's trying to maintain an identity and blend in."

"You were married once?"

"C'mon McKillen we gotta get going. Time to split."

Chapter 25

McKillen drives and smokes. I'm the passenger who fans away the smoke and adjusts his frameless reading glasses. I ride and I ride. I ride some more. I imagine we're riding through one of those full-scale museum dioramas that enshroud historical events in the encoded meaning of painted backgrounds and false perspectives. Epistemological constructs like pizza, film canisters, spools of telephone cable, orbiting lumps of frozen astronaut urine, the Mafia, skateboards, nuclear weapons, one of Australia's largest firearms importers, the giant radio telescope at Arecibo, the Battle of Berlin roll right on by at flash-cut speed. Immersed in the phantasmagoria of the living, junk begets junk time and time again until appearances become ghosts. Big deal right? You know about mirages and the obstinate questionings of a slobbering pale-skinned alcoholic.

McKillen's ten years my junior. He's coarse-grained yet contingent, not so famous though resembling the density of recognizably real human beings. He wears heavily creased Hawaiian shirts and baggy trousers. His voice is sweet and pungent by turns. Like me he hungers to know what will happen next. He knows those circumstances will be pretty weird, not in the

Hunter S. Thompson sense, more along the lines of the tragic life of Austrian philosopher Ludwig Wittgenstein.

I've told McKillen about Penny and Amber, warned him about Goldsmith, reminisced on Reshad. McKillen is an accomplice, a collaborator, nothing more, not a confidante, not a lover, not an editor or imperial proofreader. McKillen is a warrior. He has the wounds to prove he's killed many people in battles sanctioned by world governments. He's never served prison time. Nor is he considered insane or neurotic by the relevant experts. He killed at the behest of those who required such to ensure the safety of abstract ideals. I won't continue with the stale irony here. Epistemological boundaries must occupy a particular place in this story. My ignorance remains fully strategic. Can't you see? Around you are the murmur and hum of little white spaces separated by words that seek to trouble the air like clouds of swarming gnats. Those white spaces are the cancer of written human history. Thanks. I'll take a corridor of gray rooms instead.

Headlights flash in the distance.

"McKillen you gotta change the CD. I'm sick of that Pink Floyd crap. I don't wanna hear it anymore."

"Be quiet!"

I lean forward on the dashboard, barely manage a smile. A sense of light-headedness overtakes me. "Please pull over at the next motel. Let's call it a day. I need to change into some fresh clothes."

"It's only three in the morning!"

"I said pull over!"

Here's the Red Star Hotel.

The man working behind the reservation counter has the face of an astronaut who's not very comfortable with his job. He's covered with tattoos and pumped up on caffeine and other stimulants. "I want to give you both fair warning there've been multiple sightings around here of a suspected serial killer. We've had three sightings in the past two days. We know it's a young woman with weapons. The cops haven't tracked her down yet."

McKillen laughs. "Your local tax dollars at work!"

The reservationist's eyes are rheumy, unblinking. His voice is clipped and Midwestern. He reaches up, peels a tattoo of his face, tucking it into a shirt pocket. The effect is altogether disturbing.

"The authorities are concerned. A female serial killer's a rarity. It's not easy predicting her moves. There's no good baseline."

I nod my head in agreement.

McKillen steps forward. "Will our room have a functioning air-conditioner?"

"All our rooms are air-conditioned sir."

"Good. I prefer environments I can control."

"You'll be on the third floor. The nearest elevator is right over there. Should I call someone to help you with your bags?"

"We're both very tired. We'll manage. Thanks. It's been quite a day!"

The reservationist shakes his head. "I'm reserving judgment on that. The day's only a little more than three hours old."

McKillen smiles. "Let's keep an open mind right?"

The reservationist ignores him.

We walk over to the elevator.

"That guy back there at the counter's a cosmologist. He spends his nights peering into deep space."

I snicker. "Let's keep an open mind McKillen."

McKillen and I sit back on our respective twin-size beds, activate the television monitor, begin sizing up the channels. We start off with a game show host who sounds like a terminal emphysemic. We have a documentary on the arrest and conviction of the Wilmington Ten. A Sixties radical strikes his girlfriend on the head thirteen times with a hammer and claims the CIA made him do it. A bomb explodes in the baggage area of New York's LaGuardia Airport. Eleven people are killed, dozens more seriously injured. A SWAT team decked out in black flak jackets surrounds the White House. Flags are flown at half-staff in the U.S. capital. The airports are closed. No planes fly overhead. A disembodied voice announces, "The number's constantly changing. We'll let those who did not commit serious crimes go back to their work units." Afterwards a gaudy commercial for a pawnshop appears. I remember seeing those three golden balls over the shop at our own corner in the Tenderloin. How they glowed like kryptonite!

McKillen yawns and knocks the ashes from his pipe onto the carpet. "The pawnbroker's symbol is three spheres suspended from a bar. There's nothing more you and I can do about that."

"Who's your handler's handler McKillen?"

"Same as yours I suspect, a hypnotic courier, a drug mule, a Mormon wearing a black knit beret, someone suffering from a technological addiction who's more human than human yet reeks of amniotic fluid."

"Damn we're the walking-talking embodiment of a sick male fantasy with the dry-heaves!"

McKillen laughs. "I'm even programmed to empty trash bags into the toilet."

"You're not programmed to do that right NOW are you?"

"Religious technicians behind that mirror over there are activating brain-implanted electrodes to trigger Asimovian directives that are updatable and involve smoking lots of cigarettes."

"I get it. You're God's perfect marionette. The power of Christ compels you!"

McKillen laughs.

On the TV a genius scientist chases after his son's windblown toy airplane when he's struck and killed by a truck. Upon seeing the tragedy his son goes into prolonged seizures. EMTs arrive, take him to the nearest trauma unit where he's hooked up to machines to monitor serum oxygen levels. The seizures continue. Five minutes, ten, fifteen minutes later the seizures haven't ceased. The audience is forced to watch it in real time. I can no longer watch. I change the channel.

McKillen laughs. "You haven't seen the worst of it Rosenberg. He's got cysts the size of a grapefruit on his temporal lobe. Nasty shit."

Here's a one-hour special on a group of men known as the Psychic Mafia who carry out parapsychological research. One of the researchers describes himself as a planetary enzyme. I watch for awhile. I keep thinking about the son. When I change the channel back, the seizures have ended. A nurse is wheeling the boy over to a CT scanner in a radiology suite. Drs. Sapirstein and Hill are standing nearby speaking in a sinister whisper. Again I can't bear to watch. I change the channel, this time to grainy newsreel footage of rows of dull houses, grimy trees, cars with smashed and bloodied windshields.

McKillen laughs at the bloodshed, removes his transradial prosthesis. He's a below-the-elbow amputee who prefers the traditional prosthetic hook to the more trendy myoelectric prosthesis you see Iraq War veterans sprouting these days. The hook makes shaking hands difficult while obviating the need for fingernail clippers.

"Being an amputee must get real boring McKillen."

"You get used to it. Missing limbs can be replaced by phantom limbs or prosthetics or razor-sharp claws." He waves the hook at me like it's a weapon.

I shake my head. "Everything about you becomes unnatural. You become an unnatural self. You're no longer identifiable as human. You become inhuman."

"'Inhuman' is a pejorative term. We amputees call ourselves 'post-human.' With the loss of mobility comes an extension beyond the senses. We see too deep and too much. You non-amputees can't handle it."

"You become what they used to call a humanoid or cyborg, nothing more."

"The Cyborg of Vyborg. Ever read it?"

"Prosthetic technique becomes a reality unto itself."

"Ever read it?"

"You become the Six Million Dollar Man, a Bionic Woman. You become half man half machine old buddy."

I change the channel to a grainy black-and-white movie about a railway terminal man who lives in Medford, Massachusetts. Bodily fluids are seeping down from the flat upstairs, staining the walls of his kitchen. He's none too happy about it. He suspects a body is decomposing up there in a trunk stowed away inside a closet, a ghastly corpse dismembered and refashioned in the image of an idealistic man possessed by the idea of crime and punishment. Turns out the terminal man is responsible for the murder though he has no recollection of it! Why? A posthypnotic suggestion of total amnesia. Much like the famous 1960s political assassins Ruby, Sirhan, and Oswald, who received their hypnotic cues from Western Union wire transfer forms and teletype machines, the terminal man falls into a trance whenever he receives a particular email message from his handlers at headquarters. The deep-voiced narrator refers us to page 332 of the Warren Commission report.

"You're a God man Rosenberg?"

"I live in God. I live for God. I love the Bible for quotable things. I thank the Koran for forbidding pork consumption. If I didn't live in God I'd never have had the capacity to murder my own daughter."

"You believe in a One God Universe?"

"A single God beyond description and notation, beyond cause and effect yet a condition for every possible cause and effect, a God hidden at the inception. That's right. Goddammit McKillen watch your drinking! What the hell are you doing?"

McKillen spills beer onto the bed, slams his stump down on his knees before his voice skids to a halt. "Okay Rosenberg let's hear it. I wanna hear the gory details!"

"No details attend to God. That's lesson number two, which explains the Biblical admonition on graven images."

"Details about how God supports murder, including the murder you committed."

"I've been sworn to secrecy. You want me to second guess God? You want me to sit here for a second of arrested time, turn the lock on the Mysteries, make light of the substance of the world while I leave behind a skeleton of crystal bone? You'll begin to hear the wind whistling through that TV screen? Is that what you want McKillen?"

"I'm ready for it Rosenberg."

"The story begins at a point where you realize you've lost your way and gone off the Straight & Narrow. At some point you got distracted by the unimportant things in life and mistakenly raised those to the level of Ultimate Goal. That's step one. It's pouring rain in the middle of January or November."

"I can sense we're in for a real piece of bullshit!"

"Step two you start making your way back to the Straight & Narrow. You're enthusiastic, dedicated, smart. You're Jewish. You suspect the whole thing's groundless yet you're careful. You want to avert disaster. For the first time you realize life isn't a hobby. You clear out a space for action."

"Whereabouts?"

"In the Tenderloin."

"Everybody's speaking at once in loud voices?"

"Loud enough yes. Step three you glimpse the Straight & Narrow. There it is in front of you. You can point at it like it's an address, like it's a route on a map, a very concrete thing. Step four you begin following the Straight & Narrow again. The longer you follow it the prouder you become. You see those stragglers on the roadside and in the gutter who've yet to reach the Straight & Narrow. They're as lost as you once were at step one. By this point you've forgotten about step one. That's where step five begins."

"I know what you mean. Self-deception is more potent than a hog tranquilizer."

"Step five is a test of divine commitment in the face of overweening pride. You're asked by God to do something, or 'command' is a better word, something as far removed from the Straight & Narrow as anything in this world. You're commanded BY GOD to murder your own offspring. Should you succeed you'll gain two things in abundance, God's love and the wrath of humanity."

"What a trip! I'm impressed with your dignity in the face of a lifetime prison sentence."

"Confinement yes. Demonization, psychopathy, God knows how many other terms of notoriety. See where this is going? If you carry out that murder you prove to God nothing can push you from the Straight & Narrow. You're offering Him the greatest show of love in the history of the world. In the eyes of humanity you become the furthest thing from the Straight & Narrow. You're a danger to society, the devil incarnate. That's the fundamental paradox of step five."

"If only they knew you were communicating with God."

"They cannot accept or conceive of such a thing except as a form of delusion and mental incompetence. That's step six, the mitigating factor of diminished capacity arising from the fact I saw nothing wrong with the act when I committed it. Nor do I find anything wrong with it now. Nor will I ever find anything wrong with it. In the eyes of a knower, a commandment by God cannot be wrong. That leaves step seven, the final step, your escape from the medium-security institution and return to society as a fugitive from the law, your sole purpose now to turn society back towards the Straight & Narrow and show the world a Jew has guts. That's the Arab surrealist movement. Now turn off the TV. Let's get some sleep!"

Chapter 26

That first morning I remember Sophie, the Styrofoam coffee cup, and the book she was reading, a tattered copy of The Life of Mohammed by Reverend George Bush. She stood there at the self-serve coffee counter looking like a handsome young animal with a long ponytail of raven-black hair. She didn't need a pretty smile or makeup to get what she wanted in life. Her eyes flashed with fire and had the unmistakable look of race. She was the most relaxed creature I'd ever seen. Perhaps she was a sorority girl so subtle deep and full of guile with those long green skirts trailing after her and that heavy silver coffeepot in her hand. I knew McKillen and I would have to recruit her. She needed instruction from full-time professors.

First thing she says is her name's Sophia.
"What's to become of Sophia Sophia?"
"I think I burned myself on that coffee."
"Oh dear was it a burn or a scald?"
"It's liver and bacon."

I laugh, timidly looking down at her small hands. Rings of topaz and jade decorate those sleek fingers. I watch as she sweetens the dark coffee with honey. When I look up again I notice a tiny gold crucifix around her neck.

She's smiling. "I make videos, the digital ones. I can like freeze an image in a viewfinder. I study at the University of Florida."
"That's in Gainesville right?"
I notice she thinks about the question. "Yeah."
I wonder why she's lying. "You're a real overachiever." I tap her hand with a rolled-up newspaper. "How would you like a job Sophia?"
"What do I gotta do?"
"I'm not sure yet. We'll find something."
Her brows knit. I'm thinking lies are easier for her to process than enthusiastic truths. "Are you gonna like totally ignore me?"
"First there's the interview. I'm Rosenberg."

She's got a decent handshake for a woman with such small hands. Her voice is a bit husky. "Nice to meet you Rosenberg. Can I get you a cup of coffee?"

"You can handle that? Good. The entry-level position will be my handler. You know that means you don't wanna annoy the captain."

"I don't hold doors open for anyone or boring stuff like that. It's not gonna be my responsibility to make you smile." She thrusts out those pert little breasts.

"So I gather from your body language. You don't fit the classic profile. This is no time for a panic attack. I won't treat you like you're stupid. I might ask you to take off your jacket from time to time if you know what I mean."

I notice she has two piercing holes in each ear.

She feigns offense, crossing her arms over her chest. "Are you trying to make me feel bad by suggesting I've got no personal life?"

"Not against my better judgment. Relax. Work's over for today. Are you dating anyone?"

"We broke up last week."

I hand her the rolled-up newspaper. "Pretend that's a knife. Swing it at my neck, stab me with it."

"What?"

"Just do it. Don't worry."

She swings the rolled-up newspaper at me. I easily block it.

She frowns, puts the newspaper down on the counter. "That doesn't prove anything. What did you say your name was?"

"Rosenberg."

"That doesn't prove anything Rosenberg."

"Did you get a sick pleasure out of doing that?"

"No."

"Why did you swing at me with your right hand?"

"I'm right-handed."

"You could've used your left handed if you wanted. There you have it. Freedom of choice. I'm not taking any of your fundamental rights away."

She frowns, thinking about that for a moment, points outside. "I'd like to meet your friend."

"McKillen? Sure. Let's go out to the car."

I help her gather up an extensive collection of Samsonite luggage that in appearance and weight resembles slabs of glistening black granite.

We lumber outside to the cab parked beside the gas pumps.

"Hey what's going on here?" is the first thing McKillen says when Sophia opens the car door and takes a seat in the back.

"I've created a monster McKillen. Its name's Sophia."

She corrects me. "Sophie!"

"I thought you said your name's Sophia."

"Officially yes. My friends call me Sophie."

"There you have it McKillen. Sophie. What's the big deal?"

"Does she have a police record?"

"I don't know. Do you?"

She shrugs her shoulders/

"That doesn't prove anything Rosenberg. Has she had a run-in with the law?"

"I don't know. Have you?"

She shrugs her shoulders again. "Speeding and parking tickets. When I was in high school I set off the fire alarm."

"Okay nothing Miss America wouldn't be guilty of. C'mon McKillen stop drooling. Help me with this luggage. We need to get this outfit back on the road!"

Once we get going Sophie passes the time in a stupor, watching movies on the DVD player that's installed in the rear-facing cushion of the driver's seat. I throw looks over my shoulder to check up on her.

"What are you gawking at back there? Your magic eight ball?"

Sophie wrinkles her lightly freckled nose, barely cracks a smile. "I'm going to miss my dental appointment."

"Put on some lipstick. You'll look fine."

"Like the only time I ever wore lipstick was in my high school yearbook picture."

"I'm sure you were very pretty too."

"Is it true you're a Muslim Rosenberg."

I hear suspicion in her voice. "McKillen told you that during the last potty break huh?"

"You read the Koran?"

"I pray. In Arabic. I saw back there at the filling station you're reading a biography of the Prophet."

Sophie loses the poker-face and blushes.

"Why's that embarrassing? Islam's a very healthy religion for men and women."

"Is that why you're acting like you own me?"

"Don't say that Sophie. You'll drive us crazy. Stop feeling sorry for yourself. Stop chewing on those fingernails."

I put my fists to my temples to emphasize something I'm not aware of.

She stares at me with wide hyperthyroid-like eyes, does a hocus-pocus thing, causing her expression to vanish, returns to thinking about what's outside the car's windows. Lies, everything.

I get the impression Sophie lives in constant expectation of sudden violence. I bet she's very absentminded. I imagine speaking into her ancient answering machine, reminding her to feed the puppy, not to miss that important dental appointment, and to visit the blood bank for the monthly bloodletting. She'd unplug the phone from the wall. Better yet I bet she's a chameleon wearing lace bras and pantyhose, sucking down bottles of Snapple in a desperate attempt to soothe that grinding abdominal pain. I imagine her lurching over to a line of taxis. Ten minutes later she's giving the Nigerian driver a hand-job. The two of them would exchange comradely looks when he ejaculates on the dashboard. She would yank her hand away as if burned.

The cab crests a hill, nearly rear-ending an older-model Mercedes that's cruising well below the posted speed limit. McKillen cuts our speed by more than half. We're in a no passing zone.

"Shit this is why I hate taking the two-lane highways Rosenberg."

"I like how it cuts down on the chances we'll run into state troopers and cops."

"We make terrible time."

"Think of it as a twisted voyage through small-town America."

"What's the music you're playing?"

"Schubert's Sonata in D Major."

"It's getting on my nerves. You agree Sophie?"

I turn around to look at her heavenly face.

Sophie says nothing, keeps looking out the window. Again I sense she's a woman who lives in constant expectation of sudden violence. What am I supposed to do, slap her? She might bleed. I don't want that. There's something different about the way she carries herself, something malign yet academic. If she's unstable it isn't the first or last time to involve projectile vomiting.

"Sophie have you plugged up your ears again with self-loathing?"

"I'm trying to fall asleep."

"If you wanna do that first you gotta close your eyes."

I turn back around. "McKillen you get the impression we might be followed?"

"All the time. I've learned to ignore it."

I glance at my cheap Casio watch. I gaze out at the highway rushing by.

Consciousness starts fading away.

I'm becoming the proverbial blank slate.

A wicked form of paralysis sets in.

I fall asleep.

When I awaken it's dusk. A hard rain's begun to fall. Large raindrops beat against the windshield. The car's cold as hell. McKillen's got the AC going full blast. He's sweating bullets as he tries to maneuver curves in the driving rain.

"I'm getting hungry McKillen. We might want to pull over at the next exit, call it a day."

"We got plenty of time. We're still on schedule."

I glance over my shoulder at Sophie who's lying across the backseat asleep. I turn back around in time to see a brilliant silver light flashing far up in the sky.

"You see that McKillen?"

"I saw it an hour ago. It's an optical illusion, not real. It's our minds playing tricks on us."

"Intriguing. It was a strange beauty. What's that?" I point to a blurry shape on the side of the road.

"Looks like a large Labrador retriever."

"What the hell's it doing out on the highway? We got a potential crime scene here. Murdered by its homosexual lover. Hit the Jew dog on the head with a wrench, shot him in the face."

McKillen laughs.

"Maybe the woman serial killer's on the loose again. She's got an anti-Semitic streak."

"Labrador retrievers aren't Jewish Rosenberg."

McKillen's a smug lying bastard no doubt about it. The trouble with lies is they never stay simple, never exist as isolated units. One lie leads to another. Before you know it you've got a logically coherent story that's false and potentially dangerous to everyone involved, including the reader.

I convince McKillen to pull off at the next exit. We have a whole row of clean-looking eateries to choose from.

The three of us occupy the booth furthest from the entrance to ensure an unobstructed view of the entire place. I sit with both elbows on the table, my fists at my temples. Sophie and McKillen sit across from me with their backs to the dining area. Sophie's hands are fidgeting. She makes clicking noises with her teeth. McKillen elaborately cracks his knuckles.

I reconnoiter the premises. Although I don't smoke or chew nicotine gum I notice ashtrays on every table. Despite the many NO SMOKING signs.

"What's on the menu for tonight McKillen?"

"Deep-fried Twinkies for Sophie."

Sophie scowls at the joke.

"Sophie's not hungry. She's been eating fingernails this afternoon."

She doesn't like that comment either.

"You're gonna share a moon pie with both of us McKillen?"

"I will if it's good for the movement."

I look around more intently at this goddamned carnival sideshow. I watch the princely-looking waiter maneuver about the place with a tray of egg-drop soup and tea. I watch a good-looking blonde at the neighboring table remove a thin box of Virginia Slims and a Bic lighter from a Gucci purse. I watch humanoid blobs of flesh belly up to the fried food buffet. Everyone seems too young, too stoned, too loud or some combination of the three. I know they're pumped up on prescription medications.

"Call that cute Latino waitress over here McKillen. Tell her I'll take a daiquiri."

When the waitress arrives she looks a fraction less marvelous than I imagined, with a cheap haircut, a mouthful of yellow teeth, a heart-shaped locket on a golden chain, and clunky black shoes. I can see the bulge of pierced nipples through the tight-fitting waitressing uniform, the nipple tips straining anxiously through the beige linen in the direction of my stiff outstretched index finger. A clash of lascivious impulses erupts in my head.

The waitress smiles, sucks the spit off her teeth.

"Whadda ya'll need here?"

McKillen orders for us. I won't bother describing the interchange between him and the waitress. Suffice it to say the way he orders the food doesn't make a difference one way or the other to the outcome of this particular episode.

As the waitress walks away I admire the protrusive roundness of her bottom. How much alcohol does she have in her system right about now?

"Eel is quite the treat Rosenberg. There's something different about eel compared with other seafood."

"That doesn't mean it's right to eat it. Excuse me."

The men's room is cavernous and reeks of mildew. The roar of air-conditioning is deafening. An elderly man's passed out in his own vomit near the urinals. A strange mewling sound emits from his throat. Next to him on the floor a cellphone keeps ringing. Sure glad that's not happening to me! I turn the man over on his back and see that his clothing's cut down the center and peeled away to expose the body from throat to crotch. That's the serial killer's trademark, her calling card. The man's skin has a weird greenish cast to it. Three press-passes hang from his neck. That's when I realize I'm looking at a pool of blood NOT vomit. What about the attacker's fingerprints and DNA evidence? Could they pin this shit on me? The mewling sounds continue. Bile rises in my throat.

I return to the booth. "What I saw back there in the men's room's illegal."

Sophie glares at me.

"What's wrong with you? Don't be such a baby. You're not in danger."

She continues to glare, crossing her arms over her chest.

It's difficult to think of Sophie in any kind of position of authority.

I've piqued McKillen's curiosity. "What was it Rosenberg?"

"Perhaps the latest victim of the local serial killer we've been hearing about. An old man, a journalist or a reporter all bloodied up, barely breathing. The killer's on the loose again. If she has a car she could be traveling as fast as we are. She's using the back roads too."

"Why would she go to the trouble of murdering a man in a men's room? There's unnecessary risk there."

"You're asking me to psychoanalyze the bitch. I refuse. Who knows what's going through her mind. Do you have any talcum powder? I can't get this smell off my hands."

McKillen and Sophie shake their heads no.

"The soap wasn't strong enough. Where the hell's our food? This is taking WAY too long. I'm starting to get paranoid about the whole situation."

"A reporter you say?"

"He had press-passes on him."

"That's a new angle. A serial killer murdering the people who help make her famous. Think about it."

"You want me to go back in there to confirm it?"

"You understand what kind of crap I'm getting at here Rosenberg?"

"Maybe he was a drug dealer and the deal went bad. He was elderly."

"Maybe he's wearing an ancient monkey suit."

The waitress arrives with our food.

We manage to eat our meals in relative silence.

When the three of us enter the hotel lobby a fat female reservationist is intently staring at the pages of a wall calendar. When she sees us approach the desk she smiles, waves, acting like she belongs on goddamned Mount Rushmore.

"Our town's gonna have two parades on the same Friday, followed by a community picnic, according to this here pamphlet." She thrusts out the pamphlet, striking Sophie across the nose. "How many rooms tonight?"

"One room with three beds."

"Not an option sir. We got left one single room and one double both smoking."

McKillen shakes his head in disgust. "We'll take those two rooms if we got no choice in the matter. Will the rooms have air-conditioning?"

"All our rooms are air-conditioned. The doors lock from the inside."

"Even the front door?"

"Excuse me sir? Things have been hectic around here this past week. I'm a little tired."

"Is your community being terrorized by the female serial killer?"

"I doubt it."

"Why? There's nothing to do around here?"

"I'm sorry sir. I'm not familiar with your expressions."

McKillen shakes his head in disgust. "I like the way YOU talk honey-bunny. Don't you gotta haul hay out to the cattle?"

"Suck on a chill pill bastard!"

Did I hear that?

McKillen ignores the comment, turns to me and Sophie. "I'll take the single. The two of you can take the double."

"Whatever you want McKillen. You're the driver."

First thing I do when I enter the room is walk over the bathroom, push open the door, flick on the lights, stand for awhile in front of the toilet. An acidic burning has risen up in my chest. I have to suppress the urge to vomit.

When I return to the room Sophie's sitting on one of the beds.

"This harsh fluorescent lighting gave me a vomit attack. You want a drink? A beer? A cola?"

"I'm fine. I don't drink colas. Alcohol gives me hot flashes and headaches. Snapple's better."

"You're not anorexic are you?"

Sophie shakes her head, slightly scowls.

"You wanna rinse out your clothes?"

She scowls again.

I hear a toilet flush in a neighboring room. "I bet these walls are pretty thin."

I put my left ear up against the nearest wall. For some reason that relaxes me. I hear a television in the next room and the rustling sounds of a newspaper. "Do you hear a smoke alarm beeping out in the hallway?"

"What happened to McKillen's arm?"

"He lost it in Iraq. I don't know the details."

"Is that why he's rude to people?"

"I never noticed."

"If you're Muslim don't you have to pray before you go to sleep every night?"

I walk over to the other bed, sit down across from Sophie. "I do pray. I've been praying."

"I never saw you pray once today."

"It's internal. I've reached a point where prayer is automatic like a heartbeat. It happens without me having to be conscious of it. I turn in the proper direction to face Mecca five times a day."

"The words too?"

"Even the proper muscles tense up as if I were doing prostrations. If you're disciplined you can internalize the whole ritual, not bother making a show of it. God or Allah, what have you, is not interested in show-offs. God's interested in unbroken commitment to That which is One. Okay?"

"Dude you've thought this out."

"I've thought everything out. With me nothing's left to chance."

"Where are you taking me?"

"Taking you? You make it sound like we've kidnapped you. We're not taking you anywhere. You're along for the ride. You're our latest companion."

"What are you guys doing driving around the country? Don't you have regular jobs and families?"

"I haven't worked out the details of McKillen's story. Myself I'm separated from my wife. I have a daughter. I earn money as a storyteller. You sure you don't want anything to drink?"

"Why do you keep asking McKillen if we're being followed?"

"I'm careful. You can never be too vigilant, which is a religious compulsion, keeping an eye out for God."

"Are you one of those New Age types?"

I take off my glasses, put them on the nightstand between the two beds, lie back, stare up at the ceiling. "Maybe we could talk about this tomorrow. It's been a long day. This isn't the best time to get into my life goals."

"I want you to know I can't wander around with you forever. Classes begin in September. I have to be back on campus in August."

"Your call Sophie. You're free to depart at your own discretion."

"I graduate next year. How old's your daughter?"

"Seventeen."

"What's she doing?"

I sit up and glare at Sophie. "My daughter's a very smart and precocious girl. She's got psychological problems."

"Depression?"

"Voices and nightmares."

"How does that work? I wish I could have nightmares. Most of the time I can't fall asleep."

"When someone keeps an entire side of their lives secret from you it's fascinating. It's also frightening. We've had our share of family dramas. You get used to it. You learn to expect it."

Silence.

"Sophie did you know you have a sleek delicate-looking body? You were a gazelle in a previous life. Is that your real hair color? Stand up. How tall are you?"

She rises up off the bed, stands on her tiptoes, stretching her arms to the ceiling.

"Five feet four. I hope you don't think my breasts are too small."

"I've seen smaller."

"That's reassuring."

"It's better than an overly large butt. May I see them please your breasts?"

"As long as you promise not to laugh."

"Laughter's the last thing on my mind right now."

She starts pulling up her shirt.

"Here let me help you with that."

Her breasts are so firm and taut it's no wonder she never wears a bra. They point straight out from her chest like little cones. As I begin removing the rest of Sophie's clothes I feel myself responding to her nudity. Once I've whisked away the nylon yellow panties and we're naked, I draw her down on a soft crimson quilt that's laid out on the room's floor and begin making slow careful love to her. I know I have control over every limb and the digestive system as well. I feel a bit like a burglar. Never in my life have I wanted to screw anything as much as I want to screw this young woman right now. She reciprocates with vigor, thrusting her pelvis against mine as if the electrical patterns in her brain have gone quasi-epileptic. There's barely enough room for our bodies to writhe about on the floor.

As we make love I imagine the motel's supervisors have hidden surveillance scanners in every wall. Each gesture's recorded in preparation for a routine inspection of our carnal progress. I feel a surge of excitement thinking about that recording equipment, the latest triumphs of electrical transmigration cycling digits through eight or nine decimal places, a torrential flow of information. Sophie's nipples move against my chest. Her feet are pointed at the ceiling. I squeeze her buttocks until they become inflamed and bruised. By the end of our performance I have to bring a hand to my forehead to block out the nonexistent light that's blinding me. Sophie's arms are outstretched in benediction, her legs spread wide, her flesh shiny with sweat, her eyes dreamy and unfocused. Here's dramatic confirmation we've achieved something rare and unusual even on the grossest of behavioral levels. The desire is gone from me forever.

As I readjust my black Calvin briefs I notice Sophie's trembling. I nudge her with an elbow and squeeze those little fingers.

"I think you're turning nympho on us Sophie. Are you frightened?"

She makes a puzzled frown.

"A penny for your thoughts."

"I'm thinking about an old boyfriend."

"You can't filter him out like so much useless noise? Myself I'm good at severing contacts with the past."

"Shadrach. Shadrach's his name. He's this real cute real-estate agent. He's like allergic to Prozac."

Her gaze is steady. Her voice is centered and composed. I know soon that'll change.

I point at a tattoo on the inside of her elbow. "Where did you get that?"

"Paris."

"What is it?"

"A pink and white ice cream cone."

"You think I'm psycho Sophie?"

"I'm not sure."

"What would I have to do to prove I'm not?"

She starts thinking really hard. Her brows knit. A distant look forms in her eyes.

More than a minute passes.

A cellphone rings.

"Cool. You can use your telekinetic powers to make a phone ring. That's one messed up ringtone. Let it ring."

When the ringing stops Sophie grabs my dick with both hands like it's a mop handle and she's got lots of cleaning to do.

"Nice to know some things never change. Is that our new mutual friend down there?"

Sounds rush through my ears as I stare down at my erection. I wonder if I'm losing my mind.

I pull Sophie to my chest, begin kissing her. "You don't remember anything about Shadrach now do you?"

Sophie shakes her head, makes a clicking noise with her teeth. "Seems like my memory gets worse every time you screw me Rosenberg."

Her hands work vigorously on the shaft of my penis, which is eight inches long and smooth to the touch. She reaches down to massage my balls. I inhale, trying to remain calm, waiting for a recognizable reaction from my body. To be honest it's pretty scary. She makes me feel like a little boy, like I'm trapped in a teenager's body. Is this how transsexuals feel during adolescence? I shut my eyes, reminding myself I don't have to be alone ALL the time with my little peepee.

The next morning I awaken feeling as if I've been shot from a cannon. Sophie's holding dresses up to a full-length mirror that has a blue-painted frame.

"The green one's pretty."

"Puh-leese!"

"Some coffee?"

"Not now."

Sophie's spacey this morning.

"What's wrong with you? Last night didn't make you forget about Shadrach?"

"I feel better now."

"You haven't eaten breakfast. How about a swim in the pool before you settle on a dress to wear? The sign says the water's heated."

"I don't have a suit."

"Wear your panties or nothing at all if you feel better without them."

Wearing only her panties Sophie steps to the edge of the pool before gracefully diving in. I wade in from the shallow end, walk out until I'm armpit-deep.

Sophie rises up out of the water in front of me. She's holding the panties high above her head like a surrender flag.

"They're pinching me in the crotch!"

I reach out to cup her small breasts. The nipples come alive under my fingers. I follow the delicious curve of her ribcage down to where the flare of her hips begins.

"Last night didn't I make you vibrate like a violin string?"

"I was out of tune."

I pull her close, crushing my lips to hers.

Sophie pulls away, dives underwater.

Chapter 27

McKillen wants to see Pekingville for himself. He wants to see the two-headed dwarf chained to the altar in the tan-colored chapel. That can only mean we're returning to the desert. We're NOT stopping for drinks and bottled water at that noisy 7-Eleven.

Here we are in the middle of the Utah desert. There's nothing as far as you can see. I've never seen so much nothing. This is worse than tramping barefoot through a field of thistle. Sophie points out the snake tracks. I'm hungry.

We're 94 million miles from the sun, between the sun and the moon where the eagle flies between them. It's one giant step for mankind. When you talk about a woman dead for three days rising from the dead you're pushing the limits of MY credulity. I've traveled thousands of miles to be here now that bad shit's gonna happen. The banking system will fail. People will die up there. Chaos will fill the world. Knowledge incessantly remakes the whole of civilization. First Thorazine. Afterwards, Ritalin. Nothing's worse than choosing gummy bears to put on your ice-cream cone at Breslers.

"When do we eat McKillen? My fuel cells are depleted."

"How about the White Castle over there? Doesn't that sound good?"

"Let's do it."

Fifteen minutes later we're back on the road. McKillen clutches the steering wheel with nightmarish conviction. His teeth are bared, his jaw clenched, his gaze focused on the dusty desert highway.

Sophie fiddles with a floral-print pot-holder and a silk scarf made in Thailand. She's distracted. I'm unable to hold her gaze. When she tires of the scarf she opens an overstuffed leopard-print vinyl tote bag.

"Didn't I tell you to flush those antidepressants down the toilet?"

"No."

"Okay I'm telling you now."

Sophie doesn't respond. She glances down at her feet, stunned, silent.

I remove my reading glasses with a Brechtian flourish. "The future doesn't belong to San Francisco anymore Sophie. Look outside these windows!"

I make a sweeping panic-stricken gesture with my arms, again very Brechtian.

"What's out there?"

"Look for yourself!"

We pass a delivery van with a massive Snapple logo. We pass three bright green recycling trucks. We pass a gray Lexus with paint peeling on its roof. McKillen's driving very fast. Every vehicle we overtake becomes a blur. I flash the peace sign at some of the drivers we pass.

Sophie begins nibbling on filberts and brazil nuts.

"You got a pair of binoculars in that ostentatious tote bag?"

"Nope."

"Got coffee stains in there? Birthday presents? Got money in there?"

"If I do it's MY money. I'll spend it how I want."

"Your tiny little inheritance? Did you know there are underground tunnels where we're going? Underground tunnels in the middle of the desert. It boggles the mind."

A couple hours later we make a skidding entrance into Pekingville. I lose myself for an instant before noticing a whole rank of dusty Vespas lined up on the sidewalk in front of a rank of dusty out-of-order ATM machines.

McKillen points, laughs. "Where's the clowns on stilts Rosenberg? Where's the fat midget riding a dinosaur and the pissed-off gorilla? You made this place sound like a circus. There's nothing here."

"Clowns to the left us, jokers to the right."

"I'm serious Rosenberg."

"Be patient!"

Sophie continues with her sucking sounds.

"Slow down. You're driving too fast."

McKillen glances in the rearview mirror.

I glare at him. "I said watch the road!"

"There's no one here. What difference does it make how fast I drive?"

"Slow down. You slow down too Sophie NOW!"

I bite my lower lip, lightly tug at her large hoop earrings.

Sophie pulls my dick from her mouth, looking up at me for further instruction.

I jerk off a bit until I almost come. I let Sophie's mouth take over again. She's grabbing my ass so hard I can't pry her hands loose.

I direct McKillen to park the cab several blocks from the tan-colored chapel.

"Jesus Sophie where did you learn to give head like that? You know how to capture the spirit of a relationship."

"I practiced on doctors in the bathroom of the local abortion clinic."

"You naughty girl."

"It takes two to be naughty you naughty boy!"

Sophie grabs my coconuts and screwdriver again.

"You sat on men's faces where men take babies from this world?"

"I never let the interventionists clean out MY unit." Sophie tosses her head back like she hates herself for what she's about to do. She keeps that mouth busy.

McKillen turns around in the front seat. "You two finished back there? I wanna see this circus sideshow, the two-eyed midget."

"Pathetic McKillen you can be so pathetic!"

McKillen douses out a half-smoked Marlboro Light in a Snapple bottle, turns back around, stares out the window at the side of a giant dusty aquamarine delivery truck.

"We'll be done soon enough McKillen. You're free to watch if you like."

I bend over to whisper into Sophie's ear. "You think he heard me?"

Sophie resumes deep-throating.

I imagine Sophie's amazing mouth's a jagged hole through her throat. My erection's filling up the emptiness inside her. I close and open my fists to block out the deafening pulse in my ears. My legs are trembling violently. Is this what Jim Morrison meant by 'mute nostril agony'? At once I imagine dropping a brick warm, wet, and sticky on McKillen's other hand, the non-prosthetic one.

McKillen remains silent throughout the third and final act.

As the three of us walk down the now familiar dusty main street of Pekingville I conjure up two sisters hiding their maniac brother in a cellar, three wealthy men sharing a neurotic prostitute, a nude bathing partner, a civil rights activist molesting Jewish children, a harassed mailman accused of mutilating a defrocked priest, four bank tellers who fail to pull off a robbery.

Everything in San Francisco and Reno becomes another degree or aspect of some thing or combination of things in Pekingville. Everything else excluded from Pekingville's city limits shades off into a residue of hidden-culture campaign advisers, sleaze factors, talk-radio, persistent video teleconferencing, screaming corporate lawyers, National Press Club lifestyle, obscure organ music press-briefings, time-slot projections, sheer poignancy, self-limiting activity, turgid downsizing, supreme-moment regulars, cryptic visionary utterances, limitless blue skies, solipsistic worlds, disconnected atomic facts, anarchic zeal, spiritual flight, great ghostwriters, recorded impulsion, tape-graphic extremities, scavengers of antagonists, tormented human lives, divine photo-locating presence, unthwarted professional taxpayers, wide-screen single-scathing portraits, inappropriate ripple effects, hard sweetheart-deals, buzz-word ops, trickle-down acts of futility, randomness-marketing, primitive tribal chants, young liners, breakthrough feelings, hidden-edge benchwarmers, private pundits, apparent deduction-images, other-attitudes leadership, long-repressed speechwriters, watchdog circles, consultant dubs, detours over tanks, inner pronounced tendencies, choreographer-vision, mother styles, ceremony-think.

Creepy dolls and steam tunnels are the only way to go around here. That's not a euphemism for anything.

A bit later there it is, the tan-colored chapel. On the dirty ground amid the dust-covered grasshoppers and dirty old crickets lies the decaying knife-wielding Mormon woman I clobbered to death days earlier. Large quantities of blood have streamed from her head, staining the front of the light blue dress dark crimson. Her hands frozen in rigor are pressed against her skull in a failed attempt to stanch the flow of blood and pulverized gray matter. When I imagine I see her eyelids flutter open I lose my shit right there.

McKillen points. "Looks like some bully smashed her head in with a brick!"

"It was a wrench McKillen. That wrench delivered the fatal blow."

I point to a bloody wrench lying not far from the body.

"I better watch out for you in the charity kitchen."

The three of us enter the tan-colored chapel. It occurs to me a knife and a door are masculine and feminine symbols. How would you characterize a knife slicing open a package of wieners?

The two-headed dwarf's no longer chained to the altar. By God she's strapped to a wheelchair and scoffing at us! She's got robot motors inside her legs. I approach to give her a big phony hug. I reconsider. A great ugly sucking sound emits from her mouth.

This cannot be happening.

Each time the two-headed dwarf cracks those gouty knuckles her mouth winces in pain. She's a remarkable handicapped woman with milky white breasts and calcium-deficient bones.

I'm Robot Man. I'm here to disprove the reader's assertions.

Seconds later McKillen bludgeons the dwarf with a rusty pole.

Horrible high-pitched screeching echoes through the chapel. Blood gushes onto the floor.

This cannot be happening.

One of the head's eyes are half-open, watching the chapel doorway. The other head's eyes are shut. Both heads are gulping for air.

You can't take anything for granted around here. That's the point.

Pekingville fades into the distance.

Life is full of beauty again. Wonderful light and composition. Nice ambience. From the far side of the car's windows I glimpse a succession of turbulent disconnected images. Field hospitals, Red Cross carriages, refugee camps, three-dollar brick walkways, sparse pieces of homemade patio furniture, tangles of rusted bicycles, gallon-size soup tins, laundry troughs, dust-covered automobiles, crates of canning jars, toppled statuary, seed sacks, work tools, ladders, stacks of unused logs, shopping carts full of copper cable, freight sheds spilling over with rotten fruit, dried-up irrigation channels, the meager flames of candles and kerosene lamps, desolate fields where chimneys and thatched roofs are secured against harsh winds.

Haggard figures scurry in and out of open doorways as endless caravans of ragged migrants sprint along the railroad tracks, begging for cigarettes and food, beef jerky, hardtack and liquor. Mere scraps of bone and clothing. Bluish tongues poking from mouths. Trousers and jackets fashioned from worn pieces of tent canvas. With only the barest netting of flesh covering their bones the girls decorate their faces with dramatic eye makeup.

I watch wild men dragged into detention areas, shoved to the ground, kicked several times, their genitals stepped on, their legs made to work if they want their arms to function again. Skull fractures, profiles of human faces drenched in blood, old boots, uniforms, military belts. A chain gang, a column of soldiers to God knows where.

I have to remind myself this is a vanity project funded by local film school morons, a light forgettable farce, like being sidetracked in a relationship with a feeble-minded girlfriend. Granted my ultra-macho attitude is tough to stomach. This film can't build tension convincingly.

Although a few set pieces deliver, with plenty of scatter-shot gags and that much-imitated fireworks scene, the imagery rarely rises about an unpleasant improbable melodrama.

We stop for $1 Wendy's cheeseburgers. Later, a nice little jog around an 18-hole golf course.

Later Sophie vomits down the side of the cab.

We're in Colorado at a restaurant overlooking the Rockies. Sophie's slouching in the back row sipping peppermint tea. She's wearing sunglasses and a hoodie. McKillen's reading a stripper's autobiography. I'm contemplating chicken salad and Doritos. A shot of vodka would also be nice.

Hair grows out of the bald waiter's ears. Hot chicks love bald guys. Ask Sophie. Her thighs are sore.

We'll arrive at Mount Rushmore by Sunday. I intend to make my final break with God in South Dakota. I'm officially on spring-break. Sounds kinda awesome, kinda stupid. Once I arrive at my destination I'll need a place to stay, things to do. Jumping head first into a swimming pool of spiders and glass. Cooking up crystal meth.

Who doesn't love a good doggie nose print on a car window? God's shit can be nasty from the windshield of a moving car. As we drive I listen to Black Flag and cycle through endless rounds of Truth. I haven't felt this energized in a long time. I'm serving my country, volunteering for everything in sight. I can't wait to say fuck you on national TV. The video will air on YouTube for everyone to see. That's called creating value. Fantastic! I imagine well-meaning politicians strangulating starving babies. Years, decades, centuries pass. Jesus Christ is tossed out of Congress. Executives at NBC snap into action to ensure everything's precisely outlined.

The colors are cartoon-like.

Wind advisory. Severe thunderstorm watch.

I hurl greasy sausage manure into the gutter.

We'll be in Rapid City Sunday if we survive a Cracker Barrel that smells like a dentist office.

Texting while driving over 40 mph is dumb McKillen!

Why can't people drive the speed limit and learn to merge?

Uh oh. The Garmin chose a different route than Google Maps. What the hell's this goddamned fence doing here next to a phosphorescent paint stripe?

To hell with Friday afternoon traffic. McKillen's like a man recovering from a recent cataract op who lost his life savings to a Ponzi scheme. He can't make the data stand still. I need a hovercraft and

Flintstones chewable vitamins to deal with this shit. Beer and vodka are the real solution to road rage.

Why would someone steal orange traffic cones?

Two Waffle Houses at one exit!

Awesome sunset over the mountains tonight. Nice to get out to the firing range. Shoot anything? I saw two pedestrians hit and killed at a busy intersection in Wyoming. Clueless kids selling Girl Scout cookies.

The Colorado pics from last night are hilarious. I'm at a cemetery not a chicken-processing plant you moron! Can't you hear the Annie Lennox soundtrack?

We get shafted at a Hampton Inn. McKillen locks the keys in the car. It's the end of an era, time to let it go. We're tired, burnt out. We realize government's no longer the answer. In Wyoming we begin to blame the astrological calendar.

In South Dakota I take a nature walk and nearly burn the fake hair off my face. I manage to nail the local pastor's daughter behind a shitty little elementary school. Trashy goodness. It's fun using a new American Express card with a pastor's name on it. The IKEA catalogue makes Sophie totally want to redo the pastor's chapel. She's daring me to imagine new and disturbing things, like reading a book about neuroscience or pretending phone bills don't exist or looking for Orion in the night sky or drinking a fluid that burns my throat worse than this crappy vodka.

Chapter 28

I get the impression daydreaming's starting to impair my friendship with Sophie.

The bright white motel room's barely ornamented apart from the bed and several white crates, three cubes, two white plastic chairs, and one filthy yellow chair the color and texture of pubic hair.

I circle the bed before ingloriously plopping down on the stained, faded comforter.

"It's hot enough in here to fry an egg!"

"Rosenberg does this door lock?"

"Sure why not? Lock the damn thing and come over here."

Sophie fiddles around with the lock for awhile. "Who cares if it doesn't lock. We're the only ones in the motel right?"

"Don't forget McKillen's next door."

Sophie sighs, walks over to the bed, sits down. "Oh yeah. Wonderful McKillen."

"Kiss me Sophie."

"Like we're falling in love?"

I laugh. "That's right. A dreary seducer and his pale flinty lover. Very decadent. I've been looking around for a new hobby."

Sophie stands back up. "I gotta do my exercises first. You can masturbate for awhile."

"Suit yourself. Love's everywhere right? It's our job to keep the little Buddhists out there happy in little Buddhist land."

"Why do you talk to me like I'm dumb?"

"I'm telling you funny stories. You don't laugh at them."

Sophie begins her calisthenics routine.

Rather than masturbate I use the remote to turn on the TV. There it is. Images of Mount Rushmore, some black-and-white, some color, some blurry. We're getting closer and closer to the real thing. I'm reminded of one of those museum exhibits that have a TV sitting atop a classic Greek pillar to illustrate an allegory of our collective dilemma. Except in this case we're missing the zombie's rabbit ears. The motel has full-blown cable.

"Did you notice there's a full moon tonight?"

Sophie smirks at the floor.

I stretch out my legs. "I could go for some fish tacos right about now. Too bad we're in the wrong part of the country for quality eating."

Sophie continues exercising, shifting her balance on and off her toes. I turn away from the TV, watch her for awhile. I feel like I got two basketballs suspended perfectly between my legs.

Sophie looks at me. "You were thinking about kangaroos just now weren't you?"

"I don't believe they're real."

Sophie sighs. "Aren't you getting tired of driving around? I'm getting tired of it. It was fun at first. Not anymore. McKillen gets on my nerves."

"Don't tell him that. It'll confuse him. I feel the same way. We can't stop and change our pattern yet, not till we arrive at Mount Rushmore. You seem a little excited."

"Why do you think you were imagining kangaroos?"

"I'm hungry. Maybe I'm horny. Come over here. Sit down and kiss me."

Sophie lies down on the bed. "I'm sore."

"Lean forward. I can massage your back."

She leans forward.

"I like this kind of life, the barrenness of the land, the gloomy weather, the endless stream of restaurants, cocktail bars, hotel lobbies, what have you. Wearing T-shirts and jeans."

Sophie shakes her head. "I get bored. Everything starts to look the same. Food tastes the same. I can't tell whether this is supposed to be funny or depressing."

"Both. To each his own. Some men find it erotic to yell at women over the phone. I don't. I want my woman right here beside me. You got a mole here on your back." I start fondling Sophie's breasts. "You've got goose-bumps on your shoulders."

Sophie turns around, stares at me. "Maybe you should hire someone else who has a real life to be your companion. I'm a bored college student. I need to get back to school."

"Hire? Those days at Harvard I was a tall malnourished vegetarian who subsisted on astronaut's food. I used to play games when I got bored."

"You went to Harvard?"

"I graduated with a bachelor's degree in philosophy and religious studies, went to medical school for a year before dropping out, Harvard Medical School. I got an incredible score on my MCAT, applied on a whim, got accepted."

"How'd you afford it?"

"Scholarships. My parents paid for most of it. They had high-level positions in the Boston city government. Money was never an issue growing up."

"Why the hell are you out here driving around doing nothing?"

"Long story as they say. I AM 'doing something' as you put it. The short of it is I got my girlfriend pregnant my first year in medical school. We both dropped out. She wanted to have the baby."

"Were you trying to make her pregnant? Was it an accident?"

"At the time I would've said yes. Looking back on it I think there was a subconscious purpose. It got me out of the whole higher education racket. We packed up our belongings, drove to San Francisco. From that point I never got another penny from my parents. They disowned me. It was a huge weight off my back. I no longer felt like I had any obligation to them. My wife and I were happy to support ourselves clearing away dishes at a coffeehouse. It gave me lots of time to write stories and philosophize."

"What's that involve?"

"Keeping journals of your thoughts and reflections on life. It was also a stressful time. I converted to Islam. Technically not converted. Before that I didn't practice religion."

"What'd you do?"

"On our drive out to California we gave a young Muslim man a ride to Denver. Along the way he talked about Islam. That's what got me interested."

"Now you're here in a motel room doing nothing."

I laugh. "How do you mean nothing?"

"You're in trouble with the law, on the run from the cops."

"Who says I'm in trouble? Grown-ups don't run from the cops. This is my calling, what I'm meant to do."

"What about your wife and family? What about your daughter you told me about?"

"They're doing their own thing. I told you we're separated."

"You want your daughter to go to Harvard?"

"Why not? I don't want her to get brainwashed there."

"Is she like me?"

"She's younger, not as laid back. Amber's intense, too intense. That affects how she thinks about things."

"Her name's Amber? As in Amber Alert?"

I smile.

"What's your wife's name?"

"Bianca."

"I gotta get back to the campus. Don't take it the wrong way. I can't keep going around with you and McKillen. It starts to get depressing. One place is no better than any other." Sophie mimes cutting her wrists.

"Lighten up! Tell me a story, something sexy, a fable of revenge. Did you ever run away from home?"

"Once we get to Mount Rushmore I'm leaving. I should've warned you it's a summer fling. We're not married. It's not like I'm an Islamic feminist enrolled in Islam 101. Don't worry about me. I'll be fine. I'm not your daughter. I'll live till I'm ninety."

"What's that mean?"

"I don't know. Nothing. I shouldn't say that. I think I'll take off right now!"

"Are you crazy? It's dark outside, pouring rain. It's Bangladesh out there!"

"I'll wear something on my head."

"You know the story of Achilles and how he was dipped into the River Styx as a baby. His heel didn't get wet."

"Yeah I know it from karaoke."

"Bingo. There you go. Think twice about using hats and umbrellas in the rain. To hell with physical modesty. Safety's the main thing. C'mon stay a little longer Sophie. Have a Heineken."

Police car lights flash through the window.

Sophie opens the door.

The sound of pouring rain on the sidewalk fills the room. It's very Brechtian.

"Sophie don't leave us!"

Sophie walks outside, doesn't close the door, doesn't turn around, walks right up to the police car.

I remain seated on the bed.

The sound of pouring rain is deafening.

"Sophie come back here!"

Sophie's getting drenched out there. The cop's ignoring her. He's not getting out of the car. He's doing nothing. He might not be alive. He might be comatose.

I sit on the edge of the bed awhile longer. The cop car backs out of the parking lot, returns to the highway. Sophie wanders off into the night never to be seen again.

The excitement has left me wide awake.

I go next door to hang out with McKillen.

"Who's that?"

"It's Rosenberg with a message from God."

McKillen opens the door. "What's that?"

"A message from God. You want me to describe that? It's like eating a ham sandwich, like remaining in bed for a single instant, like walking up a slate path to your favorite garden gate, like wearing one of those wide ties with a loud psychedelic pattern. Need I multiply examples? You don't know how much hair you got till someone cuts it all off."

I watch McKillen remove his artificial limb. He looks irritated, like he needs his ass wiped and his balls scrubbed.

"I'm too practical for the movement. Is that it Rosenberg? The whole damn world's in on the secret except for me."

"That's putting it too strongly. It'd be a hell of a big secret to keep from you or anyone else."

McKillen agrees with me. He's silent for awhile. I notice a restlessness building behind those eyes. I notice a twitch in the limbs. The way McKillen glances around the motel room reminds me of a cranium with holes drilled through its surface and wires stuck in.

"Where's Sophie gone off to?"

"She left us a couple hours ago."

"A food run?"

"For good."

"She's not coming back?"

"That's right."

"It's almost dark! How could you let her get away?"

"What are you talking about? You're nuts if you think this is a reenactment of the Patty Hearst story. There's no shortage of disenchanted people out there. The movement can find other recruits."

"I thought she was special."

"She WAS special. We're special. What do you think that means?"

McKillen lights a cigarette, stares at me defiantly. "Cut the new-age horseshit Rosenberg!"

"This is the night before another day. Tomorrow we'll find another drifter, another drop-out. Trust me on that. The curve's rising sharply now."

"Hell so much time wasted!"

"What are you talking about? We save money. One motel room's cheaper than two right?" My heart's pounding. I'm breathing hard.

The way McKillen keeps rolling his eyes makes me nervous. For the fist time I suspect a severe personality disorder in the making. I imagine implanting forty electrodes in his brain to prevent nonviolent seizures.

I lay back against the pillows trying to relax.

McKillen stabs his last cigarette into an ashtray on the nightstand. "Am I making you nervous Rosenberg?"

"A little."

"That's normal. I expected a more philosophical approach from you."

"Cognac? Psychomotor epilepsy?"

"How's it you never give me a straight answer yet you talk about the Straight & Narrow?"

"We're on it right now. Sophie's the one who fell off the Straight & Narrow not us. Her commitment to a stupid university trumped her commitment to the movement. That's her problem. That's the practical implication of what's going on here. What's more practical than the problem of why an apple falls to the ground?"

"It comes down to gravity? It's not you who let Sophie fall off the Straight & Narrow. Gravity did it?"

"The Arab surrealist movement and the Straight & Narrow are one and the same thing? I'm serious. Think about what I said a moment ago."

"You're so goddamned reasonable I can't stand it. You've got it ALL figured out!"

"You surprise me McKillen. I've never seen this sort of temper from you. Irritable yes. High-pitched yelling no. Maybe you need your ass wiped."

"I'm gonna watch some TV! Hand me the remote."

I ignore his request, holding up a wig instead. "Look at this! What's it look like? A wig Sophie gave me as a parting gift."

"A new disguise? C'mon give me the remote."

"I carry wigs and masks for protection."

"Gimme the remote!"

"Go over to the TV, turn it on yourself if it's so goddamned important to you."

"I wish you'd stop being such an asshole."

"I wish you were heavily sedated."

I toss the TV remote in his direction. "Big day tomorrow McKillen. I can sense it's gonna be a big day for the movement."

McKillen sighs, begins flipping through the channels.

I point at him. "A very big day I tell you. You better get your ass up early."

"I'll get up when I damn well feel like it."

I check the things on the nightstand. Car keys, wallet, electric razor. "Looks like we've run out of cigarettes."

"Go get some. I'm watching the rest of this movie."

I leave the room, walk out into the lobby where I'm confronted by a man in bandages and a bathrobe.

I return to the room empty-handed. "These places no longer have cigarette machines."

McKillen snickers. "You know what thorazine is Rosenberg?"

"It's a powerful tranquilizer. Why?"

McKillen points at the screen. "That's what the nurses are giving that guy. Look."

"What's on his head?"

"Bandages."

"What happened?"

"Christ I don't know. Let's watch."

"You watch. I'm turning in."

I close my eyes, roll over. I can't fall asleep. I hear the TV's dialogue. I begin imagining my own movie to match that dialogue. How well does it correspond to the real thing?

I turn back over, glance at the TV.

There it is!

The frame freezes. There I am on TV! Who the hell tipped off the media? Never ones to miss a publicity stunt, whenever and wherever the cops find a dead body they tip off the media. It's a highlight reel. This ain't ESPN. The camera zooms in. There I am in a high school yearbook portrait. The camera pulls back. There's the Tenderloin, my corner, my flat upstairs above the three golden pawnshop balls. There's the pawnbroker himself. A woman's interviewing the bastard! What a pathetic meathead. He's telling her about Amber though using the wrong adjectives with poor inflection. Holy Christ where do they get this shit? Who the hell's the obnoxious self-righteous narrator who's casting aspersions on my so-called homicidal crime spree? The camera pans to the right. There I am in one of Goldsmith's clubs sharing a booth with fat shirtless strippers who drink Rolling Rock straight from the can. Except this time around I'm in a museum, frozen in a sculpture garden, with a fake sunset mural behind me and plastic potted palms towering over the table. I can't begin to tell you what it means. What's the difference between this and that? The meth-addicted bitch I once screwed and shared my flat with is on national TV telling everyone within earshot I once accused her of being a serial murderer. That's the culmination of what the Situationists called our Society of the Spectacle. The asshole correspondents keep calling me 'psychotic' and 'homicidal,' two words with referents I can't imagine.

The scenes become too degrading. My stomach can't take it anymore. My mouth opens and closes. I feel an overwhelming surge of sickness. Memories flash through my mind faster and faster until I'm not sure my head will ever stop throbbing. What the hell am I, an actor in a shitty Martin Scorsese movie?

McKillen's in a state of pure ecstasy. "That's you Rosenberg! They're reenacting your life on Unsolved Mysteries!"

"What can I say? I've never been good at memorizing the lines from someone's else script of my own worthless life."

"I guarantee this will be a classic, right up there with the Mysteries of the Afterlife! This is the publicity you've wanted."

"Looks like they've filed the movement under 'bizarre murders' and moved on to the ads."

"I'm proud of you! You did kill your daughter and escape from an institution and murder a cabdriver and they still haven't tracked you down! Unbelievable. I thought you were full of shit. Man was I wrong. You recognize the cops they're interviewing?"

"The whole thing's a lot of idiotic speculation. I never did any of that stuff high on meth or any other drug. At worst I was drunk. I don't do drugs anymore. I rarely did them, not even aspirin. I didn't deal drugs either. That was Penny's problem. They're confusing me with Penny. Plus the pawnbroker is so full of shit about Amber. What does he mean he was protecting her from me, acting as a surrogate father? She was his babysitter for God's sake. He paid for her to come down and sit with his daughter while he went out and screwed perverts in the bushes."

McKillen laughs. "Sounds like you're gonna have to set the record straight Rosenberg."

The show returns. The woman correspondent's now interviewing Goldsmith outside one of his gentlemen's clubs. He needs a shave. The whites of his eyes are canary-yellow. For Christ's sake how am I supposed to compete with this incoherent blather? He's calling me a psychotic drifter. That's the exact phrase, 'psychotic drifter.'

"You recognize that guy? Why's he calling you Rosenberger?"

"He's the other half of the Arab surrealist movement. Looks like he's lost it worse than I imagined. You'd think he'd show a bit of loyalty."

"He's getting paid for this interview. He's a capitalist whore. It's that easy to turn someone away from what they believe in."

Another set of ads replaces Goldsmith's talking head.

"They're devoting most of the hour to your exploits Rosenberg."

"Shut up McKillen. Shut up!"

He shakes his head and snorts. "Don't you get it? This is what you need for the Arab surrealist movement. Exposure and notoriety."

"Great. I won't ever die. I'll get older and older locked up in prison like Charlie Manson."

"What are you talking about?"

"I said shut up. Shut up!"

My neck's slick with sweat. I begin flexing my fingers. I sip the beer, staring out the window at a car passing in the parking lot.

When the show returns they're interviewing a Nevada state trooper in the parking lot of a motel outside Reno. That's where the motel manager found the body of a cabdriver who was strangled and viciously beaten multiple times over the head with a champagne bottle. You've got to be kidding me. Where the hell would I get a champagne bottle in the middle of the night? The trooper has deep dark eyes framed by a thick set of lashes. He's rakishly handsome and glamorous in that pink button-down shirt and those black wool pants. He appears nervous as he speaks.

I zone out for awhile.

Another set of ads appears.

When the show returns the credits roll, giving proper credit to the clumsy stand-in actors and derivative screenwriters.

"I never realized you had so much experience with strip clubs Rosenberg. You meet any high-profile types?"

"Not specifically. It's demanding work, keeping the girls in shape and disease-free, keeping them off drugs, keeping their energy levels high enough to convince the clients those tits are the center of their universe."

"Sounds like a full-time job. What do you think, the best time of your life? What happened?"

"What happened to me? What's happened to you? You want explanations. That'll help you make sense of me? Is that it? Don't bother. The Arab surrealist movement's never been about explaining things."

"That guy Goldsmith's your friend?"

"Not anymore."

"You okay?"

"I have lots of feelings to sort through now. My throat's killing me. I'm turning in the for the night."

"How can you sleep now? Why aren't you ecstatic? What more could you want? Your time's come."

"You're the one who doesn't get it! The whole reason the movement has a chance of working is if I'm anonymous, if I blend in, if I act and look like a loser who could never harm anyone except himself. The point's never been to lavish attention on myself and appear threatening. I only increase the chances I'll be arrested. If that happens the movement's finished."

"You've thought this through."

"Not well enough. Now my life's highlighted on a TV show. That only confirms what I suspected. The cops and FBI are on my tail twenty-four-seven."

"Fame's a Catch-22."

"It's a no-win situation." I shrug my shoulders, take another sip of beer. "You know what I mean McKillen. Now when I die the tabloids will have a field day with me. The message is lost in cheap photographs and unsubstantiated rumors. Where's the disturbance? Isn't that what everyone reads standing in line at the supermarket? How's that surreal?"

Silence.

I stare intensely into McKillen's eyes. It feels intimate not in a sexual kind of way.

I watch McKillen's lips part.

I hear him say only "Rosenberg?"

Part 4 Rosenberg

Chapter 29

"Everyday I worked there I saw Rosenberg at /../../. Nothing noteworthy about his thin body and oversized wallet. The strippers liked his company. They joined him in his favorite booth for cheeseburgers and a beer. I rarely saw him fondle their tits or check for vital signs. I asked him once why he spent so much time at the club. He said my question wasn't relevant. I remember that exactly. 'Your question's not relevant.' After that I left him alone.

"He said he was a writer. He carried around a tape recorder to record ideas as they popped into his head. He taped descriptions of everything. You'd see him going through his pockets looking for blank cassettes before he'd start talking into the recorder again, fast, not fast like a tweaker, fast like he's reading something written down. The way he did it, holding the recorder right up to his lips, staring at it the way he did, struck me as autistic, even psychopathic. I remember he had a weird haircut too and colored his hair which I thought was weird for a man that age, in his late thirties I believe.

"Rosenberg's life was an exercise in opportunistic social disturbance. That's his business. I refuse to be complicit in praising a lot of Brechtian horseshit. Students of his life know the man used the term 'Brechtian' to describe a wide range of incompatible artistic and social techniques that were meant to convey a distance between the audience and life's dramas. The frigidity of that distance left me cold.

"I remember he liked loud music and barbeque. Women with large asses fit the sequence of his fantasies. He liked jerking off from behind and rubbing your ass while he did it.

"I could never hate the guy for too long. He was such a lady's man. One night something wasn't right in his head. We were alone in one of the club's back rooms. He was getting aggressive and threatening, kept saying he wanted to beat the psychological damage right out of me. He said that a lot. 'Psychological damage.' Sometimes it was from your parents, other times from your parole officer or pastor. They were responsible for your 'psychological damage.' Another thing he liked was to repeat 'stop blocking things out bitch.' He was opinionated, made sure to set the record straight before he let you give him a hand-job. He wasn't about to risk castration.

"I ran into him once at a Palo Alto post office. Very weird guy.

"Rosenberg lived his life impatiently. I bet he still does. He was on the move, on the run, going somewhere else different from where he was, not running away, getting the hell out. He never had the time for anyone else's opinions or views. Not that he was arrogant. He was in a great hurry. He was charming too. He knew how to smile. I imagine he's never a happy man. The first thing on his mind's escaping from wherever he finds himself, even escaping from life itself.

"You could tell by the way he treated the strippers he was a born teacher. That's his true calling, not a celebrity criminal or a revolutionary surrealist or whatever the commentators call him. He's a teacher. Too bad most of the world's uninterested in his lessons and find them too confusing to understand, too painful to experience.

"Can I get you a private session with the staff anesthesiologist? Some painkillers? Can I borrow that cigarette?

"First thing Rosenberg said to me was 'Never apologize for something you never did.' He laughed sarcastic-like. Whenever he did that you couldn't tell if you were supposed to take him seriously. That was the problem with Rosenberg. You never knew whether to take the guy seriously. He undercut what he said with a strange giggle or he'd roll his eyes. How do you relate to someone like that? Is he a comedian? Is he mocking you or himself? He never seemed to be in a realistic mood for very long.

"Disruption and disturbance were his only options. He confused any form of peaceful friendship with complacency.

"Turn off your cellphone please!

"I liked the guy. He was flakey, messed up in the head. Who isn't in the Tenderloin? His voice was sharp and loud. You heard him above the background noise of the club. I remember seeing him with the older strippers, the retirees with bad boob jobs and unruly pubic hair. He enjoyed coaching them, helping them with midlife crisis stuff. It wasn't clear he was getting paid for it. My impression is he was terminally unemployed. He got on with the club's management who let him hang out there as he pleased. He drank liquor, smoked. Never struck me as a drug addict or criminal type. He sounded more educated than most of the people who frequent a club like that.

"I never understood where Rosenberg got his money. He was a big spender at the club, buying many rounds of drinks, leaving big tips. He bragged to me once he never ran up a debt. He didn't believe in tabs and credit cards. With him everything came down to cash. I don't know where he got the cash. I used to joke he was an undercover cop, a nark, a hypnotic courier. He denied everything. I'm not sure what his real name is.

"After what he did to me that night I swore I'd never kiss him again. You don't shove your dick in a girl's mouth without asking permission, no matter how much you pay her and what the camera angle. To make matters worse, his privates reeked of Lysol disinfectant. Rosenberg was like that.

He could be so passionate about dishing a girl's brains out yet worry she's gonna give him a disease. He preferred hand-jobs over intercourse and blowjobs. Not to get too technical here, the way I see it he was a misogynist with an oral fixation.

"Bottom line is Rosenberg was more of a perfectionist than a committed surrealist.

"Imagine taking a turd-stained piece of toilet paper warm, wet, and sticky out of your luggage at Baggage Claim in Heathrow Airport. Does that make you sick? It makes me sick!

"My impression was he lived alone, was a life-long bachelor, an outsider. You can imagine my surprise when I learned he had a live-in girlfriend, an ex-wife he brutalized, and a daughter he murdered. It's incredible the difference between machines and animals. Rosenberg never learned to accept the fact he was a machine with a pulse, a sex maniac.

"We suspect his sudden homicidal impulses coincided with minor attacks of epilepsy when the urge to kill usurped the entire scope of his attention. He may have heard voices commanding him to act or he may not. We can't know for certain.

"I'll never forget the night he ordered round after round of tequila shooters. It was our monthly Johnny Guitar Night. The club was packed with lesbians done up in cowboy regalia. We know Rosenberg had a thing for converting lesbians to the straight life. He wasn't homophobic. He believed wherever you are in life, whatever you're doing, Rosenberg thought you should stop doing that and start doing the opposite. That's wisdom or some such shit. That night he grabbed me by the hands, pulled me onto the floor. We did a weird swing dance to loud rock-and-roll music. For the first time in a long time I thought of myself as a woman not a lesbian. I moaned, enjoying every split second of the dance as he bounced my big ass across the floor. I hadn't been with a man for so long I didn't have a backup plan. I felt like I'd stepped into a rap video.

"The final night happened so fast it's hard to remember the exact chain of events.

"I remember Rosenberg disrupted the food line at the local homeless shelter by passing out free raisins. I told him that kind of loathsome sentimentality discredits the whole motive behind the Arab surrealist movement. He never did it again.

"I don't want to spill ALL the beans on the man. There's a lot more there than most of us have the courage to realize. He planned it that way. He was a great guy. To prove the two lobes of his brain worked independently of each other he once wrote a love letter with his right hand and a set of mystical verses with his left, both at the same time. The principles of the Arab surrealist movement are Rosicrucian in origin and permeated with the doctrines of the Gnostics.

"I never thought of Rosenberg as having a life outside those strip clubs."

Impossible, unreasonable dreams, a form of insanity! An inconceivable chaos! Rosenberg doesn't see things the way they are!

"Don't give me that literary horseshit! Pay attention! Our hero has a reasonable enough personality. He's an ambitious outsider with a burning desire to prevail in the face of several painful setbacks, a series of ungovernable mood swings, and a blizzard of lawsuits. What's unreasonable about that? The message here revolves around unstoppable character development NOT excessive sex and violence for the sake of sex and violence in accordance with the televised advertisements. I don't care if Sterling Hayden claimed writing and wandering never mix. I know this ain't the cradle of civilization or the square and compass of Masonry atop the cross of the Knights Templar. I recognize a new-age Christian altar when I see one. I'm no pornographer or criminalist. I know nothing's more pathetic than a serial murderer with a scheduling conflict."

Working writers as a rule profess very humane political and social opinions! On the other hand rebels, neurotics, psychopaths, assassins, proud-hearted profligates, poor lads clothed in black, contemptible aristocrats ALL failed in London before trying to fail again in Hong Kong. That includes lunatic asylums crammed with epileptics and ill-balanced geniuses so tight and hot the reader cannot imagine that cleft.

"The Yankee rose with the first light of dawn, dressed himself in the clothes of a foreigner, boarded a flatboat bound for New Orleans. The Gulf of Mexico beckoned."

That imagery's got nothing to do with jingoism or free-thinking materialism! Your hero's exhausted his money and now abandons himself to dissolute living. Under the crush of debts and duties forgotten and monstrous criminal fantasies your hero's overtaken by the excesses of finely honed indulgence. He's no idler though idlers surrender to dissolute living. Those nincompoops!

"Are you paying attention? Our hero works hard. He's committed. He's 'in control' as we like to say to the Emperor at the End of the Arts of Wanton & Luxurious Living. Our hero understands that religious feeling is the best safeguard against suicide, poetry and satiety of pleasure being the worst."

Lantern slides! That explains your hero's lack of deliberation and balance! Those flimsy translucent images are felt while they cannot be explained in meaningful literary or psycho-cinematic terms. Reminds me of peering out at pedestrians through a vent-hole in one of those old Parisian streetlamps.

Look over there! A Schopenhauer precursor! A lost disciple of the Buddha!

"The plight of an outsider who feels he doesn't hold a social position commensurate with his merits. An enemy of the bourgeois spirit."

My job's to pour cold water over those panegyrics!

"Having exhausted life's pleasures in a series of orgies, our hero's lived fully and is satisfied. Overheated imagination dominates his soul. The bliss of non-existence beckons. That's it folks!"

Come again? The motive underlying erotic poetry? The highest manifestation of the human will?

"Our hero conceives of an imaginary deity called Allah, Yahweh, what have you, whom he adores as an existing entity and pays regular homage to before a new-age Christian altar."

Impossible, unreasonable dreams, a form of insanity! Illusions, visions, hallucinations! Restless agitation! Unstable eccentricities! Paroxysms of uniqueness! Whatever's morbidly exaggerated! Whatever you can rip off from Celine!

"Isn't there a time in life when human genius approximates madness?"

Duplication of self notwithstanding the irritability!

Chapter 30

I'll be more dignified come tomorrow. Today I crisscross the globe like a goddamned lunatic. I'm indignant. First it's London on my way to Hong Kong only to find Los Angeles doesn't have cabs roaming the streets like New York. On a train from Gare du Nord to Berlin. Back in Paris to the Musee D'Orsay, three days in Miami, a cute little weekend in Mexico City, a cafe overlooking Sunset Boulevard. Washing it down with booze and cold beer. I'm in Bristol. I have a massive migraine. £4.15 for a vodka and coke, £2.10 for a can of Red Bull, 59p for a pack of Chewits.

I study a place before I visit, scribbling notes, speaking into a mini-cassette recorder, thinking deeply, sleeping poorly. Every night I drink at least four bottles of beer and two shots of vodka before I nod off. It doesn't help that this wristwatch is adjusted to Mexico City time.

Come to Qatar the weather is awesome!

How's unmarried life?

Ketchup and hot sauce belong on scrambled eggs.

My customary life continues. The work is the same, same complex and monotonous existence bearing me along as it does everyone else. Everyday the sky shines like a waxed piano. Now and again memories of

Penny and Amber come boldly back to me. Other times strangers and things motivated by Money-Sex-Greed-&-Power appear shadowy and distant when I go out among the crowds. Pedestrians have fangs and wear masks similar to those worn by the rock band Slipknot. They express interest in serial murder, vampires, suicide, cannibalism. They've contributed to the delinquency of minors, violated their paroles. Many bear names scrawled across the semen-stained pages of the local sex offender registry. They've joined covens. They want your baby. Last week the cops found a dead infant wrapped in newsprint in the basement.

Pardon me I have to be on my way.

I love flights that aren't full. Having an empty seat beside you is awesome. I forgot my noise-cancelling headphones at the hotel. How the mind locks up from stress and trying too hard! Packing light would be easier if I didn't lug around ../../../../. God I'm terrible at this career development thing. Hitler no longer scares the shit out of me. Let's shove a camera in your face, take photos of everyone everywhere! I have lots of blackmail photos. Smile and wave. I'll change your life forever. Buy me a puppy I'll love you even more. I hate the UK. I wouldn't mind if the whole goddamned place burned down. Including Swindon. It's not a real country. Philadelphia's amazing. Everything there goes better with coke. The lines at Starbucks never end.

Mirrors cover three walls of the interview room. I face the fourth wall. My interviewer has long very straight wheat-colored hair braided and pinned to the back of her head.

"Don't try any funny stuff Rosenberg."

"I love children. I could never ../../../../."

"Let's begin with the goals of the Arab surrealist movement."

"You ask what the Arab surrealist movement's about? I assure you it's not about the sudden and violent disintegration of buildings and the persons within them. If it were, in ninety-five percent of deaths an autopsy reveals the cause of death on the same day. Where's the surprise and disruption in that?"

"I notice you use the word 'disruption' a lot."

"I've seen lots of movies. That's how I think. Frame by frame with narrow black bars disrupting my vision twenty-four times a second."

"That's weird."

"Disruption is a way of waking people up, rousing them from slumber and degradation, preventing the same scenario from occurring time and again. If we're amusing ourselves to death, it's not that we're watching too much TV. We're failing to seek out painful and confusing situations. The great French writer André Gide said a culture born of life kills that very life. I step into the picture to offer a novel form of resurrection."

"Is that insurrection? Now that you've 'made the scene' as they say how does it feel?"

"It feels one-hundred percent painful at the beginning of every new era. That's good. The situation's getting critical. We're heading straight for disaster. Try to figure that out! The artist Brion Gysin said abrupt word-withdrawal can be a life-shattering experience. There you have it, the Arab surrealist movement in a nutshell. No talking. Stop what you're doing, take everything out of your pockets, put it on the ground before you. What do you see? It proves the movement doesn't like people who hide money in their shoes to purchase progress and reduce the pain in their lives."

"Let me get this straight. You're traveling about the world giving interviews and lecturing on how the next era will begin with silence, with the total absence of words and activity?"

"I know it's paradoxical. I can't help behaving that way. Wandering is giving me horribly ulcerated feet. Once the movement's generated sufficient momentum I plan to retire to a more sedentary occupation. My core competencies include abstract reasoning and blindfolded screwing."

"You should work with computers. You have the right mindset."

"Computers are very proud. They're distracting humanity with easily accessible online pornography. Where's the grand idea in that? We want to search out and confront pain and confusion, not protect ourselves from those things."

"Let's change gears and talk about your past Rosenberg."

"That thing upstairs is not my daughter!"

"Excuse me?"

"Did he fall or was he pushed? That's the question behind every human action. Did he fall or was he pushed? Can we put the blame on the force of gravity rather than the force of a shove? See where I'm going with this? It's an incredible gamble. The stakes are your very own life."

"Tell me Rosenberg how does one become a member of the Arab surrealist movement?"

"You eat the entrails of an animal while its heart's still beating."

"What does that prove?"

"Gotta do better than that scumbag!"

"What?"

"Your questions. You better improve the quality of your questions very quickly. You're lulling me into complacency. C'mon get up in my face! Try to beat the shit out of me!"

Silence.

"There you have it! Disruption. See how it works? That's the Arab surrealist movement in a nutshell. I use disruption to trigger a state of confused silence in the audience. Did I mention I scored 800 on both the math and verbal SAT while suffering from a bad hangover? Though not as disturbing as taking a leak off the Golden Gate Bridge or ass-fucking the community demonologist or American combat units thirty miles east of the Harz Mountains in central Germany."

"I know where you're going with this Rosenberg. I don't like it!"

"You don't know! You guess! What the hell do you know? You don't know shit! You're a media punk who doesn't know her mouth from an asshole in the ground. You get pad for this entertaining bullshit?"

"That's not the type of behavior we agreed on when we sat down to do this interview!"

"I'm too painful and confusing to you and your audience. Your only excuse is you've got a face like a cat's ass. That's right. I forgot. We're supposed to have an interview today. Aren't you supposed to have questions ready for me? That's the first rule any interviewer should know. You think you can handle that? Where's my bottle of Southern Comfort?"

Silence.

"Once again there you have it. Disruption. See the mechanics of it? That's the Arab surrealist movement in a nutshell. Nothing personal I assure you. Suffering and confusion are God's two favorite wake-up calls in this mundane reality."

Silence.

Painful disruptive revolution's spreading.

Tonight my Bullshit Tolerance Level is quite low. I'm up late in an airport Hilton reading novels off Kindle, watching the Discovery Channel. We wanna become nations of fanny-packing people?

No One calls from Tokyo. It's International Woman's Day. She's learned the Japanese words for *exfoliate, mousse, chafing*. She loves cats and tattoos and Dance Dance Revolution. She's not blowing chunks anymore and instead listens to the Beatles. No One's my first real contact in Tokyo.

Next morning I awaken with my mind in the gutter. Holy shit. How's it 6am? Did I get food poisoning? Did I get a job offer from Starbucks? Goddamned Kopfschmerzen gehen einfach nicht weg. This ain't Germany. The most important relationship you can have is with yourself in the next train car.

My iPhone lights up the room when I realize I just had sex with myself. Oops. You're not gay I hope you don't wanna screw me.

Bijna weekend in Holland. It'll be sheer perfection. Landed in Amsterdam. Congratulations on your new citizenship! I'm not wearing any pants. Hell yeah I feel woozy. I need an illuminated keyboard. Ah the simple pleasures of a chocolate chip cookie. An amazing cardio and weights workout. A seven-hour flight from Dulles to Amsterdam. File those under things I'll never understand. Like child rape in Swindon. That scares the hell out of me more than the female passenger who hit 5,000 Tweets yesterday. She needs to create shit where it don't exist. She reminds me the lesbian thing ain't the worst idea after queer proms. I love her new avatar pic.

Trying to listen to Blondie and chain smoke and read Blender. I have a weird shitty pain in my right hand. There's hardly any onion on this onion bagel. If you had to buy one bottle of vodka on a commercial airliner what would it be? The smell of smoke's no metaphor though fire fills every window of the fuselage and Slayer plays on the soundtrack. Bronze pigs dance in the air. Someone hand me the mic! An eleven-hour flight to Adelaide. Twenty-four hours without Internet's insane.

Summertime in Europe. Good morning everyone! I'm driving to Austria to put some fuel in the car and see a man about a horse. It's gonna be a productive day. Three adults, three dogs, a malnourished baby, plenty of skeletons. I'm on top of my shit. I look a bit drunk. Why can't I return to Reno this weekend for the gun and cigar club show?

I'm in the Nashville airport in route to Little Rock. Layover in Memphis. When's this journey end? I feel like a Red Sox fan at a Yankees game. Is this an anthropology assignment? Excellent use of the word 'bamboozled'! Ever consider not yawning? I might be in Delaware or New Jersey by next Wednesday.

I watch for falling rocks the next three miles.

I stop at a Burger King for a Whopper, America's all-purpose mood stabilizer. My mind's in the gutter. I'm too young to be hanging out with these old overweight women.

I may be drunk on the express train from Ditmars to Queensboro Plaza. I enjoy holding other people's babies. I can quickly hand them back. I'm stuck in crowded collage though I'm trying NOT to touch the person sitting next to me. Today there's double the people in one train car.

Finished sampling wine at Whole Foods. Can't remember the last time that happened.

I need a new ringtone for this iPhone.

Queens is depressing. It has more churches than Jerusalem.

No. No. No. No. No. No. No. No. No. No. Nooooooo. No. No. Dunkin donuts forgot to put sugar in my coffee!

Moments later I'm northbound on the Metro-North. Hudson Line. I'm heading for Toronto to be interviewed in a documentary movie. A genius piece of bullshit. I hate Canadian winters. I hate rocking out on YouTube to Judas Priest. I'm gonna puke if that lady doesn't shut up about her son's gross skin problems. She's having a mini-freakout. Half-Dominican. I bet she sucks at parking.

Ten minutes later I'm caught in the middle of a gay guy panic. I think I need absinthe. I thought it was illegal. A chocolate porter? The conductor announces a delay for a moron who jumped in front of the train. When you hate your job Mondays must suck. No take-backs there.

Here's the lovely city of Pittsburgh. I think I'll buy some property, hire some whores, jerk off a character from Star Wars. Mmmmm. I love that wet paint smell. Kool-Aid tastes great. Cheese steak or tacos? Suicidal or intensely sexual? I can't finish these soggy fries. Car-seats on trains suck. As do suspicious objects. Why do old people bitch so much to every passenger in earshot? Wish I were sorry you lost your baby ma'am. World history sucks.

Wanna start a blog?

I try to imagine going to Cardiff next month for a surrealistic black mass. The woman sitting across from me keeps staring. I glare back. Stop with that high-tech shit! You're creeping me out bitch! I imagine candles and kerosene-powered space heaters. It must be an authentic black mass. Another English power outage.

Egg-and-cheese bagel? To hell with the food. Order those women to stand in line along the edge of a glass coffee table. Remind them we come from the Goddess.

The Eurostar has a hypnotic effect on me until I reach Lille. I awaken from a stupor to find I'm no longer in St. Pancreas. I love when drunken midget passengers call me bitch. It's such a turn-on. Even Hitler had a girlfriend though her head hurt mightily. Dancing with her doesn't mean I'm a Nazi sympathizer. Geez Adolf! Good little girls like to shake their little Aryan asses and vomit beer all over the beer hall. Why are you racists making me so mad today?

Silence!

With train passengers the best offense is a great defense. Like Germany in the 1920s. On the Shanghai-Beijing train I break out my FDA-approved phone sex operator voice. Toot toot. In six days I'll be in Vietnam. I need to find the perfect travel bag. I need to sit in a hotel lobby comparing the girths of American and European tourists. Too bad I have to work. I hope my boss doesn't know about Twitter yet.

Chapter 31

Here the editors force me to suppress a shocking phrase.

What kind of frightful literature is this?

Thursday night I'll get revenge. Beware! I'll fashion the means to an end. Let's make Part 4 as approximate as possible to a divine instrument.

Tonight I watch the patterns of red taillights reverse themselves over the motion of bats fluttering through darkness. The freeway's crowded. Every freeway's crowded at 2am on a Friday morning. Behind the steering wheel I carefully hold up a candle and a brass-handled hand-mirror. Looking into that mirror I see images of human beings turning into giant centipedes with narrow black eyes, high jutting cheekbones, tan skin cool and moist.

FREE INFLUENZA NEXT EXIT

For more than a month I've bullied myself into believing the Arab surrealist movement has accomplished its goals. The Straight & Narrow's second-nature, effortless, autonomic with me now. Tonight I realize we have the oldest brand of conundrum here, something more ancient & profitable than your favorite shaggy dog story. Am I going crazy or is the world around me nuts?

My fondness for fun's begotten many anecdotes. My fondness for solitude and wandering's generated legend and myth. By now I should be secluded in nirvana, laughing up my sleeve at the ways of the world. I've got lots of volunteering to do before I put on the monk's cowl.

Every thing leaves its imperishable impression including the rubbish heaps of scientific and theological opinion. Every transient thing gathers detritus through the ages. Books copy from books, movies pillage movies, songs quote songs, churches build on churches. The truth needs no augmentation here. Nor would there be family if we founded empires on the habits of monks and nuns. Why should we regenerate this world? Isn't that where the distortion begins?

I drop anchor at a rundown Holiday Inn Express. Overhead, the cackling of geese. Behind me, the crackling of burning logs in an open field. At the front desk, a chorus of dry laughter and sibilant whispers.

As I collapse onto the bed a whiteness in the sheets far below flashes out at me. I'm consumed by flames falling through a dream.

The next morning I lift my head from the pillow, blink in the dim light of the motel room. I don't like the room's cornball pale green curtains or that sticky nastiness in the corner. It smells like Bigfoot spent the night in here.

I lie back on my elbows, stare up at the ceiling, watch armies of shadows advance from the east and west to clash at the center. The soldiers' uniforms are in shreds, spotted with blood and mud. No flags fly at the heads of the columns. I watch until the shadows touch, swallowing one another whole. The image blurs. That's not slaughter. That's martyrdom.

I crawl out from under the blankets.

I stand up, walk over to the casements, throwing them open to let the velvety morning air flow into the room. I'm greeted by the sounds of mourning doves right outside the window and the resonant humming of bees on steel cables.

Overhead, pillars of cloud. Before me, pillars of flame in an open field.

They've laid the whole state of Arizona out on a stretcher.

God what a stupid day!

I close the casements, step back, turn away from the window, walk over to the smudged mirror, yank the pull-cord, inspect my reflection.

If I'm a Muslim at heart, my face is cast in the purest of Hebrew molds. Fear coils around my heart. My body aches from anxiety. The room's harsh fluorescent lighting catches my breath.

That succession of faces has begun to reappear, nodding and swaying from side to side with an odd sort of rhythm. The eyes are curious, the ears pierced, the mouths carrying numerous trinkets, lead pencils, safety pins, beads, black bones. The voices are very loud.

I mean the abstraction of humanity defiling itself before God if not before their fellow man. Travel-stained types cycling through generations, social group to social group, tome to tomb, tomb to tome. Babylon during the reign of Cyrus the Great, the Quarries of Zarodather, the memoirs of Comte Allesandro Cagliostro, Franz Graeffer's Recollections of Vienna, a mysterious Muscovite adviser to the Dalai Lama, a millionaire pickle manufacturer, the last Grand Master of the Knights of Malta, Count Cobenzl the Austrian ambassador at Brussels, the ghostly Benfratelli, the Wizzard of Marblehead, Count de Bretteville the Maltese ambassador at the Holy See, the monk Wenzel Seiler, the son of Prince Rakoczy of Transylvania, a valet and a certain Father Atansio, Caesare Cantu librarian at Milan, the protection of the last of the Medici Gian Gastone, the anti-Nicean fathers, a mock funeral similar to what's given the English adept Lord Bacon.

Everything leaves its imperishable impression on the collective imagination before departing for its tomb.

I step back from the Universal Storehouse, turn away from the mirror, walk over to the smudged TV, plug it in, turn it on, adjust the rabbit ears, inspect its unique brand of imagery.

Ready to benefit the primitive races of humanity?

The President of the United States is speaking. His words are clear and distinct though not an adequate substitutes for sunlight and reflection. He serves our country. Do you know how much he earns per day? Please don't touch him. That's illegal!

This America of ours is big, very big, its patterns and external illusions as intricate as the double-letter S.

Is that why you're leaving our nation behind? I have a dream, a dream of freedom from every form of writer's block.

I start the car, return to the highway.

My fingers flex nervously.

A plaster-of-Paris Cupid shoots an arrow at me from a billboard.

Prepare to charge!

The highway ascends a hill out of a pool of mist and dusty hedgerows into the muted afternoon sunlight. Long trestle tables run the length of the highway. Grotesque heaps of clerical clothing lie about. That's the strangest part of it all. Where ARE they?

Through the deserts.

Across the moors.

Past forests and streams.

Like the spokes of a wheel each highway converges on the same central city.

Everyday it's the same, the same stench, the same noises and doggerel rhymes, the same moral chronology, the same pedestrians with armbands swarming over the same pavements beneath the infernal roaring of elevated trains.

On the account of one man all are lost. Gamblers in tired-looking shoes curse the dawn, their eyes vague as opal. Yellowish wax-like cabdrivers overdose on Jamaica. Strippers in luxurious robes with golden tassels specialize in the nonhuman diseases of mankind. They speak of being beset by the devil. They worry about the existence of SOMETHING ELSE. That's medical science sir not Paracelsus throwing medicine to the fire. Great Pan is dead. None of what you imagine here is slaughter or martyrdom. It's Walt Whitman's grocery list. That's liquid manure on the ground. That's NOT my handiwork!

I honk the car horn, corner sharply, nearly run over a nun. Her hood conceals the back of her head.

She's a witch!

Oh shit! The traffic cop rushes to her side, takes her by the arm, drags her down the sidewalk past wonderful shop windows. She scowls like an angry bear otherwise not a word. She's an American citizen with shooting pains in her limbs and tears zigzagging down her cheeks. More cops charge down the street. The nun's position is a perilous one.

I lean out the cab's window, call out to those cops by their first names. They wave, smiling at me. They see nothing except a mask.

I park the car, cut the engine, get out, step across the sidewalk, enter the nearest shop front.

Up two flights of stairs, through musty halls, past closed doors with china-white knobs.

I step inside the flat. A hand grabs my shoulder, pulls me aside.

A throaty voice sounds out.

"Do you know what a perpetuum mobile is?"

An alarm clock ticks menacingly on the mantelpiece.

"Do you?"

I pull the mask from my face with a Brechtian flourish.

The audience gasps.

"Let me off right here!"

The surgeons are preparing to amputate my limbs. Too bad that doesn't mean me. I've got lots of volunteering to do before I put on the monk's cowl.

I'm west of Truckee on I-80, making the descent toward Sacramento. The brakes are barely working. My fingers flex nervously. I'm asking myself over and over gain, Is the poet in the poem or the poem in the poet?

Those aren't mutually exclusive!

Allow me to tell you a Sacramento story.

I want this to be amazing. If you can't picture the Middle East picture Sacramento, California. Picture a battered taxicab taking an exit off I-80, screeching to halt in downtown Sacramento. Who do I encounter on the sidewalk? Goldsmith holding out an open manila envelope. He's dressed in an olive-green three-piece suit. He's acting like a goddamned brain surgeon who's too impatient to prep his latest victim. By strange coincidence we're spending the night in the same motel. By stranger coincidence we're both in a very inspired mood.

"Surgery can handle that Rosenberger!"

"Handle what?"

"Penny and Amber. I've prepped them. They're lying on the operating table. I've shaved their eyebrows, rubbed disinfectant on their wounds."

"That's code for something?"

"Does this look like a hospital emergency room? On the other side of that wall are six empty cubicles. The Reality Magicians live over there. They have followers, slaves who prep the patients and hide little oil lamps beneath their cloaks. They wear masks, carry daggers and pistols in their belts."

I walk over to the wall, start pounding on it with my bare fists.

I scream at the tip-tops of my lungs. "I'm still good! I'm a team player! I'm still good. I swear I am! Goddammit I'm the best volunteer!"

Goldsmith grabs me by the neck. "Listen to me closely Rosenberger!"

"Goddammit Goldsmith my real name's Rosenberg!"

"Listen! I got Penny and Amber stashed over there in two of the six cubicles. There's no law against that. It could get much worse. Got it?"

"How can I know you're not lying?"

"You can't. You must trust me. The slaves who hide the little oil lamps beneath their cloaks are keeping watch over Penny and Amber. They're doing fine. For now. Though now never lasts forever does it?"

I walk over to the wall again, start pounding on it with my bare fists. "I'm still good goddammit! I'm a team player! I'm still good! I swear it! Goddammit I'm the best volunteer!"

"What's with the sudden fervor? The movement's gone stale Rosenberg. It's no longer wedged between the public affairs of nations and governments. It's a bunch of preachy pamphlets. I detect a case of the moral funk, a handicapped imagination too."

"What ever became of the documents missing from the documents vault? Were those recovered?"

"The long lines of motors will continue rolling along regardless of the documents. We're no longer trying to recover them."

"Not a single one of those long cloth-covered ledgers? Not even The Confessions of the Yellow Cat or The Indiscriminately Across the Column Ruling?"

"We've given up on finding any of the mustard-colored documents and ledgers. They've vanished, evaporated, what have you."

"Who's this 'we' anyway?"

"Who do you think? You and me and the rest of the team, the cubicles and surgeons on the other side of that wall. Stop banging on it please!"

"You're suggesting a new name for the movement? A new focus? New membership requirements?"

"Those would make for a fresh start. Ever see black powder smoke in the moonlight?"

"God no!"

Goldsmith snaps his thumb and forefinger with a didactic flourish. "That's what we need Rosenberg. By gracious That's the ticket! We need an epidemic. We need a disease to spread, a disease of political confusion, economic mutilation, religious catastrophe. You can play the role of a Typhoid Mary who escapes the institution and finds his way back to the city proclaiming a new chapter in the movement. A more relevant chapter that appears on the evening news rather than getting lost in underground chapbooks. You're the disease they'll hail as a cure!"

"You wax eloquent. You prepared that script?"

Goldsmith pauses, his lips working vacantly.

Silence.

I swear I can hear the sounds of many pins dropping in a fair and steady breeze while the wall across from me looms ever larger and gray. I imagine Penny and Amber on the other side of that wall lying motionless on gurneys or something similar. I pray to Allah or Yahweh, what have you, to intervene, to kick Goldsmith in his respective balls and send him collapsing to the floor in pain.

"You said something about a disease spreading. Go on."

Silence.

Goldsmith bends forward to examine the floor. For the first time I notice an unspeakable birthmark on his scalp. Moments later he stands back up, adjusts his suit.

"I said go on!"

Silence.

I pull the revolver from my jacket pocket. My trigger finger flexes nervously.

Goldsmith steps back, slides over to the wall, turning his back towards it. "Rosenberg you'd never be fool enough to shoot at your own shadow would you? Nothing's more embarrassing to posterity than a murder-suicide."

"I said tell me something warm and sunshiny about what we need and why the movement's gone defunct while I've been out there busting my ass."

"Paranoia's gotten the best of you, a persecution complex. It's you with your cops and agents in tow."

"What you said doesn't sound warm and sunshiny. It sounds like shit."

"You're forgetting this is a performance. You've fallen off the grid of higher sense, lost the proper perspective. The yellow cat's sitting on the wheel-box as we used to say."

"I'd like to see you out there alone day after day driving hundreds of miles, picking up strangers, passing out pamphlets, inciting disruption and disturbance. If anybody's moving the movement it's me! I'M the incorruptible sentinel around here!"

"What about Penny and Amber? What about Sophie, McKillen, Bachir, Reshad? A total of six!"

"Go on. I see you're trying to tell an actual story here. I feel funny inside. You've got my attention."

Goldsmith lifts up a hand as if to shield his eyes from a shadowy bullet. That gesture's not a sign or a stain or a scrap of clothing or anything else I care to mention. There's not a trace of the Arab surrealist movement in that gesture.

"Go on Goldsmith! Is there any figure in your budget to prove you're not a bad chap after all? If I'm forgetting this is a piece of drama why are you cowering from a bullet right about now? Why do I feel like I'm stranded in the last ten days of Hitler?"

Goldsmith turns his back to me, starts pounding on the wall. "Let me out of here! Come get me off this stage!"

"That's enough Goldsmith!"

Silence.

Goldsmith turns back around to face the gun and the audience. His back's pressed against the wall. He squints.

I swear I can hear boots stamping around on the other side of that wall. Instead of stagehands I imagine the sounds of the Back Ward, Reshad's realm, where Bachir's taxicab arrives out of nowhere in the middle of the night to cart away the unfortunate escapees. I hear Sophie whistling outlandishly in a block of roadside moonlight. I imagine the puncture wounds about McKillen's forehead, those big black eyes.

"It's time to go ashore Goldsmith. You can come with me or you can step to the other side of the wall and hunker down in your piles of manuscripts. That's how it works around here. That's the bravery of personal expression."

"I haven't slept in three nights Rosenberg."

"I haven't slept in three months!"

Silence.

For the first time I appreciate this Transmigration Of Souls Thing is an uncanny business.

"Have you given any deep thought to taking a final trip to New Jersey?"

I awaken from the dream, rise from bed, wash, dress, check out of the room.

That concludes the Sacramento story.

I'm west of Sacramento on I-80 rapidly approaching the Bay Area. I tell myself not to worry, I'll be there soon enough. You might as well relocate to Canada. No. Thieves live there too, thieves live everywhere, thieves and their slaves who hide little oil lamps beneath their cloaks and dig little tunnels to help them sneak into houses. It takes them five seconds to climb through your open windows. You never notice.

I'm in Marin County heading south. The fog's burned off. The sunlight's exceedingly bright. Every nook, ever cranny of material existence stands out in relief, every shade of color, every nuance of nothingness, every bulging borderline between neighboring regions of solitude and somnolence. As I descend through tiled tunnels I know I'm approaching that singular time.

Last night's dream dawns on me. Six cubicles on the other side of that wall, two cubicles occupied by Penny and Amber, the other four empty.

There it is.

I'm crossing the Golden Gate Bridge. Try as you might you cannot swerve an automobile over the side of the Golden Gate Bridge. No one's ever succeeded. The best you can do is swerve into oncoming traffic though that rarely amounts to more than the standard 911 ambulance call.

I'm on Van Ness heading south toward the Tenderloin. Thieves crowd the sidewalks on their way to the latest bloody reality performance. The Reality Magicians feed those thieves, inducing them to command their slaves to bring silver & gold treasure back to the thieves who pass it on to the Reality Magicians living elsewhere underground or in that hilltop mansion over yonder. Along the Way I've learned about that hierarchy. There's no longer any question where I fit in. I'm the guy who wears sunglasses and a fake white beard. I'm beyond the pedestrians' mildest or wildest dreams. I see their patterns. I know their hangouts. They can hide from each other. They cannot hide from me. That fact alone should ease the reader's mind at the outset.

Left turns are rare around here. Parallel parking's a bitch. I park the cab in an angled space across the street from Penny's diner. I lean over to open the glove compartment, remove the mini-cassette recorder.

I step out of the car onto the sidewalk.

My fingers flex nervously.

Is that the smell of dog shit and diesel fumes?

I press RECORD.

Greetings from the Arab-Israeli movement!

Part 5 Ivan Johnson

Chapter 32

There it is.

Something worthless has been ripped right out of my chest.

I push the bloody manuscript across the table as far away from my bleeding torso as these long trembling arms allow.

You know me. Every time you turn a page you recognize the two colors. I'm that voice speaking directly to you leaping right off the page.

I stand up from the writing nook. Wearing only white boxer briefs, I stagger out to the balcony.

There it is. The Mediterranean stretching out to infinity. Many stories below our beachfront flat are the crowded Tel Aviv beaches. The globetrotting beachgoers look so small from here yet it's more pleasant than scary to watch them from a high-rise. They can't escape from these prying eyes. They can't know what I've accomplished. They can't imagine how yellow and snippety this latest story is. I imagine they're dolls with jointed limbs and ratty swimsuits. God help them if they fall into my clutches.

How relaxing to breathe in the hot salty air and feel the warmth of the morning sun on my face. I tilt my head up, push back my mane of white hair, smile. Amazing isn't it? Over there behind that piece of blue sky is a country that thinks it owns the goddamned planet.

I back away from the balcony railing, return inside, walk into the adjacent room where Rachel sits on the sofa beside a portable dialysis machine. She's reading a sparkling green German-language newspaper. I walk over, kiss her on the forehead. I run my fingers along her jawline. Only an expert can appreciate the width and depth of those breasts.

Much like Rosenberg and Penny, Rachel and I first met under strange, literary circumstances.

"Goddammit Goldsmith My Real Name's Rosenberg! is finished."

"Did it turn out the way you wanted? How are you feeling this morning?"

I shake my head. "Pretty much how I wanted. A crazy world within a crazier world, everything saturated with sex and four-letter words."

"That's the one about the enlightened psychopath?"

"The one that takes place in America yeah. I need to find a translator to get it into American English."

"You speak American English great. You do it."

"I don't write American English great. I need someone who can write fiction in English and Hebrew. That's not me. I'll never be able to do that."

"You're in a sour mood."

"I want the novel to be an easy read. I want to fool readers into having a good time of it before they go bonkers. What else can I say? I feel like shit for awhile after I finish a novel."

"Was he killed?"

"Rosenberg? I don't think so. You can't tell what happens to him."

"All you have to do is choose an outcome."

"I'm ninety-nine percent sure he's alive."

"Did he get his final wish?"

"I think he did yeah. It's an upbeat ending."

"What about Rosenberg's handler? You said he's murdered."

"He may have gone insane or killed himself. He wasn't murdered, not by Rosenberg. That much is certain. Rosenberg leaves him to his own devices in a mysterious Sacramento motel."

"What's Sacramento?"

"A city in northern California."

Rachel returns to the newspaper.

I walk into the kitchen, head straight for the coffeepot, pour myself a cup of straight black coffee. I'm a bit agitated. I pace back and forth on the kitchen tile lost in deep thought.

Once the English translation of the novel's complete I'll be required to visit the United States. That makes me more nervous than visiting the Old City. I've never been a friend of the ordinary. I'm compelled to write these frantic bizarre stories. From the beginning I knew the Rosenberg story would be set in the United States, an unordinary, perhaps extraordinary, psychopathic country I've never visited though I will very, very soon.

You've noticed the baroque surrealistic style. I don't write bedtime stories. These are free-stream creations whose purpose is to drive the reader mad, revealing to him something he prefers to ignore. In previous episodes I convinced readers I was a thirty-two-year-old Mossad bodyguard and that I once took part in the historical mission of the modern European proletariat. That was a long, long time ago.

Chapter 33

By the end of the following week I manage to find a Hebrew-to-English translator on Craig's List. I hire him to translate Goddammit Goldsmith My Real Name's Rosenberg! into American English. He does a very good job, with the proper compression of expression and unorthodox use of punctuation marks and fonts. At my request he's careful to avoid using semi-colons, colons, hyphens, dashes, parentheses, brackets, italics, bold lettering. The final translated text looks beautifully uniform and classical. As a bonus he also translates the novel into German.

I take the English-language version of the novel to a publisher in Tel Aviv. I represent myself. The publisher gets back to me within a week. He's enthusiastic about what the story stands for. If he and his editor underlings are confused and disturbed by the narrative, they recognize that state of mind as a good thing, something that could change their lives in a positive way and alter relations between Jews and Arabs in the Middle East. If only every man, woman, and child read the novel and allowed its message to wipe clean their narrow-minded religiosity.

The publisher gives me a five-thousand dollar advance, promising to publish a hardback edition in the first quarter of 2010. The publisher promises to pay for Arab- and Russian-language translations. By 2011 the English-language version will be distributed worldwide.

I burn the Hebrew-language draft, my first draft, and wipe the electronic versions from my hard drives. The original version of Goddammit Goldsmith My Real Name's Rosenberg! now no longer exists. The novel becomes an endless series of copies and facsimiles.

Chapter 34

In the summer of 2009 a one-way ticket from Tel Aviv to San Francisco with a connection in New York City costs about $2000 on Delta Airlines. The duration of that trip is a little over 30 hours. I buy the ticket.

These are new times. We're living in a restless age. The world may not need another Jewish Nobel Prize winner or marvelous Negro athlete.

I pack lightly, carrying with me a single tote bag that contains two manuscript copies of Goddammit Goldsmith My Real Name's Rosenberg!, a hardback copy of Brecht On Theatre, a shaving kit, five changes of clothes, a variety of simple disguises, including fake beards, mustaches, and a rubber Halloween mask. In my money belt I place one hundred one-hundred-dollar bills, American currency.

In Ben Gurion International Terminal 3 I pass some time trying to identify the plainclothes airport security officers. I browse the duty-free shopping rotunda. As I walk through passport control I wave Rachel goodbye. Neither us knows when or if I'll ever set foot on Israeli soil again. I look at myself in a wall-length mirror. That's Ivan Johnson on one side of a two-way mirror. I'm wearing a dark gray overcoat, a red silk scarf, a fake mustache and beard. My posture is formal. I look like I pay more taxes than anyone else in the whole terminal.

On the flight I decide to write my next novel entirely in the third-person. I'm no longer interested in first-person narration. After Goddammit

Goldsmith My Real Name's Rosenberg! I'm sick and tired of first-person literary indulgences. I want fewer interior monologues, less explanatory nonsense, more suspense. I want a situation where the reader learns about characters from their external actions and behaviors, where phenomenology replaces psychology, where internal states are absent from the story altogether and social intercourse is reduced to alternating states of machinelike regularity and unpredictability. The next novel will be set in the United States, in the Midwest, not on the West Coast or East Coast. I know the opening sentence of that novel will read, 'Three men in three separate cars descend on a small college town along three of the four cardinal directions.' Once again I have murder on my mind.

Chapter 35

The flight over Europe and across the Atlantic is uneventful. I have no problem making the connection at JFK. For several hours I watch the North American continent glide by beneath me. At 2:55pm our jet pulls up to Gate 42, Boarding Area C, Terminal 1, San Francisco International Airport. We're right on time.

First thing I do after disembarking is go to a restroom. I peel off the fake mustache and beard, put them in the carry-on bag. Those will come in handy later. I splash my face with water, rinse my mouth out with mouthwash, check my skin for flaws. No doubt I look great.

Outside the airport I hail a cab at the cabstand and instruct the Middle Eastern-looking driver to take me to the Tenderloin district of San Francisco.

The driver has an odd aura of intensity about him. When he asks me where I come from and I tell him Israel, he winces. Maybe not. Maybe for the first time in my life I've witnessed a so-called 'enigmatic smile.' In America! I'm not paranoid. That man doesn't like Israelis.

I ask where he's from.

"Jordan originally. I've lived in America for many years. What brings you here?"

"I'm looking for you. It's been a long time. I'm sure you don't remember me."

"Excuse me."

"Just kidding. I don't mean to be such a mystery. I'm a travel writer. I'm on the go most of the time. When I stay put I live in Israel."

We exchange glances in the rearview mirror.

"Is smoking allowed in taxis here?"

"In my taxi yes. I'm a reformed smoker myself."

"I know I should quit. We don't need to have that conversation."

I look out the window for awhile. The heavy traffic on the 101 Freeway north into the city looks very much as I imagined it. Nothing new there. I imagine the cab is outfitted with bulletproof windows, anti-mine floorboards, armor-plated sides.

"Is this same 101 Freeway they have down in LA?"

"It is. I used to drive down there too."

"Will this take us to Reno?"

"Reno, Nevada? No not directly."

We drive much of the rest of the way in silence. The driver's very distracted and annoyed by his dispatcher.

We exit the freeway onto Van Ness Avenue.

I point to a glassy-eyed African American gentleman at the side of the road. "Is that a homeless man?"

"I don't know. Maybe."

"That's how I imagine they'd look, homeless people in America."

"Sometimes it's difficult to be sure."

I point to a car in front of us. "Is that's a policeman's car?"

"SFPD yes."

"Except for the color scheme and lights on the roof that could be your car."

"This car was retired by the city police department. It's not unusual."

I laugh at that remark.

The driver smiles slightly. "What's so funny?"

"I'm imagining I'm sitting in the back of a police car being taken to jail."

"What do you think of the city?"

"It's much as I imagined it. A city destined for wealth, power, and beauty."

"Are you planning to do some sightseeing?"

"I'm planning to live here. I hope to see lots of different and unusual things. Where's the Tenderloin? Drop me off there."

"We're heading in that direction."

"According to my map we'll need to turn right off Van Ness. Right there. You passed Turk Street!"

The driver frowns. "That's going the wrong way sir. I know how to get to the Tenderloin. We'll be there momentarily."

"It looks like if you're not careful it'd be easy to block a driveway when you park around here."

"Hail a taxi!"

"That's shameless advertising."

The driver turns right on Eddy St.

I gesture to the facades moving past our window. "This is the Tenderloin? It doesn't look as rundown and dangerous as I expected. Where's the dirt and trash? Most of what I'm seeing has a historical museum-like feel to it."

The driver glances at me in the rearview mirror. "Where in the Tenderloin sir?"

"I'm hungry. Can you direct me to a diner? I need to find a place to eat, a diner on Turk or Taylor or Eddy Street. Something like that."

"There's one right there. Another over there."

"Okay drop me off here. I'll walk the rest of the way."

I give the driver a substantial tip.

"Thank you sir. That's very kind of you. Good luck!"

"One last thing. Do you think I need to wear a disguise in this neighborhood?"

"How do you mean?"

"Forget it. That's my business. I'll figure it out. Thanks again for the smooth ride."

"Goodbye sir."

With the carry-on bag slung over my shoulder I go from diner to diner, bar to bar, eating establishment to eating establishing inquiring about Penny. At each place that has a counter I sit down and order a coffee or a Coke and strike up a conversation with the counterman or bartender.

"Excuse me sir do you know when Penny's shift starts?"

"Who?"

"Penny."

"No one by that name works here."

I drink my coffee or Coke in silence, pay, go to the next diner. "Excuse me sir do you know when Penny's shift starts?"

"There's no Penny works here."

"Never?"

"Not since I worked here."

Late afternoon turns into evening. At the tenth place I enter, a beautifully rundown diner that reminds me of American things, I ask the counterman about Penny.

"Penny? You mean Peggy?"

"Yeah Peggy. Sorry I mean Peggy not Penny."

"Her shift starts at ten o'clock."

I glance at my watch. That's about two hours from now.

"Okay thanks I'll return."

I spend the next couple hours wandering the streets of the Tenderloin. It's an interesting place, very much as I imagined it based on hundreds of photos I downloaded from the Internet over the past six months. The sounds, the smells, the pedestrians, the architectural details more or less conform to my own inner vision. I can understand why Rosenberg and Goldsmith and Penny feel at home here. I feel the pull of the poverty, the exciting unpredictable lifestyle poverty carries with it. I don't miss the beaches of Tel Aviv.

At 10:15 I return to the diner, sit down at the counter.

Peggy turns out to be a down-and-out-looking perhaps formerly beautiful large-breasted black woman. I wonder if she's on drugs of some type.

I introduce myself as Ivan Johnson from Tel Aviv.

Peggy frowns slightly, slides a refilled cup of coffee in my direction, says nothing.

"I said I'm Ivan Johnson."

"What do you want me to do about it?"

"You're Peggy right?"

"Yeah so?"

"When do you get off your shift?"

"What's it to you?"

"I'd like to make your acquaintance."

"You're not from around here are you?"

"I said I'm from Tel Aviv."

"Where's that."

"In Israel."

"You're a tourist?"

"I am at the moment. I want to live here forever."

"In the city?"

"In the Tenderloin. I'm hoping you could help me with that."

"How am I gonna do that?"

"We'll work together on it."

I spend most of the night and early morning sitting at that counter talking to Peggy as she waits on the few customers who enter the diner. Every customer orders coffee. Most look gloriously hungover or stoned. Most are black.

By the time Peggy's shift ends, the day's first sunlight is cutting through a light fog that envelops the Tenderloin.

Peggy invites me back to her place, a multistory single-room occupancy building with a beautiful façade on Turk Street. On the ground floor we walk past a social worker office and a large open room intended as a common gathering area. As we ride the elevator up to the fifth floor Penny lists off an impressive number of health problems and personal grievances, including a chronic cough, a chronic shortage of money, a husband who's in jail for attempting to commit a felony with an unregistered handgun, and a mildly retarded six-year-old son she leaves with the neighbor when she's working at the diner.

She calls her home a 'unit' not a flat or studio or apartment. Her unit consists of a single room with a sink, refrigerator, microwave, and various cabinets. I'm impressed with how clean the place is. I walk over to the window, pull up the shade, look out. One hell of a view. Down below, across the street, a junky-looking electronics store could easily pass for a pawnshop.

I point across the street. "What's in that beautiful building over there?"

"More low-income housing, for street youths and handicapped people and people with AIDS."

"Amazing. You have it good here."

"I have to get some sleep."

"My internal clock's screwed up. I'm still on Israel time. I'm wide awake. I think I'll explore the city. Do you mind if I put my stuff here?"

Peggy frowns. "Sure go ahead."

"That carry-on gets heavy after awhile. I'll pay you to allow me to stay here. I have money, lots of cash. I'm not, what's the word, a freeloader."

I borrow a key from Peggy to let myself back in without waking her and return to the streets. Not only am I not tired, I feel great. Everything about the Tenderloin appears pretty much as I imagined. I could change my name to Rosenberg and Peggy's name to Penny and short of committing a murder I would've stepped right into the novel I wrote while living on the other side of the planet with no prior experience of this place.

You ask What does that prove? It proves your imagination is more than a mere distraction. What if I let these sentences dwindle away until the reader's confronted only with the stark whiteness of a blank page?

The air on the sidewalk smells of stubborn cigarette smoke, stale beer and stale piss. I'm thirsty. That means I need a drink. I walk over to the next block where I find a poorly lit bar. I enter, order a honey-colored glass of beer. I do love how alcoholic liquids satisfy my thirst anywhere on the planet. I make small talk with the bartender. He gives me a primer on North Beach strip clubs. He offers recommendations on restaurants and cafes in Chinatown.

I spend much of the day wandering around, pretending like I'm an old Tenderloin local, half drunk, out of work, alternately bored and enraged with the pedestrians I pass.

What separates me from Rosenberg is that my behavior is a conscious act. I'm not truly bored or enraged. I'm in a great mood. I'm able to put myself in an angry frame of mind and sustain that mood indefinitely, much like a method actor.

You ask, What does that prove? It proves your feelings and emotions are little more than intrusive distractions that control and destroy your life. None of the characters in my next novel will have the rich inner life I ascribed to Rosenberg. They'll recognize the useless nature of drama and attend to their tasks with a minimal amount of positive or negative feeling. Without constant emotional distractions, those characters will accomplish their tasks efficiently and with great success. Their behavior will have a machinelike quality to it. They won't be automatons. Conscious choice will underlie their every action. I imagine the resulting story will read much like a social engineering manual and perhaps seem boring to a reader more accustomed to the screaming, yelling, and killing that accompanies intense literary drama. I'm done with drama. That's so yesterday.

I return to Peggy's unit at 3pm. She's in the kitchenette preparing macaroni and cheese. Her son Bobby's sitting on the floor beside her playing with an unremarkable toy. I rush right up to her, put my arms around her, give her an enthusiastic kiss.

"Peggy you look terrific!"

"Cut the crap."

"I'm serious!"

Peggy's shocked when I remove the fake beard and mustache. She bursts into uncontrollable laughter, says she's never met anyone who wears a disguise except on Halloween. I tell her in Israel everyday is like Halloween. Everyone wears a disguise when they go out on the street.

I help her wash and towel off the dishes. "What's that noise I keep hearing in the hallway?"

"Carl. He's got mental problems and slams the door over and over again."

"What door?"

"The door to his unit."

"Lots of people in this building have mental problems?"

"I think so."

"Before I took the elevator up I saw one guy rocking back and forth on a fire-escape."

"On the building across the street right?"

"Yeah. You've seen him too?"

"He's out there in the afternoon. I'm not sure if he's drunk or high or what's going on."

"It was hilarious for awhile, until it got boring to watch, until it got depressing."

"I gotta get ready for work."

After she puts on her tight-fitting waitressing uniform Peggy takes Bobby across the hall to the neighbor babysitter. When she returns ten or fifteen minutes later, we both know what's on our minds. Peggy lets me remove that tight-fitting waitressing uniform. I'm half naked. We make love for the first time on a leftover rug Peggy removes from the dining area and lays out on the carpet next to the sofa. I pretend she's Rachel. I imagine Peggy pretends I'm her imprisoned husband waving around an unregistered handgun. I've never made love to an African American woman before. I enjoy it immensely.

Chapter 36

Weeks pass.

"Are those butterflies on your dress hand-embroidered?"

"I think so. I bought it at the Salvation Army store."

I pick up an object from the kitchenette's counter and wave it at Peggy. "What's this?"

"A clay dish Bobby made in pottery class."

"What are you supposed to use it for?"

"Hold things like paperclips and chalk."

Peggy and I have a regular arrangement. I pay half the rent. She cooks our meals. We make love regularly, otherwise sharing little of ourselves. When she's not working at the diner she's visiting her friends across the hall or attending to her son. When I'm not wandering around the Tenderloin visiting bars and the occasional strip club I'm hunched over a laptop working on a first draft of my next story.

The hardest part about living in the same room with someone is keeping anything hidden. Besides the occasional domestic dispute and drunken brawl, my only complaint with staying in the SRO is a bad Internet connection that makes downloading online photos of Midwestern college towns laborious and time-consuming. I've never set foot in a Midwestern college town. I need those photos to provide the story with local color and detail. What I don't need is to wait ten minutes to download a single image only to find it's not what I'm looking for.

I point at the kitchenette's red-and-white-checked wallpaper. "I bet no one ever told you why the designers chose that particular pattern for the wallpaper."

"No they didn't."

Peggy nervously wipes her hands on a rag hanging from the refrigerator's door handle.

It turns out Peggy has a meth habit. Lots of Tenderloin residents do, including the Chinese doll maker across the street. His one-eyed German shepherd tried to attack me last week. I angrily wagged my finger at the mangy bastard.

I point at the sunlight pouring through the little white curtains and making patterns on the rug and sofa. "Nice day outside. You ought to come with me when I go for my afternoon walk."

"Maybe."

Peggy walks across the room to a large chest of drawers with bright brass handles. She opens the top drawer, looks inside, removes nothing, closes the drawer, walks over to the sofa, sits down, starts crossing her legs back and forth.

She knows I'm studying her behavior. The way her limbs twitch and move reminds me of Polonius's comments on Hamlet's 'antic disposition.'

"We can take Bobby with us too if you want."

"He's with the babysitter."

"I know. We can go get him if you want."

Peggy frowns. "Maybe."

"Walking would do us some good."

I've expanded the scope of my solo walks, ranging north into the affluent Nob Hill neighborhood and east into North Beach. I have so much energy it's hardly enough to spend the entire day strolling up and down the hills of San Francisco. Taking a page from Rosenberg, I carry a voice-activated mini-cassette recorder, speaking into it whenever story ideas occur to me. Unlike Rosenberg I'm uninterested in suffering from writer's block. That doesn't suit the image I want to project here. Not yet.

Peggy leans over my shoulder. "What are you writing about?"

"I write about very unusual people, outsiders."

"People you met?"

"People I create entirely in my mind. I call it fiction. The people I write about can exist only in my mind and your mind too if you read the story."

"They're stories."

"Yes they're stories. Like Moby Dick and the merry adventures of Robin Hood."

"I remember that one from grade school."

Peggy walks over to the sofa opposite my writing table, sits down.

I look over at her. She knows I'm studying her behavior.

"When I'm finished you can read this story too if you like."

"I don't read books."

"I'm not surprised."

I gesture at the meth pipe sitting on the kitchen counter.

Peggy glances over at the pipe, starts licking her lips.

"You can think of reading books as a mind drug."

"Maybe." Peggy starts pulling at her chenille housecoat.

"What's wrong Peggy?"

"I'm tired."

"You don't act tired. You look the opposite, fidgety, nervous."

Peggy shrugs, stands up, walks over to the kitchenette, sits down on the floor with her back against the refrigerator.

One day on a whim I buy a large useless wooden propeller at the junkshop across the street from the SRO. Peggy helps me carry the object up to her unit where we display it in the middle of the living room area.

"Isn't it in the way if we put it there?"

"That's the point Peggy. It'll keep us on our toes."

"Maybe."

"If you forget it's there you'll trip over it and fall down. See my point? It teaches you to be alert."

"Bobby could get hurt on it."

"He's a big boy. He knows to watch where he's going."

I point at a large red circle on the wall calendar. "What have you got planned for that day? Meeting a friend in the Amazon?"

Peggy looks at the circle for awhile. "Not sure. I forgot why I put that circle there."

"Why's it a red circle?"

Peggy looks at the circle again. "Don't know."

"Do you have any other color marker?"

"Maybe."

"No you don't Peggy. You have a red marker. That explains why the circle is red."

A couple days later I buy an old red-white-and-blue Schwinn bicycle at the same shop. I take it up to our unit.

"Check out my new bike. I found it the old-fashioned way, at the junkshop across the street."

Peggy blinks uncomprehendingly. "You're gonna ride it around here?"

"Why not? I can teach you how to ride too if you want."

"I know how to ride a bike!"

"Why haven't you taught Bobby?"

"I don't know."

I walk over to the sofa, sit down. "You wanna make us an afternoon cup of coffee?"

Peggy walks into the kitchenette, starts rifling through the cabinets. She becomes agitated.

I fish the meth pipe out of my pocket. "Look over here Peggy. Is this what you're looking for?"

Peggy turns around, sees the pipe. "So that's where it went."

"I asked for coffee remember? Shouldn't you be looking for coffee grounds and a filter maybe?"

I put the pipe back into my pocket.

Peggy returns to the cabinets.

I'm alternating my walks with bike rides around the Tenderloin. While peddling along the sidewalks and through the alleyways I'm in high spirits. The Tenderloin has defied my expectations. Perhaps I'm not looking in the right places, perhaps my definition of crime is more restricted than the definition favored by the American criminal justice system. I find the Tenderloin to be a remarkably crime-free neighborhood. While drunken brawls and domestic disputes are common, as are street-corner reefer deals, I've yet to observe any evidence of rape, homicide, infanticide, false imprisonment, arson, or mayhem. That's not as I imagined the neighborhood based on Internet news stories and photographs.

I haven't met a single person in the neighborhood who remotely approaches life along Rosenberg's lines, balancing European philosophical erudition with a uniquely American psychopathic perspective. None of these pedestrians has the imagination to understand anything outside his own experience. I'm concerned Americans won't find Goddammit Goldsmith My Real Name's Rosenberg! a compelling read if the main character impresses them as a genetic and cultural impossibility. Thankfully Middle Eastern readers should have much less difficulty accepting Rosenberg as genuinely American. Most of them will never set foot in the United States.

Peggy leans over my shoulder. "What are you writing about now?"

"Same thing as before. Strange, unusual people, outsiders."

"Doesn't it ever get boring? It looks boring."

"If it were boring I wouldn't do it."

"It sure looks boring."

I haven't landed a regular day job, as Americans call it. I don't need the extra money. I live cheaply with Peggy in the SRO, smoking only cheap cigarettes, drinking bottled water rather than beer. My expenses are covered by royalties from previously published novels. Writing and researching my next story is what I care about. I'm reading widely, focusing on 20th Century American and European serial killers. I've assigned myself the unmanageable task of imagining a new breed of serial killer, a highly efficient machinelike murderer who dispatches her victims without any emotional involvement. She's capable of murdering hundreds if not thousands of people in a single lifetime without feeling guilt or arousing anyone's suspicion. I'm concerned readers won't embrace such a flawless serial killer if she seems like a genetic and cultural impossibility. How can we sympathize with her and share in her moral plight if the serial killer lacks a tragic flaw? Very good question. The exams are over. You can leave.

Chapter 37

Months pass.

"Are those butterflies on your dress hand-embroidered?"

Peggy cranes her neck to look me in the eyes, says nothing.

"Are those butterflies?"

"Yep."

"Where'd you get that giant gold cross around your neck?"

"Clark gave it to me."

"Clark the social worker downstairs?"

"Yep."

"The social worker's turned Jesus freak on us?"

"Maybe."

"You think Jesus will save you?"

"Maybe."

"Maybe's right."

I walk over to the open window, point outside. "Jesus saved those people out there too, including that gay prostitute over there preying on homeless kids."

Peggy glances out the window. "Who?"

I point out the window again.

Peggy glances out the window a second time, turns to me. "You're not Christian are you?"

"Not lately. I'm not affiliated with any religion since I came to San Francisco. I'm a big fan of Islam though."

"Doesn't Israel have a religion?"

"Not anymore. They once had Zionism. It's fallen out of favor with the locals."

"Clark says religion is a good way to keep yourself on the straight and narrow."

"The straight and narrow? Do you think he knows what that means?"

"I think he does."

"I think I do to. I doubt he and I would see eye to eye on that. It's a lot more than confessing your guilt. The differences between these religions are superficial. At bottom they have to answer the same questions. Do humans have a soul? If so, how can they liberate it? Everything else, the rituals, scripture, what have you, is window-dressing and a pretext for bloody conflict. Are you following me Peggy?"

"You've thought this through."

"The only way out of that mess is to intermix those differences until you're left with shades of black or white."

Peggy works the same shift at the same diner. Her meth habit has worsened over the intervening three months. By my estimate her level of consumption puts her in the hardcore tweaker category. Her complexion looks fine. She hasn't developed meth mouth yet.

Peggy's in the kitchenette, leaning against the counter. She has lipstick stuck to one tooth.

"What's with the makeup?"

"I have to meet with Bobby's teacher today."

"He's in trouble?"

"No he's fine. The schools have meetings with parents."

"You want me to come along, pretend I'm the father?"

Peggy giggles. "You're white."

"When whites and blacks have kids they can have a dark complexion right?"

"Maybe."

"I've seen it."

"Bobby! Time to go! C'mon get dressed!"

I've remained on U.S. soil longer than what an Israeli passport allows without a visa. I risk being deported. I'm not nervous. Everyday I'm excited, filled with creative energy. One of Peggy's Italian friends has promised to forge me a California driver's license. He suggested I use a false name. I refuse to use an alias. I'm not ashamed of my name. I'm proud of who I am and where I live. I'm not moving till the first quarter of 2010.

Shaving my head has made wearing disguises more convenient. I change wigs and beards regularly, adopting different hair colors and hair lengths depending on the day and my mood. I've become hyperaware of sounds inside and outside our SRO unit, sounds of food cooking, families murmuring, footsteps in the hallway. I spend most of my time indoors pursuing mental and literary explorations. As long as I keep receiving royalty checks from Rachel I'm not complaining about anything.

I've made progress on my next story, the one about a gorgeous highly motivated serial killer who redefines American standards of criminality while terrorizing a Midwest college town. I haven't given her a name yet. The killer's become the anti-Rosenberg. She's efficient and ruthless, single-minded in her devotion to killing, her inner life devoid of interior monologue and introspection. Unlike Rosenberg, the killer understands that talking to herself is a stupid waste of time. Nor is the killer's head cluttered with erudition and opinions that, as we know from Hamlet, only undercut decisive action. The killer's drive to kill is unstoppable, her focus one-hundred percent accurate. She kills any living thing that stands in her way, men, women, children, animals. The new story is a litany of gruesome killings described from a cold clinical inhumane third-person perspective. Rather than the surreal study of duality and madness that comprised Goddammit Goldsmith My Real Name's Rosenberg!, the new novel's pure journalism. Rather than dramatic events and flashy characters filled with self-disgust and anger, the new novel consists of minute descriptions of defensive gestures and movements of life-threatening objects. Rather than the comical foulmouthed weirdo we know as Rosenberg, we now have a tightlipped serial killer who's a homicidal maniac disguised as a sober-minded traveling salesman. She's a genuine and terrifying figure. I can't wait to hand off the first draft of the new novel to a Hebrew-language publisher here in San Francisco.

Peggy leans over my shoulder. The giant gold cross around her neck dangles in front of me. "What are you writing about?"

"A murderer."

"Want some scrambled eggs for breakfast?"

"Sure."

Peggy walks into the kitchenette.

I reconsider. "No wait. I'll take fried eggs instead. Scrambled eggs are for old men."

"So what does the murderer in your story do?"

"She kills people."

"She?"

"That's right. She kills people."

"Why?"

"It's her sole purpose, why she exists. She's a genius at killing people. No one can stop her."

"What does she kill them with?"

"Whatever's handy at the time."

"How does the story end?"

"With a beauty pageant how else?"

"After that?"

I reconsider. "No wait. Not a beauty pageant, a bodybuilding contest."

"She's bodybuilder?"

"She's a contestant yes. She's classically beautiful. A genuine feminist."

"What comes after the ending?"

"Not sure yet. I'm working on what comes after the ending. My guess is it'll be another beginning."

"Isn't tomorrow your birthday?"

"It is. You remembered. I forgot I told you."

"I saw it on your fake driver's license."

"Maybe everything on that license is fake."

"Your name's right."

"Be sure to make those eggs over-easy."

"You want toast?"

"Wheat toast slathered with butter."

"What's that?"

"You know how to do an egg in the basket?"

"Customers at the diner order that sometimes. You want eggs in the basket?"

"No, no. I wondered if you'd heard of it. You know how to box the compass?"

"What's that?"

"What are you making for yourself?"

"Eggs. Like you."

"You're chipper today. You're not tweaking?"

"I'm trying to stop."

"Don't try to stop. Stop! There's a difference you know. Who's in control here you or the drugs?"

"Me."

"Good. Keep it that way."

Peggy brings the eggs over to the table, sits down beside me, straightens her blouse, leans over her plate, starts mumbling under her breath.

"What are you doing?"

"Praying."

"Which prayer?"

"Our Father who art in heaven hallowed be Thy name."

"Clark taught you that?"

"I knew it. He mentioned it to me the other day."

"Is that his new thing, Christian prayer?"

"Maybe."

"You don't think it's ridiculous?"

"I guess not."

"These are good eggs. Did you know your brain can't feel pain?"

"No."

"That's right. There are no nerves in your brain."

"Is that good?"

"Maybe. Could you bring over the orange juice?"

Peggy gets up, walks over to the refrigerator, returns with a carton of juice. "You don't like Clark do you?"

"I don't know. I never introduced myself. I see him downstairs hanging out and drinking tea in the lounge."

"That's his job."

"Wish I had that job."

Peggy stands up, walks over to the TV, turns it on. Thanks to my royalties we now get cable. She flips through scores of channels before settling on a documentary about exorcisms.

"You can't get enough religion can you?"

"Let's watch this!"

"Go ahead. I don't care what you watch. I gotta get back to writing."

"Watch it for awhile with me. Please!"

"Thanks I'll pass. I've seen The Exorcist. That's more than enough."

"This is the real thing. It happened. Look! That's an ordained Jesuit priest and that's real holy water."

"How do you know? It could be an actor on a set."

"I know."

"Can you tell me how a TV works?"

"No."

"How can you know it doesn't do something else?"

"I know."

I roll my eyes.

Peggy fixates on the TV screen.

I walk over to the rickety little writing table, power up my laptop. Demonic possession, hearing voices, unexplained blackouts, fugue states are no longer on my list of research topics. I trod that ground in Goddammit Goldsmith My Real Name's Rosenberg! I don't want anything more to do with characters who aren't in complete control of their bodies and minds.

Chapter 38

It's November. I've been living in the Tenderloin for five months. Peggy and I now embark on the American holiday season.

I immensely enjoyed celebrating Thanksgiving in Israel. Celebrating Thanksgiving at a homeless shelter in downtown San Francisco is breathtaking. Hundreds of us share long trestle tables laden with turkey, dressing, mashed potatoes. Peggy sits across from me. Two beefy ruddy-faced men sit on either side of me. A small rat scampers across my boots.

I pretend I'm truly poor. I have no money, no resources, no hopes, no figures of speech. Out of financial necessity I've reduced my literary technique to the two-dimensional geometry of a line bisecting a plane. Every single sentence must begin with a noun. I'm the happiest man alive. Who needs revolution or surrealism when you've fulfilled your fantasy of complete downward social mobility and hit rock bottom? I'm elated. I've stumbled into a Henry Miller novel. I know this pretentious feeling can't last forever. I'm told nothing does. I know I'll soon be traveling by bus to a small college town in the American Midwest.

I've nearly finished my next novel. I've given the serial killer a name. Maria. I imagine her voice on the telephone. I imagine her purposeful lips sucking down a bottle of Coca-Cola.

I often ride my bike to Golden Gate Park. While I do I daydream about Maria the serial killer. Maria and I will keep in touch. We'll walk barefoot across the hot asphalt to a vacant telephone booth, one of the last booths from an ancient hippie era when you couldn't put a phone in your goddamned pocket. You had to search one out if you wanted to establish a connection over a long distance.

Next Monday I'll put the finishing touches on my next novel. Its title is MARIA WILL. Rosenberg makes a cameo long enough for Maria to bash his brains in with a monkey-wrench. She travels from town to town, carrying traveler's checks like we used to in the olden days, traveler's checks in a special little waterproof pouch. You don't want traveler's checks? Take this cash. Get lost! Maria hardly sleeps, barely eats. Unlike Rosenberg, who was difficult to distinguish from the other characters surrounding him, Maria stands out against the backdrops and set dressings. I gotta shield my eyes from the glare.

A secret plan among people to do something illegal or to achieve a legal end via illegal means is called a conspiracy. I've never understood why the mere act of planning a crime IS a crime. Regardless of what you plan to do, if you don't attempt to carry it out, how are you endangering yourself and others? Maria wants to know and Maria WILL know. End of story.

I'm sitting at the table waiting for Peggy to return from the kitchenette and serve our dinner. When she returns I tell her the surprising news. "I'm gonna be leaving San Francisco soon, at the beginning of the new year, after the Christmas holidays."

"Where are you going?"

"To a small college town in the Midwest."

"You're going back to school?"

"No. I have to see the town for myself. I have to see with my own eyes how the reality matches what I've imagined."

"I don't understand."

"Why do you think I came to the Tenderloin from Tel Aviv six months ago? For the same reason. To measure my imagination against reality. In this case the Tenderloin turned out to be very much as I'd imagined it."

"What if you go somewhere and it's not as you thought it'd be?"

"Sometimes it is, sometimes it isn't. It's a matter of degree. There's no right or wrong answer here. It's my job to bear witness to the difference that exists between imagination and reality."

"Why leave now?"

"I've nearly completed my next novel, the one that takes place in a particular small Midwestern college town. It's the story about the female serial killer I told you about. Part of the protocol is once I've finished a story I have to visit its setting in the real world."

"How long will you be there?"

"As long as it takes to write yet another story set in yet another locale on the planet. Once that's completed, the cycle begins again. Off I go to another place."

"You get paid for doing this?"

"I collect royalties from my past stories. How else could I afford to live here and help you pay rent?"

"I knew something's wrong."

"Trust me it's not. That's the function of my life."

"What if I want to see you and talk to you again?"

"You can. No one's stopping you."

Early the following week I find a publisher in North Beach who specializes in Hebrew-language experimental fiction. He reads MARIA WILL, promises not only to publish it in Hebrew. He'll also hire a Stanford graduate student to translate it into American English.

Chapter 39

On Christmas morning I give Peggy one of my two English-language manuscript copies of Goddammit Goldsmith My Real Name's Rosenberg!

"Peggy I want you to have this. You're the inspiration for a character in this book."

"You know I don't read books."

"Please give it a try. For me. I think you'll enjoy it."

"This is your new serial killer novel?"

"No. This is the novel I wrote prior to that one, when I was living in Tel Aviv. I brought this copy over from the other side of the world. Feel that paper. Genuine Israeli parchment."

"You didn't even know me."

"You'll notice similarities between yourself and the character named Penny, also similarities between Bobby and another character named Amber. I think you'll be surprised."

"Maybe."

"Please read it. I'm sure you'll recognize some of the places too, like the Tenderloin."

"Okay I'll give it a try. What do you want for breakfast?"

"Thanks. I'm leaving now."

"Right now?"

"That's right. My bus to Reno leaves in an hour. I need to get to the station."

"You're leaving?"

"Sorry to be so abrupt. I was awake last night thinking about things. I realized my time is up here."

"Where are you going?"

"I told you last week. To a Midwestern college town. I can't be any more specific than that."

"How will I reach you?"

"For now let's see how things go. I know your number. I'll contact you when the time's right."

"Promise me!"

"Ah c'mon Peggy. Let's not make this into a drama. How can I promise you in good faith? I have no idea what I'll find there and what'll happen."

"I don't want to read this stupid book!"

"Please read it. It'll explain what I'm doing better than I can in this conversation. Once you better understand my life's mission you may not want to keep in contact with me."

"What?"

"Read the book."

"Are you running from the cops? Have you killed somebody?"

"Don't be ridiculous."

"Where's Bobby? Have you killed my son? Bobby! Bobby!"

"Read the book."

"Why do you keep saying that? Where's my son? Are you the serial killer?"

Bobby walks into the kitchenette wiping the sleep from his eyes.

Chapter 40

Often it's best to say nothing about the dead.

As the bus travels east on I-80, I anticipate seeing the other California and Nevada locales I imagined and wrote about in Goddammit Goldsmith My Real Name's Rosenberg! Sacramento, the Sierra Nevada mountains, Reno. Given my track record I might encounter a two-headed dwarf chained to the altar of an abandoned chapel in the Utah desert.

I'm increasingly preoccupied with the American Midwest and what's happening there. I imagine Maria's voice on the telephone. I imagine her purposeful lips sucking down a bottle of Coca-Cola.

From my carry-on bag I remove Brecht On Theatre. Here's where the rubber meets the road, as they say in America. Here's where you remind the audience they are indeed an audience.

It might seem that one episode must begin right where another ends. It's not so. Reality and imagination form a continuum without end in space and time. A book's front and back covers create the illusion of a beginning and ending.

By definition the life of the Wandering Jew never began. Nor will his life ever reach an end. His course is fixed along the circumference of what's possibly conceivable. You must thank God for that.